Jung for Kittens

Glyn K Green

Jung for Kittens

Published by Showborough Books

Copyright © Glyn K Green

www.jungforkittens.com

Showborough Books
Showborough House
Twyning
Gloucestershire
GL20 6DN

Disclaimer

This is not intended to be an academically rigorous treatment of the work of Carl Gustav Jung. It could be viewed as positively misleading on the subject of kittens.

Chapter One

We all have a journey to make through this world – given the good fortune and the perseverance to stay alive – and at some point in this journey, sometimes sooner, sometimes later, we may find that living the unexamined life is not working out for us. In order to progress in a manner that we at least find acceptable, we need to know who we really are.

For Arthur Loveday, this point arrived on September 31st 2010 in the North London offices of Carruthers Sloan estate agents where he had worked, with moderate success, for the previous ten years. Lately, however, there had been a hiatus in the business of property dealing – a state of affairs that was generally attributed to the current government and the prevailing banking system. But Carruthers Sloan felt the need to attribute it more specifically than that, and so they laid it at the door of two or three of their more moderate employees. Three days after his thirtieth birthday, Arthur Loveday was 'let go'.

For a small orphan kitten, the unexamined life came to an end slightly later than this (ten days) and somewhat farther down the high street (seven doors) in the window of Happy Paws pet shop, where it found itself miaowing desperately through the plate glass with absolutely no idea of how it had got there or what its purpose in this bewildering world was supposed to be.

So the truth is that, far from one being a redundant estate agent and the other being just a kitten, the pair of them had a lot in common from the very start.

*****

But, whilst the owner of Happy Paws would not even hear the kitten's cries, Carruthers Sloan were not entirely deaf to the lamentations of those they had just jettisoned into the job market and so, in accordance with the latest in 'caring business' models, they provided, for each one, a full forty minutes of emotional compensation from a very experienced and succinct counsellor.

This counsellor was distinguished by a doctorate in psychology which had been largely acquired by putting unsuspecting volunteers into bogus situations, observing their reactions and statistically analysing the resulting behaviour. With complex experiments such as these, he had proved that men like beautiful women, that women like brave men and that the unconscious mind, given quiet unencumbered space in which to operate, will produce more successful and creative solutions than the conscious mind. He was thus in a perfect position to show wretched people, who have been flung by circumstance from the frying pan into the fire, how to get out of it. And in just forty minutes.

It was, of necessity, counsel without coffee. Counsel, in fact, without anything you'd hope for – such as sympathy, reassurance and a contact list for alternative employment.

There was, however, an inkblot test. Shown pieces of card with decorative splodges in the middle, Arthur Loveday saw ducks, a buffalo, an upside down lobster and two people kissing. This had dire consequences. It went on to reveal not so much what he was, as what he wasn't. And he wasn't, apparently, a great many things – exigent, resolute, aspiring, centred, high octane or focused. He was, in fact, seemingly devoid of what you could call drive. But then, a few years of trying to shift 'desirable bijou residences' against an adverse economic tide could knock the wind out of any but the most terrier-like of salesmen. And 'terrier-like' was another of those things that Arthur Loveday patently wasn't. Nor was he a smooth talker, a nod-and-a-wink man or a spinner of yarns, so unfortunately …

"From these results, Mr. Loveday," said the counsellor slowly - using 'Mister' was a piece of distancing terminology that made it easier for him to tell people of brief acquaintance things they didn't want to hear - "From these results," he repeated, "I would deduce that you are not cut out for selling things. Or acquiring things. Or sniffing out deals which are intended to sell things. Or acquire things. Or bringing such hypothetical deals, were they to materialise for you out of the goodness of their hearts, to a successful conclusion. In fact," he sat back in his chair and surveyed the heavily corniced ceiling and wide six-panelled door with its elegant brass furniture (and this just a branch office of Carruthers Sloan) "I would say that this is not your world at all. Nor anything like it ."

Arthur could think of no adequate response to this regrettable chronicle of his insufficiencies. Concluding his consultation with the décor, the counsellor shuffled through his notes. "This test, Mr. Loveday, was a psychological projection test which I went on to use in a broadly Socratic manner."

Arthur had no idea what he meant .

"In a psychological projection test, Mr. Loveday, you are presented with a field of ignorance into which you endeavour to project your own psychic activity. This gives me a speculative access to the contents of your head. And then we talk about them. Or we try to. Unfortunately," the counsellor looked up, "there is scant indication in any of this as to where your talents actually lie. I find myself unable to make one solid recommendation pertaining to suitable future employment for you. Whatever your bent is, Mr. Loveday, it has stubbornly refused to declare itself." He ruminated silently on this for long, disappointed moments.

This was an experienced counsellor so he had to know that there was a rabbit loose somewhere. An elusive rabbit that forty minutes wasn't going to be near enough time to snare. For though Arthur Loveday was certainly no testosterone-driven alpha male, neither on paper nor manifest in pumped-up action hero flesh, there were things about him that began to catch at you the longer he sat there. He had, for instance, a particularly attractive gaze - one of those bluey grey, far horizon gazes that was ... yes ... heavily clouded just now, but surely capable of doing great execution should the moment and the mood come together. In fact, he was in possession of some pretty good looks that, unusually for good looks, had apparently failed to stimulate in him any inclination to capitalise on them. Or any appreciable measure of self-regard. His preponderant response to adverse comment was a weary and reasonable courtesy. But that alone meant that he had to have more good qualities that could be considered and catalogued to his advantage. So why was he failing so comprehensively to bring them forth for scrutiny and suggestion?

The counsellor sighed. "A personality," he explained, "has

to be suited to the job you are asking it to perform. And this, I feel, is the challenge that this redundancy poses for you. You need to find out who you really are."

Arthur was not convinced that another disappointing perusal of his inner self was what he needed just now. He had not been raised to undertake painstaking examinations of personal distress. "So quite straightforward then," he said. "That's something at least."

"Irony," observed the counsellor with some satisfaction. "Not necessarily a bad trait. No use in business, of course. Businessmen have to say what they mean. Though not necessarily mean what they say." He gave a chuckle. "The Mad Hatter, I believe."

"He could well be here," thought Arthur.

As his chuckles faded away, the counsellor lapsed into silence, arranging his fingers in a poised tent and studying a point on the far wall. Maybe he was actively ransacking the farthest reaches of his brain for something that could be of help. Or maybe, he was just sitting there wondering what he was going to have for supper, letting the unconscious do the work, waiting for lightning to strike. Either way, he suddenly said: "Are you acquainted at all with the theories of Jung?"

Arthur shook his head. Jung was not a name he had ever conjured with and he was still much exercised with wondering how, exactly, seeing buffaloes and lobsters and ducks and a perfectly innocuous kiss, had brought him to this pass. But, the counsellor had put the buffaloes to one side. "Carl Gustav Jung," he said, "has a strong claim to being the father of psychoanalysis. He really honed the process. He coined the words introvert and extrovert and so on and so forth. All the better to analyse you with, you see. But, over and above that, he came to believe that the goal of psychological

5

development, indeed the goal of life, was individuation. The finding of self with a capital S. Unfortunately, it's not the work of a moment. Nor the work of forty minutes. Plus, Jung was ... well, to be frank, he's not entirely my cabbage patch. But I married a Jungian ..." he paused, as if this were the first time he'd been seriously struck by the notion. "Unusual people ... disturbing even." He stared reflectively out of the window. "This morning, for instance, I cooked eggs while my wife speculated aloud on why it could be that she had devoted a considerable portion of her dreams to the killing and dissection of the dog. Most people tend to keep quiet about that sort of thing, you know. Have you ever cut up the family dog during the night, Mr. Loveday?"

"We never had a dog," said Arthur.

The counsellor nodded, smiling faintly. "It's a funny thing, but I really think that Jung could serve you well." He went silent again then, as if to allow this idea to take root in Arthur's head, and then suddenly he was all business - leaping to his feet, straightening his jacket, pushing his chair back with an air of finality. "And now, Mr. Loveday," he held out his hand, "I believe our time is up."

"Thank you," said Arthur. It was one of the most confusing and dispiriting forty minutes that he had ever spent.

As he passed, for the last time, through the reception area of the premises, the young woman manning the desk said, "Goodbye, Arthur. Come back and see us sometime, won't you? Let us know how you get on." Understanding, of course, that he never would. She was, in truth, more distressed to see him go than she cared to admit, even to herself. She stood over six feet in her precipitous fashionable footwear but Arthur stood a satisfying two inches taller. It gave her a disturbing pleasure to stand next to him but she had never looked too closely at this pleasure because she could see that Arthur's heart beat for someone else.

Equally conscientiously, she had suppressed the desire to observe some of the looks that he directed towards this enviable someone else because now and then she'd caught in them something that was as brief, but as dazzling, as the flash of sun on glass. A love that made her heart turn over. And some other parts of her as well because Arthur Loveday, caught in the right light as it were, seemed to have the potential to be … well … something he was apparently unaware of. And yet, over and above that - and a certain wayward preoccupation with minor details like breadth of shoulder and strong-looking hands, and hair that was dark but not too dark and curling in a rather satisfying way at the nape of his neck - even above all of that, what touched her most were the repeated flickers of desolation in his face. She shook her head. Why this love of his was neither thoroughly revealed nor clearly rebuffed was a mystery because it looked prepared enough for either eventuality. In the meantime, it was obviously running such an interminable gamut of agonised possibility that it was painful to even watch. Why didn't one of them do something? And why wasn't there a third woman in the office with whom this could be thoroughly discussed? The secretary suddenly decided that she ought to be relieved that Arthur Loveday was leaving, because having to be the sole, frustrated juggler of thoughts like these had started to get between her and the endless smiles and irreproachable civility she was paid to produce. Smiling now, she held out a farewell hand.

Arthur was still capable of managing a smile himself. Just. He had a smile that could have been a heartbreaker - even now it was something more than a gesture - but at this moment Arthur Loveday's big smile, like that of the Cheshire cat, was pretty much all that remained of him. Still courteous, he shook the secretary's proffered hand. "It's been nice ... "he tailed off.

"It could have been," she said.

Arthur met her eyes briefly. If he understood what she was implying he gave no sign of it. When he stepped out into the wet, wintry high street he felt peculiarly empty as if the redundancy, followed by the ink blot test, had jerked the cork from the bottle and let everything drain away. But the truth was, that Arthur had been leaking for a long time - losing life force, drip by drip, under the welter of workaday annoyances and frustrations that was his daily fare. Lately, it had become harder and harder not to recognise the fading of the dream and to weather, without acknowledging the wear and tear, his portion of defeat and failure.

Now, he walked a pre-programmed automaton's walk to the tube station. But the programme had evidently developed a glitch because somewhere, in this most familiar of routes, Arthur took a wrong turn. He felt a brief frustration and glanced at his watch. Why? There was no hurry. He had nowhere to be. He looked down at his pinstriped legs and shiny Oxfords. He felt colourless. Indistinct. Nothing more than a generic Fritz Lang figure, dark suited and tidily barbered, mere background for Routemaster buses, Household Cavalry troopers and Trafalgar Square lions. And now, with no job and no place to be, he wasn't even authentic background.

He came to an uncertain halt and looked around him. A sudden autumn gust whipped his trousers against his legs. He shivered. Where was he? What shop was this? He looked up. Krishna's Second-hand Book Emporium.

"Many titles. Many, many titles."

An Indian-looking gentleman, presumably Mr. Krishna, was occupying the doorway in a proprietorial fashion, eating a doughnut and dropping jam down the front of a fine, maroon, velvet smoking jacket with frog fastenings.

"Thank you," said Arthur. "But I'm not really in need of a book."

"I think you are," said Mr. Krishna, putting his head on one side in an ostentatiously thoughtful pose. "You have the look of a man who needs to be transported to other lands, under other skies."

"Not really. But thank you."

"I have coffee. You at least need coffee."

The alluring smell of freshly ground coffee suddenly wended its way into Arthur's nostrils. It was unusually compelling.

"Maybe I do," Arthur said. "Thank you." And he followed Mr. Krishna into the gloom of the shop. The interior smelt musty and the floorboards creaked, and an enormous tortoiseshell cat sat on the counter next to an old-fashioned cash register and watched him through half-shut eyes. As powerful coffee pummelled him into life, Arthur began to take in the astonishing size of the place. Stretching away from him was such a length of bookshelves that their serried ranks actually had a vanishing point. So many thousands of volumes yet, curiously enough, he found himself seated in an armchair that put him eye to eye with a line of works by Carl Gustav Jung.

"You are familiar with Dr. Jung?" asked Mr. Krishna, filling up Arthur's mug with yet more syrupy, black liquid.

"Not familiar." Arthur looked into his mug. This stuff was good but he was starting to feel a little odd. He felt as if things were opening up inside his chest. Vortices. "Vortices," he said aloud and somewhat to his surprise.

"They'll pass," said Mr. Krishna dismissively. "But Jung?"

"Somebody just recommended him to me," said Arthur. "That's all."

"Just? As in just now?"

"Yes."

"I am a man of words," said Mr. Krishna, "and some small erudition so let me quote to you from Samuel Butler: 'Do not hunt for subjects. Let them choose you, not you them. Only do that which insists upon being done and runs right up against you, hitting you in the eye. This calls to you and you had better attend to it and do it as well as you can.'"

Arthur didn't respond. The vortices had set up quite a distracting thrumming.

Mr. Krishna prodded him. "So, you know who Dr. Jung was?"

"Psychologist? Psychiatrist? One or the other."

"He was a doctor!" exclaimed Mr. Krishna in scandalised tones, as if Arthur had somehow impugned Jung's credentials.

So he was a psychiatrist then. And a onetime colleague of Freud's. Except Jung. And younger. Though also dead. Arthur had to work hard to maintain concentration. He took another look in his coffee cup.

"But Freud is sticking in the mind more," Mr. Krishna pointed out with some indignation," because everything was a phallus to Freud. Modern thinking, you know. Everyone is very much on side with the phallus."

Arthur nodded. That seemed predictable. "Facile!" Mr. Krishna shouted in his ear. "Facile!"

Arthur jumped. Mr. Krishna pressed him back down into the chair. He seemed determined to make Arthur understand that Jung, in spite of deconstructing the human personality into its various working parts with typical Swiss precision, had not been just a superior type of watchmaker. "That was only his start because we are not being watches, are we?"

Arthur felt able to offer confident agreement. He was experiencing some extremely odd feelings but he was pretty sure that he was not turning into a watch. And Jung, apparently, had also come to the conclusion that people were not watches. And the upshot of not being watches?

"Well, for beginnings, the watchmaker was never blind," said Mr. Krishna. "Absolutely, never blind."

"That's nice," said Arthur. "For the watchmaker. Must have been a big relief." He suspected that there was a reference in there somewhere but he just couldn't get it. "Now, what's happening here exactly?" He looked down. Mr. Krishna had started selecting works of Jung and piling them up beside him. Out of politeness only, Arthur opened a couple and scanned the writings. "This is very ..." he searched for a word "... dense."

"Good for the brain to take on something new," said Mr. Krishna briskly. "Staves off the old timers' disease."

He wiped a leather-covered volume with his sleeve and then began distributing the books he had selected between two stout paper carrier bags with string handles. "A balanced load," he pronounced with satisfaction.

"Looks an expensive load," said Arthur, renewedly aware of his jobless status.

"Ten pound the lot," said Mr. Krishna.

"Really? That seems excessively cheap."

"Dr. Jung is not selling well. Everybody here in the U.K. wants to be better with a pill before breakfast, two stretching exercises and a minute in front of the mirror saying: 'I love myself.'" He shook his head sadly. "But it's not working like that."

"How does it work?" asked Arthur, since this seemed to be of some relevance to him.

Mr. Krishna shook his head again. "No good asking me such questions. I am just the wayside inn that supplies for each his roadmap. Here is the knowledge ..." He gestured into the crepuscular gloom of his shop. "And also here ..." He tapped lightly on Arthur's head and then on his heart.

"And here?" Arthur looked into the two carrier bags.

"Very much so. Very much so." Mr. Krishna nodded vigorously and then he stopped. "Although, even the great Dr. Jung referred to himself as 'just a spoon in the kitchen'. He recognised the unfathomable. Even the cleverest of us, and that's not you and me, sir, far from it, could just be sitting in Plato's cave."

Arthur made a conscious decision not to ask about Mr. Plato and his cave. A man can only cope with the onslaught of one messiah at once.

"Ten pound to you, Arthur." Mr. Krishna was back with the carrier bags. "And that's a good price, even for fire-lighting material."

Arthur took ten pounds out of his wallet and handed it over. It was the line of least resistance – the path he was most familiar with. He did not even register that, during his sojourn in the shop, he had not once divulged his name. Mr Krishna patted him contentedly on the shoulder. "Finish your coffee now. No hurry."

Presently, Arthur set off with his books. At the end of the street he paused. Mr. Krishna, watching from his Emporium doorway, shook his head. There goes a young man who has seriously lost himself. "Left, for goodness sake," he shouted, waving his arms. *"Turn left!"*

So, Arthur turned left. And there was the tube station.

Chapter Two

Arthur had no sense of homecoming when he arrived at 29B, Acacia Avenue, N3. His basement flat was one of those places that people take for six months, while they look for something better, and then become too moribund to leave.

Yet, it had its conveniences. It was within five minutes walk of a tube station, two minutes walk of groceries, fried breakfast, the I Ching Chinese restaurant and Bhagavad Vita takeaway Indian delicacies. Moreover, 29B formed the basement of a house of substance in a respectable road. Had the place come onto the market as an integrated whole, Carruthers Sloan would not have turned up their long and self-important noses at the commission on the sale.

It was just that the flat was heavy with the cumulative sadnesses of people who had failed to make their way in the world. The very walls had begun to sigh with weariness and frustration. At first, Arthur had brought his newly acquired estate agent skills to bear on finding something as affordable and conveniently placed but ... well ... more optimistic. A place that at least felt as if it had witnessed a degree of joy. He'd found nothing.

Over time it had come not to matter. He worked long hours and such free time as he had he filled with the mundanities of civilised life: tidying, laundry, dry cleaning and the purchasing of ready-to-eat food. And, while he slept, the flat gained a spider's web hold on him.

Now, as he juggled with his briefcase, Mr. Krishna's carrier bags and the door key, Arthur felt the leaden weight of despair filling his chest. A cold autumn wind whirled dead leaves round his ankles. Some blew inside to join an accumulating pile in the corner between the gas cooker and the old Belfast sink. There was a pronounced essence of scullery about Arthur's kitchen - which was unfortunate because it had to double as the entrance hall.

He moved on into the living room which was large but gloomy with dark, faraway corners, cumbersome old sideboards and a dusty velvet sofa. There were no symptoms of personalisation or decoration. Most of Arthur's symptoms were still in boxes in his parents' garage. Piles of books - Arthur C. Clarke, Philip K. Dick, Douglas Adams - were holding up one end of a workbench, lining nests for mice and getting slowly siphoned away to adult reading centres and those public-spirited racks in Homebase. CDs were left entombed in silent plastic storage, the heady whine of a Slash guitar solo no longer able to reach him. Hiking boots, ropes and crampons – never the heart of his life but once capable of giving him space and perspective and a fine view when he needed it - were now reduced to an indecisive shunting between his mother's charity pile and the under-stairs cupboard. He no longer noticed or felt the absence of these things, nor did it strike him that he had failed to replace them with anything else since leaving home.

He dropped the carrier bags of books onto the sofa and sat down beside them. He sat there for twenty-four hours, moving only to light the gas fire, get a drink and a packet of biscuits and go to the bathroom. After thirty-six hours he changed into a jumper and jeans and opened a copy of Jung. After forty-eight hours he decided that Jung's ideas were a concept beyond what most people would consider probable - even assuming that they could understand them. After seventy-two hours he glanced in a mirror for the first time. Now, mirrors are magical devices and people who consult them are frequently shocked at the outcome. Arthur saw not a weary and redundant estate agent - a worn out version of the bland, accepting man he'd become - but his aboriginal self, mired in atavism and uncomprehending.

His smartly barbered hair had been replaced by porcupine quills and boar's bristle; his scrupulous clean-shaven look by the bronze glint of Iron Age stubble and his eyes, far from that rather distant grey, were now as prominent and as red as a couple of radishes. Something that resembled the tail of a small rodent was hanging from the corner of his mouth. He leapt backwards with an involuntary yelp.

Arthur was insufficiently acquainted with Jung to view this horrific reflection as a form of progress - as the shedding of a non-viable, stuck personality which had bungled its rites of passage and failed to progress in a worthwhile way. He could not see, in the unimproved Neanderthal in the mirror, anything that smacked of a new beginning. With an appalled groan he lurched back to the sofa.

For ten years he'd worked at selling houses, conscientiously if not inspiredly. He'd smiled, most times genuinely, sometimes mechanically. He'd been reminded, sometimes humorously, most times brusquely, that his purpose in life was not to help people find 'happy places' but to sell them the houses that Carruthers Sloan had on the books.

On Saturday nights he'd been occasionally sucked into the slipstreams of old friends that he was beginning to see less and less of; of gung-ho impresario colleagues that he'd like to see less and less of; and of that inevitable, fluctuating flotsam of fly-by-night acquaintances that he would never see again. More and more frequently, these outings resulted in nothing but a punishing headache and a leaden sense of futility.

Sundays were not always rest days. Corporate clients favoured Sunday viewings. Relatives were enthusiastic about including him in family gatherings. His father and brother-in-law, carving contentedly away at large roasts, asked questions like: "Any big sales in the offing?" His mother and his sister, a more intimidating pairing, asked: "Any girlfriends in the offing?" And his small niece and nephew said, in terms of deep and sympathetic seriousness: "If no ladies like you, Uncle Arthur, you won't be able to have any babies, will you?" Was this his entire life to date?

He glanced around at the scattered tomes provided for his edification by the extremely odd, but confidently firm, Mr. Krishna. Carl Gustav Jung – there was a man who knew about crises. If only he were more ... prescriptive. But Dr. Jung liked to treat each patient as an individual. Moreover, there was the possibility that he hadn't been entirely sane himself. Not all of the time, anyway.

Arthur was not a young man whose natural recourse had been to street corner pharmaceutical products. They'd circulated in his vicinity, of course, getting smoked, swallowed and sniffed, but he'd never seen them as helping his problems in any way other than to add some unsettling, hallucinatory edge to them. The one time he'd tried something, there had been disturbing visuals and a certain amount of vomiting so he'd never bothered again. But, it occurred to him now that this might be the time. His mind could be soothed and therefore sharpened and his pain could be dulled. Yet, even in desperation, he wanted his drugs to be legal, to operate within a scientifically plotted range of predictability and to be dispensed by the medical profession.

He rang his doctor. Because he was not obviously about to die within a prescribed time, he had to wait for a week. This meant that he had not managed to realign himself before the mandatory sympathy visit from the office. Damien Price was more or less who Arthur was expecting but, by unfortunate coincidence, the person he least wanted to see.

Damien wore very dark, navy blue suits with bold white pinstripes like chalk lines. His hair was slicked back and his shoes were a little too pointed. He had a characteristic manner of speaking that was widely held as blunt, except when he was dealing with clients when it came across as charmingly frank. Confidential even. It was a mode of discourse that sold houses in the face of some pretty stiff competition, so Carruthers Sloan had retained his services.

He planted himself in a commanding position in front of the gas fire and took in Arthur's appearance with some interest. It bore about as much resemblance to a mild-mannered ex-estate agent as some vagrant busker would to a spinster piano teacher.

"What guy without a serious drug or alcohol problem looks this way?" he asked.

Arthur didn't respond.

"Anastasia was going to come," Damien went on. "How fortunate we are that she didn't."

Arthur made a gulping sound – it could have been on account of another rodent's tail but, in fact, he was gulping on something a lot more painful. Tears came momentarily to his eyes. Damien, clapping him helpfully on the back, divined that he was choking on unrequited love. Which, among other things, he was. And his chances of getting it requited had been extremely slim, even when he'd had a job - which Damien, ever helpful, felt obliged to point out.

"Forget it, Arthur", he said. "You're a frog and Anastasia is never going to kiss you. She might sound like a straightforward English girl, except for her name, of course, but these descendants of White Russians consider themselves vaguely royal, definitely rich, and not at all in the same social grouping as people who try to call them Stacey in order to make them seem more accessible. Whatever spell it is that keeps this putative princess at Carruthers Sloan is bound to wear off soon . Which is irrelevant, in any case, as you are no longer employed there. You've got to stop this, my friend. Stop weeping on the lily pad and find yourself another pond to take a turn in."

It was an unfortunate thing but Arthur frequently felt like a frog when he was with Damien. Jumpy. Damien had one of those powerfully active slipstreams and if, at the close of business on Saturday night, Arthur found himself hanging around alone and fatally passive he could rarely resist the suction. But he rode along in the full knowledge that in some indefinable way, at some point in the evening, he would be made to look foolish. It had happened so many times that Arthur had begun to think he must have been gifted a lifetime's role as the idiot. A guy who gave other men the opportunity to shine. When foolishness presented itself to Damien he simply didn't accept it. Drunk in a traffic cone hat, he remained one of Carruthers Sloan's best operatives. Arthur envied him this from the very depths of his soul.

He ruminated upon it now, with some despair and a fair

amount of accumulated animosity, as he stared at the way Damien's trousers fell into a perfect single break before they hit his highly polished shoes. Damien, in turn, was taking a desultory survey of the books that comprised Mr. Krishna's recommended reading. He selected a couple at random and flicked through them without comment, before dropping them dismissively back on the sofa. Then he took out a navy blue handkerchief with white spots and flicked a cobweb from his cuff. Arthur guessed that, operating as effectively as he did on some well-honed, not to say feral, instincts, Damien would regard Mr. Krishna's dusty and extremely weighty guidance on how to repair and beautify a bland and broken life as incomprehensible and faintly ridiculous. Not that Damien was averse to serious thinking, Arthur reflected wearily, it was just that his serious thinking ran more along the lines of scheming. But then, on his own telling, he was a product of the school of hard knocks, where the underdog was not cosseted or counselled but repeatedly kicked until he got up. And, if he was a dog of any calibre at all, he did get up and then he made damned sure that he never went down again. Ruthless natural selection and a lot of dead and damaged dogs. But Damien was a survivor. After some impatient grunts at the cobweb he stared down at Arthur for a few silent moments and then, gesturing towards the books, said: "These ideas are never very useful in the real world. You seem to have an endless capacity for self-sabotage." Returning to the cobwebby cuff, he glanced at his watch. "Clients to meet. Sorry."

At the door he turned round. "Another pond, Arthur. Smaller, fewer sharks. Get up. Go out. Find it."

As the door closed a jackdaw flew up from the stairwell with a squawk. Perching on the outside windowsill for a long moment, it looked in on Arthur with one beady, white eye. Then it wheeled away, down the street and over the rooftops. Twisting his head to watch it go, Arthur shivered suddenly and violently as if some cold downdraught from its wings had blown right through him.

Chapter Three

Dr. Ibeg Boona was a locum. Of pronouncedly African extraction, he was more than competent at modern medicine but he wasn't entirely in thrall to it. Sometimes, he believed, a little of something else was needed. After a momentary consideration of Arthur's complaint he said : "So, Mr. Loveday, you want a pill to make you cheery about your redundancy?"

"Cheerier", suggested Arthur.

Dr. Ibeg Boona inclined his head thoughtfully. "I can offer you mild, short term pharmacological cheer, Mr. Loveday, but for long-term cheeriness …" he paused. "Tell me, were you a cheery person before you lost your job?"

"I …" now Arthur paused. "I was employed," he said finally. "And …" He stopped altogether.

"And the days passed?" suggested Dr. Ibeg Boona.

"Yes."

"In quiet assiduous contentment, Mr. Loveday? Or in quiet desperation?"

Arthur said nothing for a moment or two. "They passed," he said finally. "I didn't think too much about it."

"I see." Dr. Ibeg Boona opened his desk drawer and began ruffling amongst the contents. "Misery is easy, Mr.

Loveday." He shot a quick upward glance. "But happiness takes effort. People think it is just an absence of misery, like dark is an absence of light, and so they concentrate upon deep, analytical dissections of misery. And now, Mr. Loveday, we are in a situation where misery has become the only literary, scientific and experiential credibility." At this point he finally produced from the drawer a very large sweet which he proceeded to unwrap. "Bonbon?"

"No, thank you."

"The great Carl Jung recognised that unhappiness was the overwhelming neurosis of the age." The doctor raised his eyes from his unwrapping and looked hard at Arthur. "Are you familiar with Jung at all?"

It would be an understatement to say that Arthur was surprised. He had come expecting to see the slight, twitchy and egregiously uninterested Dr. Robinson, and to this end he had prepared, in the waiting room, a few terse sentences using phrases like 'recent economic downturn', 'unforeseen redundancy,' and 'short-term support'. But he'd found himself delivering them to this astonishingly large black man with a lavender striped shirt, a spotted bowtie and a manner … well, Arthur couldn't really boil it down to a manner, it was more a presence: an overwhelming, beneficent presence that filled the entire room and to which the accoutrements of modern medicine – blood pressure machines, stethoscopes, ophthalmoscopes and the like – were mere irrelevancies. And, through the smiles and the nonchalant astuteness and the bonbons, Arthur felt the grip of a powerful inevitability.

"Hmmm…" Dr. Ibeg Boona put the bonbon in his mouth and sucked studiously on it for a minute before tucking it into one of his capacious cheeks. "So, you know the recipe for long-term happiness then." It was a statement, not a question, and halfway through it he suddenly started to chuckle. "Myself, I am eternally grateful to the great doctor for pointing out to Sigmund Freud that all men do not want to marry their mothers. Evidently Jung had seen mine!" The chuckle suddenly turned into a huge laugh.

Then, equally as suddenly, Dr. Ibeg Boona became sober. "Oh, yes indeed. Dr. Jung recognised that unhappiness was a great and general neurosis. He knew that there is no real meaning in the world of material possessions that has become so important to us. That to discover real meaning and purpose we have to re-establish contact with the cultural mythic and religious symbols latent within our psychic nature. Using these, Jung believed, we could realise our capacity for wholeness. You must follow the process, Mr. Loveday. It's all about the process."

"Which brings me conveniently to the trouble with Jung," said Arthur. "He is very hard to understand. I need a psychologist to explain him to me and right now I am in no position to pay a psychologist to explain him to me."

"And, right now, Mr. Loveday, the great National Health Service, fine British institution though it is, is in no position to pay a psychologist to explain him to you. In addition to which," the doctor moved the bonbon to his other cheek, "... Hmm ... You do not want to be put in a pigeonhole, do you, Mr. Loveday?"

Arthur agreed that he certainly did not want to be put in a pigeonhole.

"Put in a pigeonhole and prescribed for life," Dr. Ibeg Boona shook his head. "Categorised according to some modern psychological theory that has been projected onto you. A theory that will be based upon the belief that you are just a synthesis of neurological processes. Only a brain. Jung was all against it. As far as I can see, Mr. Loveday, you appear to have no burgeoning sociopathic or suicidal tendencies. But you desperately need to find yourself. It's all about the finding of self with a capital S."

"So I keep hearing," said Arthur.

"Uncanny, isn't it?" agreed the doctor amiably. "But now come the caveats. You must be very clear about what the search can involve – bearing in mind that Jung was a man of faith as well as a man of medical science. Not religion, Mr. Loveday. Faith. He believed that we have a spiritual nature. That we are more than a highly differentiated pile of protoplasm. More than a complex biochemistry." He looked at his watch. "I'm allowed to run a little late," he said, "because these days they think it's racist to whip me." And he gave another of his great laughs. "So, I'm going to take a few moments to simplify Jung for you, Mr. Loveday."

"First there is the self with a small s. Basically, this is who you think you are. The man that got sacked. The chap who can't get the girl." He gave Arthur a shrewd, sidelong glance. "But Jung believed that we have another self, with a capital S. A higher Self. With an investment in the biological, of course, but a connection to the spiritual and the numinous. Some people may equate this with the soul. An integration of the two is really who you are and why you are here. Here on earth, not here in the surgery, although it is, of course, that as well."

Dr. Ibeg Boona fell to finishing off the bonbon while he studied Arthur and Arthur wondered what numinous meant.

"This higher Self," the doctor then went on, "communicates with us through the unconscious. The unconscious mind is not just a dumping ground for the unthinkable, or a sorting office for sensory overload. The unconscious mind is that from which consciousness arises. And it's a gateway, Mr. Loveday. A gateway."

"A gateway", repeated Arthur in a tone of appreciation because he felt he had to say something.

"Gateways have great symbolic significance," said the doctor. "Though what is beyond may be magnificent, there is often a price to be paid for the passing."

"A price?"

"No free lunches, Mr. Loveday. No free lunches. Not even in the world of the unconscious."

"No," thought Arthur a shade bitterly. "There just wouldn't be, would there?"

"And now for the big one, Mr. Loveday. Are you ready? Dr. Jung's idea of the collective unconscious. How can I explain this to you?"

The doctor mused to himself for a moment or two and then he asked: "Are you a learned man, Mr. Loveday?"

"I've had brushes with learning," replied Arthur. "Not conclusive. Not, in fact, concluded."

"Tell me about this learning. What were you going to do?"

"Nothing of significance."

"You're sure about that?"

"Yes."

"Oh dear, Mr. Loveday. These things we don't want to talk about. They will be heard, you know. They will cry out to us as heart attacks and cancerous growths and their cries will kill us in the end."

Arthur didn't respond.

"Very well, Mr. Loveday. You do it the hard way. Now, back to Jung. Let me see, would you understand the phrase, a neuropsychic ground?"

"Not really," Arthur thought about it for a second. "Using

ground like field? As in magnetic or electrical field?"

Dr. Ibeg Boona obviously felt that a breakthrough of this kind called for another bonbon and began rummaging enthusiastically through his drawers again. "Exactly, Mr. Loveday. Exactly! We could define Jung's collective unconscious as an innate neuropsychic ground from which our behavioural characteristics as human beings arise. It contains the archaic heritage of humanity in a series of archetypes, which is why, even though we come from opposite ends of the earth, you and I have comparable myths, analogous legends and similar symbols. We all do. Now I think you can get it."

"Maybe," said Arthur cautiously.

"Jung and the physicist Wolfgang Pauli posited the 'unus mundus theory'," the doctor went on. "One world, Mr. Loveday. All is one. Not individual, isolated psyches but one vast, shared, interacting energy from which we have arisen and which contains all that we can be." He paused. "Now, are you sure you don't need a little sugar, Mr. Loveday? I fear I've made you somewhat whoozy." He held out a big red-wrapped bonbon.

Arthur shook his head.

"Hmm … very well. And the highway into this unus mundus, Arthur? … I do think it's time I called you Arthur, don't you? … Dreams and visions, Arthur. Dreams and visions. Even fantasies. These are the means by which the unconscious and the collective unconscious make themselves manifest. This is how we communicate with them, and if we can interpret what they are saying to us, we can improve our experience of life immeasurably. We can become whole. Jung was not a popular young man but he became something of a well-loved guru by travelling into his unconscious in search of his true nature. But," he held up a hand, as if to prevent Arthur from taking a headlong plunge towards becoming well-loved, "these journeys in search of Self are not to be undertaken lightly. What is the modern line now? Search for the hero inside of you? Is that it? If only it were so straightforward. The hero is not all that can step through the open doorway. With the light comes the shadow. It always has to be so. And while you, Arthur, what you think of as the real you, is looking and struggling to discover, the unconscious other can begin to manifest in personalities and powers that thrust themselves upon you. Archetypes, Arthur. They want to be realised. And the true Self, Arthur, is not so much found as extracted. Extracted and built - created from what is encountered in the unconscious. The bad as well as the good."

During his years of listening to people argue about wardrobe space, Arthur had developed a fine line in blandness. He passed no comment so the doctor continued: "This means that the quest for self-realisation can be a long and perilous road with many dark cul-de-sacs and no neighbourhood policing. And no one can tread this path ahead of you to clear the way and kill the bad fairies. These things you must do for yourself."

"Fairies?"

"As you see it, Arthur. As you see it. Jung became very closely associated with an old man who had kingfisher's wings. It could disconcert a lesser person."

"I think maybe I'll have that bonbon, after all," said Arthur.

Silently, Dr. Ibeg Boona handed him the large, red-wrapped sweet. Arthur gave it some consideration for a few moments.

"I should take the wrapping off and put it in your mouth," the doctor advised. "They taste better that way. Now then, you are a single man, aren't you?"

"I am."

"Parents? Alive?"

"Two."

"Would they be a source of support and strength?"

"Not in the face of an old man with kingfisher's wings," said Arthur.

The doctor gave a little sigh."In spite of your attentive politeness, Arthur, I suspect you think this is rather amusing. And you're quite correct. I'm deliberately trying to keep it … what shall we say … light? … for the very reason that it's not. Believe me, you will not be laughing."

"That's assuming I decide to do it, "said Arthur."Follow the process, I mean. Maybe a few tablets will do me fine. "

Dr. Ibeg Boona gave a great hoot of laughter. "Now who's the comedian?" he exclaimed. "Oh, yes, yes, very droll indeed."

"What's funny, exactly?"

"The fact that you think you have a choice." He held up a hand to stifle protest. "I haven't got endless time, Arthur, so we must concentrate on the important things. The conscious mind, for instance. The conscious mind must not be damaged in all of this or wholeness and resolution can never be reached. And, if I may say so, you already look a little ragged."

Arthur had developed an acute awareness of this during what had transpired as an increasingly isolated sojourn in the pariah's corner of the waiting room. He'd been late getting out of bed - in spite of the fact that bed was merely a place in which to toss and turn and have dark, fractured dreams and bitter awakenings. He'd spent a hurried few minutes in front of the mirror, scratching away at a week's worth of stubble and staunching blood flow with still adherent pieces of toilet paper. He'd flung on a pinstripe suit that had spent its days since the final outing to Carruthers Sloan balled up in the corner of the sofa, and underneath it he wore the black T-shirt that he'd slept in. In the gloom of the flat he'd pulled on one blue sock and one grey one.

"Something is needed for the blackest moments," said the doctor. "Something to give you strength and clarity. Some sort of talisman."

"A talisman? Not tablets?"

"Talisman. Charm. Charms are good psychological tools. Charms and ritual. Stage actors and sportsmen use them because they help the mind to focus. But talismans now ... a real talisman is a horse of quite a different colour ..." The doctor looked thoughtful.

"Some sort of special rabbit's foot?" suggested Arthur.

"Deary me, no! Really! Much too generic! It most emphatically will not do. An effective talisman is aligned to a quest. It is beyond special. To our poor eyes it is, in essence, magic. We must hope that one reveals itself to you, quick time. How's the bonbon?"

Arthur gulped.

"Good. Now, as the next step, I'd like you to pay a visit to this lady. She's a cousin of mine and owes me a favour or two. She is in a position to petition for help for you."

He laid a business card on the desk in front of Arthur. It read:

Madame Ibeg Boona, B.A.(Hons.), M.Sc..
Expert in esoteric psychology
and the varieties of religious experience.

"No faces now, Arthur. Most patients are just begging to be referred to a consultant. It's really quite depressing. Meanwhile, in case my cousin is out of the country for a time …" he began tapping away at his computer keyboard "… take one of these morning and night. If your fingers go numb, I should desist, but it's up to you."

"What sort of help," asked Arthur, "would your cousin petition for?"

"I believe we'll leave that up to her," smiled Dr. Ibeg Boona. "And now, I'll bid you good day and good luck. I'll be surprised if we meet again."

Arthur left the consulting room in something of a daze. Before he left the surgery he spoke to the receptionist. "What happened to Dr. Robinson?"

"Dr. Robinson suddenly felt the need for a holiday", said the receptionist. "A bit out of the blue, but then being a doctor is a very high pressure job. Did you like Dr. Ibeg Boona?"

"Charming," said Arthur. "I found him utterly charming. And more than a little disturbing."

Chapter Four

The chemist's shop was busy. People were queueing to receive pharmacological palliatives for their pain, their sicknesses and their desperation. Arthur handed in his prescription and then crossed the street to begin his fifteen minute wait time by considering the options available in an expensive chocolate shop. As palliatives went, chocolate rated highly with him. He bought an indulgently extravagant box of chocolate animals and roamed the street eating them. He scanned, without interest, the contents of shoe shops, stationers and florists, carefully avoiding estate agents - particularly his erstwhile employers. He wished that he had registered with a medical practice nearer to home and therefore less near to Carruthers Sloan. He contemplated changing – and not entirely on the grounds of location. He wondered what Dr. Ibeg Boona said to his other patients. The ones whose socks matched.

But, above all, he fell to wondering why he was out here at all, exposing himself to the chance of being spotted by people he had a fervent desire to avoid. And one he had a fervent desire to see . But not today. He ought to be skulking inside the chemists, presenting his back to the world whilst apparently taking a long and possibly overdue interest in men's hygiene products. But he wasn't. And, before he had a chance to wonder why he wasn't, his attention was suddenly captured and held. Above the noise of the traffic, a toddler's tantrum and the somewhat feverish working of his own jaws, he became aware of persistent and plaintive cries. Over the previous ten years Arthur had become somewhat inured to plaintive cries. Potential house buyers in the hands of Carruthers Sloan made them all the time. Yet, this time, he was given serious pause.

He swivelled his eyes curiously. They came to rest on the window of a pet shop. Amidst the dog beds and the rubber bones and the carpet-covered scratching posts stood a tiny kitten with its front paws braced against the glass. It was staring at him. Miaow. Arthur pushed a headless chocolate animal hastily into his pocket.

Miaow.

It was a strangely compelling summons.

Miaow.

Arthur stepped nearer.

Miaow.

Reaching forward Arthur put one hand flat against the glass of the shop window, meeting the kitten's two minuscule pink-padded paws.

He stood like that, as if hypnotised, for long moments and then he withdrew his hand and walked purposefully into the shop. "That kitten in the window…" He stopped suddenly, realising that he had no very clear idea of how he'd intended to go on.

The girl behind the counter viewed him for a vacant moment or two while she consulted with her chewing gum. "We don't sell kittens," she said, finally. "It must have been a hamster."

"Really ?"

The kitten came scrambling over a sack of all-in-one dog food and fell onto the shop floor.

"Would you look at that," said the girl with a degree of surprised irritation. "It has to be time I dusted that window display."

Arthur picked the kitten up. It was white and round like a particularly fluffy tennis ball and, in the manner of tennis balls, it didn't seem to have much in the way of legs or a tail. When it miaowed its large, bubblegum pink miaows, it had the tiniest teeth imaginable.

The shop girl continued to be unimpressed. "It's a feral," she said with dawning conviction, "from the back of Antonucci's Big Breakfasts. He fed the strays because they caught the rats, so then they stopped catching the rats because he fed them. So, he poisoned the rats and that killed the cats. Funny how things work out, isn't it?"

Arthur didn't think it sounded at all funny.

"Well," the girl picked up a large feather duster and headed for the window, "seeing as how you found it," she waved the duster dismissively at the kitten, "you can take it to Cat Rescue. The address is on the notice board."

And she clambered up among the dog beds.

Arthur put the kitten on the back seat of his car. There was no means of securing it or, indeed, limiting its free-ranging predispositions in any way. But, short of developing some perverse desire to wedge itself under the control pedals, there seemed little chance of a tiny kitten bringing the pair of them, or the car, to any serious grief.

The car was a veteran Morris Minor convertible. Arthur had bought it in a spirit of self-mocking showmanship on becoming a newly licensed driver at the age of seventeen years and three months. He'd paid for it with the proceeds of some seriously overworked and ferociously cold weekends spent at Alfie's Garage. At that time it had appealed to the geek in him to poke around under car bonnets - a thing he only did now if recalcitrant engines positively demanded it of him. These days, the Morris spent most of its time under a tarpaulin in the driveway of number 29, benefiting from the old-age concession of reduced road tax, but threatened by the government's increasingly advanced views on exhaust gases.

Arthur drove it mostly to visit his parents out of town. This morning he had used it entirely upon a whim. He had been surprised at the alacrity with which it had sprung into life. At the moment, however, its most pertinent feature had become its leather seats. The kitten slithered and slewed around on the back one, complaining vehemently about the lack of grip, the dearth of anything resembling food, and the general inhospitable draughtiness of the entire interior.

"It's an old convertible," said Arthur. "What on earth can you expect?"

The kitten finally plopped onto the floor and took refuge under the passenger seat - still giving voice in a series of reproachful miaows. Arthur drove as slowly as was consistent with not being attacked by fellow motorists.

Cat Rescue turned out to be a collection of huts and cages in the back garden of a Mrs. Bunce, a strapping lady in Wellingtons and a brown smock who advanced upon Arthur with an uneven gait that was the consequence of shouldering a twenty kilogram bag of kitty litter. Her passage was marked by beseeching miaows and the desperate beckoning of long, supplicating, furry arms extended through wire-netted holes.

"Well, what have we here?" Mrs. Bunce dropped the bag of kitty litter with a satisfying, grinding bang on Arthur's foot.

It took a bit of dislodging and Arthur looked from his dented toecap to Mrs. Bunce's meaty forearms with deep respect.

The kitten was starting to wriggle so Arthur put it down on a patch of grass. It began to chew industriously on a green blade or two.

"Worms," announced Mrs. Bunce with gusto.

"In the grass?"

"In the kitten."

"Really?"

"Yes. Worms."

"It was a stray," said Arthur. And he explained.

"Blue eyes," said Mrs. Bunce. "Two."

Arthur had never undertaken an investigation into cats' eyes but he'd rather assumed that, much like humans, they would have two of them and that these two eyes would be, in ninety-nine per cent of cases, the same colour. "Isn't that usual?" he asked politely.

"Not if you want them to hear."

Arthur wondered why he had started to meet so many odd people, and why he had such difficulty in understanding what they were saying to him. Had he paid a little more attention to what Jung had had to say on synchronicity, he might have been experiencing more alert curiosity and less bemusement but there we are, maybe few of us would get, at the first time of telling, that there are moments in the great scheme of things when chance and causality are simply dispensed with.

"White cats," said Mrs. Bunce, enjoying his bafflement. "Two blue eyes and they're deaf. Two amber eyes and they can hear. One blue eye and one amber eye and they're deaf on the blue side."

Arthur took a moment to let this sink in. Mrs. Bunce repeated it because it was a potentially entertaining thing that she could enjoy saying twice and white cats didn't come her way very often.

"He can hear," said Arthur.

"Be extremely unusual."

Arthur pointed out that the kitten was already unusual, having been for sale in the window of a pet shop that didn't sell kittens.

"Happy Paws?"

"Yes."

Mrs. Bunce made noises. Bulky, disparaging noises that more or less oozed out of her ample chest. "They don't know what they sell there. Cats, dogs, komodo dragons…"

"Komodo dragons? Really?"

"*No, not really.*" She gave him a look followed by a frankly despairing sigh and then carried on in those slow instructional tones that are normally reserved for children. "This kitten is much more friendly than a feral ought to be. That's evidence of deafness-induced insecurity. The animal wants to be next to somebody who knows what's going on." She took a look at Arthur again. "Not that a kitten is necessarily much of a judge."

Arthur began to feel defensive. "He can hear!"

"Sometimes it's like babies. Difficult to tell."

"*He can hear!*"

"We'll see." Mrs. Bunce swept the kitten up in chunky, determined hands, turning him over and over in search of ear mites, fleas, all sorts of things. The kitten set up a prolonged, protesting miaow. Arthur made a sudden grab for it but Mrs. Bunce was quick. "Naughty, naughty," she tut-tutted, whisking the kitten up in the air.

Arthur wanted the kitten back. He felt a strange empathy with it, but he didn't relish a physical entanglement with Mrs.

Bunce's large bosoms so he stepped away and said: "I'd like to keep him." From the very start he'd thought of the kitten as 'him' and now he was thinking of him as Mike. Largely, it has to be said, because he wished he'd been called Mike himself - practical sounding, unpretentious, masculine and succinct. He thoroughly disliked being called Arthur. Though, as a name, it had a great lineage back to where it was magically coupled with swords in stones and the most famous wizard of all time, it totally failed to convey any of this. Somehow, it was a complete phonetic failure without even the questionable advantage of being in fashion. It was his Grandfather's name and it felt like it and sounded like it. Mike, on the other hand, sounded ... well ... yes ... practical, unpretentious , masculine and succinct.

But the problem of having chosen such a masculine name for such a very succinct cat was that it might not have been at all appropriate. If Mrs. Bunce had a deficiency, it was that she was no great shakes at telling very small male kittens from very small female kittens. Even Mike himself was beginning to suspect, from the length of time he was spending upside down, that she was having a hard time choosing between the two available options.

But, being guessed at is a burden that many kittens have had to bear and, though disappointed, Mike was prepared to bear it with due grace. Unlike Arthur, he hadn't read Jung on gender awareness, but he had a suspicion that he had a masculine side and a feminine side, and he just didn't want to get the most appropriate side shaded completely out while he was busy being the other one.

Mrs. Bunce, meanwhile, was being no help at all on the matter. In fact, she'd veered away from the subject, as it were, by turning him the right way up and producing an enormous worm tablet from her smock pocket. She broke it in half but, even so, the inserting of it into his protesting gullet caused so much of a kerfuffle that the gender question got completely forgotten.

"He doesn't like that," said Arthur anxiously.

"They never do but it's necessary. Now, I'm going to find a nice cage for it."

"No!" Arthur gasped in horror. "I want to keep him. You can't put him in a cage. He won't ever ... er ... develop like that." Arthur used the word develop because he couldn't think of a more appropriate one. He wasn't entirely sure what the kitten needed to do that it couldn't do in a cage ... chase balls of wool, climb up curtains ...?

"It's best off in a cage," said Mrs. Bunce. "It's helpless. And defective. It's not up to coping in the world."

"He is!" The vehemence with which this burst out of Arthur surprised even himself. "I would really like to keep him," he added more quietly.

Mrs. Bunce gave some long and pointed consideration to Arthur's crumpled suit and odd socks. "Well, I'm not convinced that you're fit to be responsible for an eight week old kitten. You don't seem to be doing much of a job at looking after yourself."

"It's a temporary aberration," said Arthur. "I'm fine. Normally."

"Well, come back then. When you're normal. There are things to be looked into. Forms to be filled out."

Arthur made as if to turn away and then whipped round and snatched the kitten from Mrs. Bunce's grasp. She set up a great yelling but there was no one at hand to help her. She had many good points but she wasn't fast and Arthur might have had his bad points but he was. Without even considering the gate, he was onto the dustbins and over the wall with the proficiency of a practised cat burglar. He'd had to park at the end of the street but he was there in a flash, and they were shooting away from Cat Rescue with its wooden huts, its wailing occupants and its oversized antihelminthic tablets.

As the old Morris roared through the streets, Arthur glanced fitfully in the rear-view mirror. He half-expected police pursuit. What sort of a criminal record did one get for stealing a kitten? But then, he reasoned, the kitten was no more Mrs. Bunce's than it was his. Cat Rescue couldn't have been granted dominion over every kitten that had lost its way. He glanced behind to see what Mike was making of all of this. He was doing magnificently - digging his claws into the leather seats, determined to remain upright, determined not to vomit up the giant worm tablet and determined to fulfil this new and strange destiny.

Some people go out and buy pets, and some people have pets thrust upon them, and the upshot of Arthur's trip to the chemist was that he now had a kitten but no mood enhancers because, whilst caught up in Providence's web, he had forgotten to go back for them.

The other thing that got forgotten in haste was kitten food. Back in his flat, Arthur stared thoughtfully into his kitchen cupboards. He felt exhausted and inclined to improvisation. He opened the fridge. A chicken McNugget left over from the previous evening couldn't hurt, he reasoned. Not compared to, say, Antonucci's left-over breakfasts or rat poison. He discarded the outside of the nugget and chopped the rest finely. Nausea forgotten, the kitten ate it - a touch inefficiently but with great enthusiasm. Then, it proceeded to reacquaint 29B, Acacia Avenue with the concept of joy. It roared up and down the rug, hurled itself at the sofa and flung itself upon the cushions. Its eyes grew rounder and its whiskers grew curlier and its tail, such as it was, stuck straight up in the air. It was eight weeks old and nine inches long and for the past few hours it had been roughly manhandled by unthinking Fate. That such a negligible creature had maintained this level of courage and fortitude made Arthur feel suddenly ashamed. He had, he realised with a sudden flash of insight, been sent the perfect talisman. Far from unthinking, Fate had been conspiratorial. He got out Madame Ibeg Boona's card and stared at it for a long time.

The kitten hauled itself onto his knee and studied it too. And then, apparently content, fell asleep. Lifting it carefully to one side, Arthur picked up Jung's Modern Man in Search of a Soul and began to read.

Presently, the kitten woke up, stretched, took a couple of steps and had a little think. What are we doing?

Now, it was Arthur's turn to have a little think. Not a big one because that, he instinctively felt, could lead to all sorts of bother. Unnecessary anxiety and such. Possibly panic. What was it that Dr. Ibeg Boona had said? Something about the talisman being a horse of quite a different colour?

"I'm reading a book," he replied finally. "You're standing on the words."

The kitten looked down for a moment or two, and then got off the page and back onto Arthur's knee. Are they interesting words?

"Well," thoughtfully, Arthur turned his attention back to the text. "This writer, this Dr. Jung, his words say a lot of things, in a lot of different ways, in a lot of different books. And he builds these words into some pretty incredible hypotheses. The main one of which suggests that we, human beings, possibly kittens, I don't know, he doesn't specify, have lost touch with who we really are. And so we need to find ourselves. In a spiritual sense. And that way, we come to happiness and contentment."

The kitten studied Arthur carefully. So, it's a book about quests?

Arthur took another moment or two in which to register a degree of inner surprise but when he spoke, it was quite levelly: "I suppose it is", he said. "In a manner of speaking. One enormous quest."

And will I be coming when you go in search of yourself? Could we go in search of ourselves together?

"Every quest needs a talisman," said Arthur. "Apparently. Maybe you're supposed to be mine."

I like that. A talisman called Mike. It sounds an exciting thing to be. I was just a kitten before, you know.

Chapter Five

The introduction of a kitten into one's life requires certain adjustments and one of these adjustments involves litter trays. For a day or two now it had been involving Arthur's rugs which, old as they were, still held scope for deterioration. Arthur knew that there was an evolutionary process that Mike needed to go through: from carpets, to litter tray, to door, to catflap, to garden. And he knew this because when he'd introduced the word kitten on the telephone to his mother, she had promptly said 'litter tray'. It was like one of those word association tests and it revealed a lot about Mrs. Loveday.

So, Arthur was in need of a litter tray and some litter. It would never have occurred to him to take a kitten shopping, but Mike was determined to come because he was evidently of the opinion that abandonment would result, through some series of vague and woolly events, in his getting misplaced in a pet shop window. And, if Arthur left him behind, more vague and woolly events might overtake him. Moreover, as Arthur was on a quest, he was in a position to be overtaken by vague and woolly events himself. And wasn't it the job of a talisman to protect him from that sort of thing?

The correct answer to that was, of course, 'yes' but, as

Arthur pointed out, he was only going to get a litter tray and some food. It was a routine task that he ought to be able to pull off without too much trouble. Mike was not convinced. Dressing oneself was presumably a routine task, yet Arthur was wearing odd socks. Again. It seemed an untrumpable argument.

Arthur went to change his socks. The kitten trotted after him in order to stave off vague and woolly events. What's a litter tray?

"A litter tray", said Arthur, looking through his drawers, "is a toilet for kittens."

Whilst Mike had a fine, indeed a surprising, grip on a lot of things the toilet concept was not amongst them. He looked around the bedroom. It wasn't immediately obvious why, amidst the heaps of discarded clothing and dried-up slices of pizza, his few little additions - discreetly buried as best he could - should be expressly singled out for criticism.

"This is not the back of Antonucci's Big Breakfasts", explained Arthur. "So, neither man nor kitten should be making puddles – or worse – on the floor. We have a bathroom for that sort of thing, and that is where your litter tray will go until you get big enough, and the weather gets warm enough, for you to follow the usual procedure for cats, which is to go in the garden. Or, more specifically, other peoples' gardens. Mostly my father's, I gather. It's all very simple for a kitten of your calibre. You'll see."

Mike was obviously upset that he'd transgressed so early in his new career. Arthur said that he himself had taken at least three years to get the hang of a bathroom, so a few days was nothing . Mike cheered up immediately and began to get excited about the expedition.

In fact, he was so excited that Arthur felt obliged to go

someplace where shopping could actually be exciting. After all, how expensive could a litter tray really get? Pretty expensive, he suspected, as he gazed in a mixture of alarm and unbelief at the display in the window of Pet Shop To The Stars. But Mike thought it was magical. And it *was* magical, insofar as it was full of things that no ordinary person would even conceive of, let alone set out to buy. Little doggy dresses with fur trim and diamantes round the neckline; tiny pink trainers in sets of four; rhinestone hair slides clipped to the heads of fluffy, stuffed Pomeranians. And the collars!

Mike saw a black cat dummy, wearing a silver collar studded with red jewels, and nothing would suffice but they had to go in for a closer look. Unfortunately, it turned out to be one of those shops where 'just looking' was not the procedure. One had to be looking *for* something, and the natural corollary of this was that one had to be *shown* something. Neither was it the procedure to have anything as reassuring as price labels.

Fortunately, Mike's criteria for collar selection were not exacting. Colour was crucial. Brightness, bejewellment and a degree of luminescence were all to be preferred. Of prime importance, however, was a spot from which to hang a disc engraved with his new name and address. Mike didn't think that he was having an identity crisis, exactly. He was a talisman called Mike, that much had been established, but over and above that it seemed important that he lay down some pretty clear statements about exactly who he was as a kitten. Being small, he felt that these statements had to be bold and eye-catching and visible by night. The fact that they were rather a poor fit at the moment could, he pointed out to Arthur, be surely remedied with a snip here and a snip there. Not that the word snip was sitting comfortably with him. It resonated in a way that he couldn't quite define. Snip wasn't a good word he decided. And two snips ... *snip, snip* ... felt even worse. He gave an involuntary wriggle. These were complicated thoughts, obviously.

Arthur had reservations about cat collars, drawn from nothing but his experience with jacket pockets and certain types of doorknob. This narrowed the field further to collars with elastic inserts, which, judging from the assistant's expression, took them immediately into the cheaper range. Even so, by the time Mike had formed unbreakable attachments to four different collars the bill would have fed them both for a couple of weeks. On the plus side, the selection procedure had occupied a substantial portion of a chilly, damp day.

Understandably, it had not been satisfying in quite the same way for the manager of the shop who had finally been moved to ask rather coldly: "Does this kitten always have to be so extensively consulted about its shopping?"

It was a Saturday in mid-November and retailers were on the countdown to Christmas. Arthur, with his stubble and his old overcoat with the hem coming down and his alarming predisposition to bizarre one-sided discussion, was not holding people on the premises. Nevertheless, the remark cost the manager the sale of a spectacularly expensive litter tray and some accompanying gold dust litter.

But, from Mike's point of view, the purchasing process had been a very rewarding experience and one that he was keen to repeat. Up an alleyway, opposite Petshop To The Stars, he had spied a window full of tailor's dummies dressed in strappy leather and velvets heavily embellished with studs and buckles and chains. One of the dummies held a mace, another a sword and another a set of black fur handcuffs.

Mike was entranced. He thought all of this looked the perfect clothing for Arthur to wear on a quest.

"The people who wear this stuff are on quests," said Arthur. "Just not the same sort of quest, that's all".

Fortunately, before he had to expand on this, Mike caught sight of a box full of luminous socks in the back corner of the window. In spite of all the evidence to the contrary, people on quests apparently drew the line somewhere, and the luminous socks had fallen foul of it. Consequently, they were for sale at a prominently discounted price – for which Arthur would normally have expected to get a pack of three. Nevertheless, Mike's belief in their perfection was unshakeable. Their colours, for instance, were so distinctive that even Arthur couldn't mix the pairs up. They were pretty well guaranteed to bring an almost savage degree of clarity to his early morning process. Furthermore, a couple of pairs matched Mike's new collars exactly, and he saw nothing but advantage in colour co-ordinated quests and glow-in-the-dark mysticism.

It meant, among other things, that he and Arthur would always have a point of reference in dark places when there was no other illumination to be had. Driven by the theory that nothing too bad could befall them as long as his collars and Arthur's feet glowed in unison Mike contrived, once again, to land the pair of them in a totally unsuitable shop.

The window display was open at the back and Mike scrambled right out of Arthur's arms and dropped into the box of socks. Unlike Petshop To The Stars this was a business which followed the principle of leaving customers to their own devices unless a purchase was expressly imminent. And, since the usual run of customers was rarely of a nervous or stuffy disposition, unbalanced vagabonds were largely disregarded. Arthur found himself standing next to a male dummy wearing a black spiked collar. He reached up, curiously, and felt the spikes. They were reassuringly blunt.

"So, Arthur," said a voice behind him. "Do you think it will suit you?"

Arthur swung round. He'd known, of course, the minute he'd heard his name. The way Anastasia spoke it was indelibly printed upon his brain. Seeing her was simultaneously excruciating and heavenly. On the one hand, he was looking indefensibly ridiculous. On the other, she was all that his tired and starved senses pined for. And, when she looked at him, it was like dying – only in a good way. Nevertheless, used as Arthur was to Anastasia catching him off guard, this situation was a humiliating novelty that, given the choice, he would have gladly foregone. He smiled. The only thing about him that had not gone disastrously downhill was his brilliant teeth.

"I caught sight of you sneaking up here," Anastasia went on. "This is who you really are, is it?"

From the first moment, Arthur had been making desperate mental casts for a plausible explanation. Lights in dark places were more easily reflected upon than spoken of. As were spiked collars for men. Nothing of logic entered his mind. Anastasia frequently had that effect upon him. And today, parched as he was of her presence, and lovely as she looked in a dove-grey suit of exquisite tailoring, she was particularly paralysing.

She took his breath away as violently as she had done three years ago when she'd walked into the office accompanied by a self-satisfied Harvey Carruthers. She'd been employed, it transpired, because of the perceived advantages to the firm of her fluent Russian, her fluent French and her fluent Mandarin. Russians, in particular, spent big money on London property and, as long as they weren't Bolsheviks,

Harvey Carruthers was of the opinion that someone called Poliakof would be perfect at helping them commit it in the right direction. If he thought that her stunning good looks would increase sales he didn't mention it.

Anastasia had dark and bounteous hair, but the light of Siberian skies shone in her eyes as powerfully as it had illuminated the lives of her distant ancestors. When she looked at Arthur, she disturbed him to such an extent that she always had to drive whatever discourse they were meant to be conducting. Strings of the stupid, inarticulate remarks that he'd addressed to her over the years flooded into his mind now. Rerun, they sounded even less like the product of human intelligence than they'd done at the time. Everything he had wanted to say had stuck in his throat, whereas everything inane and facile had fallen over itself to get out. Nevertheless, the love he felt for her had grown in power to such an extent that he could barely contain it. It was an incredible thing – the only incredible thing of which he felt himself capable. But, it was a love that had had to thrive at a distance and on a largely abstract scale. He could never bring himself to give it a chance. Whenever he thought about doing so, reality somehow inserted itself and he was reminded that Anastasia was quite beyond his expectations. He was repeatedly left feeling awkward, deficient and wanting. So, eventually, he'd stopped deluding himself that he would one day ask her to dinner and settled for simply loving her. But, at the least excuse, acute longing would flare up like some recurring fever.

His smile was starting to get a little stiff. "I've acquired a kitten," he said finally "… for my niece …" He wasn't quite sure why the acquiring of a kitten for himself would make him seem even more emasculated, after the thorough and selective emasculation procedure that had been the redundancy, but there it was, he'd felt impelled to tell a little lie. "... and I dropped it ... *no* ...." he corrected himself hastily, "I didn't *drop* it, I just wasn't holding it firmly enough and it scrambled out of my arms and ran into this shop, this window display ..." He looked around.

Anastasia looked around too. At the pronounced absence of kitten. "Damien," she began gently, "said that you didn't seem quite your normal self when he called the other day ..."

"It wasn't a good time," said Arthur. "I'd been drowning my sorrows and I was perhaps a little maudlin ..." Another lie but, fortunately, Mike chose this moment to surface obligingly in the sock box. (Where it's just possible that he'd had a little accident but kittens, unlike people and puppies, don't allow that sort of thing to show on their faces.)

"Oh, I say, isn't he wonderful!" exclaimed Anastasia.

For one wild and lovely moment, Arthur felt how it would be if the words had been intended for him. If Anastasia had seen through the obscuring stain of his inkblot personality, and the current raggedness of his appearance, to the Self that Dr. Ibeg Boona had talked about. And if, moreover, she had seen there something that she could ... The moment went in the lightning fashion in which it had struck.

"Can I hold him?" Anastasia asked.

Arthur almost said: "You'll have to ask him." Fortunately, without waiting for an answer, Anastasia picked Mike up. He gazed at her with concentrated enquiry as she held him up in the air and talked to him as if he were a baby.

"Are you working?" Arthur asked.

Anastasia pulled a face. "Christmas shopping. This is probably the last Saturday I'll have off."

Arthur nodded.

Anastasia turned her attention from Mike to him. "We missed you at Carruthers Sloan. No one brings us cappuccinos and muffins for breakfast any more."

"Healthier, I expect."

"But not happier."

Arthur had often brought in breakfast for the whole office but, because he loved Anastasia, there were other ways in which he'd tried to make her life easier and more pleasant. Small efforts to do with phone calls and difficult clients and evening viewings, but, as is the tragedy of quiet endeavour, it had gone mostly unseen and unsung. If he'd ever found himself in a position to be thanked head-on, as it were, he'd produced nothing but his usual mumbles. An inability to capitalise. The psychologist had got that one right. Arthur imagined asking her to go and drink a cappuccino somewhere with him now, but ... there was an infinite number of 'buts' that inevitably thrust themselves forward and, right on cue, the biggest one suddenly emerged, princely and proprietal, from the crowd of ranking humanity on the pavement and put his head in the shop. Ignoring Arthur, he protested his abandonment, the manner of his abandonment and the fact that he had had to tread the street at least six times on a search.

"Nonsense," said Anastasia. "I've only been in here a minute or two. I came in to talk to a friend. And his kitten. This is Arthur. We were colleagues."

Arthur said hello. The prince nodded briefly. Anastasia naturally attracted princely types and, in Arthur's experience, they were all perfunctory in their greetings. They'd called in at Carruthers Sloan on occasion – an irregular succession of them, all looking as if they travelled the world or owned the world, whilst managing to make everyone else feel that their job was just to carry it obligingly on their shoulders.

Anastasia handed Mike over. "Look after yourself, Arthur," she said. "And keep in touch. Please." Then, she stood on tiptoe, kissed him on the cheek, not as briefly as she could have done, and left.

Mike watched her go. She likes you.

"She feels sorry for me," said Arthur.

There was something more than that about the way she kissed you.

"It was a mercy kiss."

What's a mercy kiss?

"It's all part of the feeling sorry for me business. Which socks are we having?"

She obviously sees something in you.

"No, she doesn't," said Arthur. "So, please don't go there." He was aware that he could not go on in this way, loving her so uselessly and achingly. "Stick to socks."

Very well. As you wish. Let's have the lime green ones, the pink ones and the purple ones.

Arthur picked them out of the box without comment and paid for them at the till.

Chapter Six

Mike developed a taste for tinned red salmon for breakfast. Arthur, with a cupboard full of commercially produced kitten food, had no idea how. He assumed that it was something to do with empty tin cans behind Antonucci's Big Breakfasts but Mike, who had no recollections at all of the back side of Antonucci's, took a loftier view. He thought that he was merely growing into his role as a talisman, as directed by unseen and financially extravagant forces. In truth, he seemed as much attracted by the colour of the salmon as by the taste. Mike's preferences in the matter of colour had come as a surprise to Arthur, who had some vague notion that animals were colour blind. Too vague a notion to actually voice, he should have realised. Mike received the concept with an air of offended dignity. Felines, of course, have more dignity to offend than most other species of animal. A scientifically unproven but self-evident truth that Arthur had not yet learned to work around.

"Fine," he said. "So commercial cat food is the colour of mud. But we must eat up what's in the cupboard."

His bank statement had arrived. It lay, unopened and smelling fishy, under the empty tin of John West's.

"Also," he added (not really intending to provoke but

made just that little bit irritable by Barclays' timely reminder of the realities of life), "there are occasions when I think colour blind would be better."

When?

"Well, the luminous socks didn't do a lot for my image. Neither the buying of them, nor the wearing of them. And the dream diary episode almost ended up with a trip to a police station followed by a trip to a hospital."

But it didn't. Besides which, if you'd been taken to the police station you would never have been offered an opportunity to go to the hospital.

Snorting irritably at this blatant abuse of the word opportunity, Arthur picked up the dream diary. The hard cover featured a unicorn flying through a magical forest heavily encrusted with psychedelic, metallic colour. Running alongside the unicorn, picked out in a particularly shiny and eye-catching gold, was a quotation from Alice In Wonderland: 'If you'll believe in me, I'll believe in you.'

The diary had been inspired by Jung, selected by Mike and bought by Arthur. The opinion of the girl cashier on glittery dream diaries and the men and kittens who go shopping for them is not a matter of record but, with the cold eye of retrospect, Arthur could vividly imagine it. A queue had built up while Mike had made determinedly independent, though not particularly efficient, attempts to get into the carrier bag at the same time as the till receipt. With the express intention, so Arthur gathered, of getting a better appreciation of the glitter by looking at it in the dark. In vain, Arthur had tried to deter him by pointing out that the glitter would not show up at all well without a source of light. It worked by reflection. Mike insisted that of course it would show up because some of his brightly coloured collars did. Arthur explained that the collars

53

were photoluminescent. They took in photons when they were in the light and subsequently released them, making them visible when they were in the dark. For a period of time, it was as if they were actually generating light. The glitter, on the other hand, only reflected light. Mike knew that he himself reflected light because he had a tapetum lucidum which Arthur, being a mere human, did not and so if cats' eyes could see better in the dark and, in fact, showed up better in the dark because they reflected light, why couldn't the glitter?

"Neither the glitter nor the tapetum lucidum either create or release light." Arthur had started to sound a little tense. "Neither of you are in any way photoluminescent or bioluminescent or any other sort of luminescent, so your whole argument is null and void. The fact that you can see better in the dark than I can will not make the glitter any more glittery. It will be less glittery. Not as less glittery as it would be to me I admit, but ..."

At this point, the people behind him, who had, it was true, been temporarily diverted by a grown man trying to explain the principles of reflection to a kitten, began to get a little restless - not to say slightly alarmed. A security guard had drifted across. "What's going on here, then?"

The girl cashier explained that there seemed to be some disagreement about what should, and what should not, be getting into Arthur's carrier bag.

"And did you pay for these things, sir?"

Since the things, or rather the thing, being talked about was actually Mike, Arthur replied, with punctilious and insane honesty, "No." This 'no' was then followed by various 'buts' and 'becauses' and other belated and obviously uninteresting attempts at clarification. With a security guard either side of him Arthur was not exactly manhandled, but certainly hustled under pressure, to a bleak office behind the scenes. A bare table, hard chairs and high windows lent an air of prison visiting to the ensuing interview. By this point, the more senior of the security guards had taken possession of the carrier bag and with a quick gesture he emptied out, onto the aforementioned bare table, a dream diary, a till receipt and a small white kitten. There was something of the magic trick about this, but whatever the security guard felt about it - surprise, bewilderment, disappointment, quite a range of options must have presented themselves to him - he remained professionally inscrutable. "And is this your kitten, sir?"

"Yes," admitted Arthur.

The junior security guard had been standing silently, back against the closed door, gazing intently at his feet. His shoulders gave one small suppressed heave. His superior shot him a quelling sidelong glance.

"And would you care to tell us how you came by it?" he asked Arthur.

A quick vision of snatching Mike from Mrs. Bunce and bolting from her premises suddenly flashed across Arthur's mind. He shifted uneasily on the hard chair. Barely shifted, really, but the security guard was trained to notice these things. "So you stole it?"

"I found it," corrected Arthur. "In the window of a pet shop."

"So you *bought* it?"

"No."

"So you *stole* it."

"No."

The security guard shuffled his heavily shod feet under the table. "Watch my lips, sir. *Why … didn't … you … pay … for*

... the ... kitten?"

"Because ... it ... wasn't ... for ... sale."

"So why was it in the pet shop window?"

"It had just wandered in there."

The security guard looked at Mike's negligible legs and said: "Now that doesn't really sound likely, does it?"

Mike seemed unperturbed by all of this. He was sitting on the bare table cleaning himself up with such grandiose grooming gestures as he could contrive with his negligible legs. It was a method of counteracting the disrespectful way he had been unceremoniously tipped out of the bag. A type of displacement behaviour. His interest in the glitter on the front of the dream journal had apparently abated.

"This is all your fault," Arthur said to him. "If you hadn't made that ridiculous fuss about getting into the carrier none of this would've happened."

I was merely trying to get into the bag. You are the one who managed to make it look as if I was being stolen.

"Really?" Arthur snorted. "You're really going to just sit there and offer excuses? Just imagine, for a moment, that you are a *real* talisman. Imagine that this is actually a fairy story of some kind and you and I have been captured in a forest by brigands. Or, maybe, we have wandered into the gingerbread house and are about to be eaten by a wicked witch like happened to Hansel and Gretel."

Mike was a little fuzzy about brigands and Hansel and Gretel but it sounded as if they could add up to an interesting tale ... Go on then. What happens next?

"Well," said Arthur, "the next step should really be yours. You are the talisman. It would be your moment to do something. You were the one who actually pointed out that your role was to protect us from this kind of thing."

What kind of thing?

"*This* kind of thing. Being set upon by brigands."

So what should I do?

"I was kind of assuming that you would know that."

Mike turned this over in his mind. Nothing occurred to him. He looked around for a moment or two. You think this is a gingerbread house?

"Are you on something, sir?" asked the security guard heavily. "Drugs of some sort?"

"No," said Arthur. "Because I forgot to pick them up. The day I got the kitten I was supposed to pick up some medication. It seems obvious to me now that I should have left the kitten and settled for the tablets."

"So you are supposed to be on doctor's medication?"

"It was more of a suggestion, really," said Arthur thoughtfully. It had struck him a couple of times lately that maybe he ought to pop back and pick up that prescription. A kitten but no tablets wasn't working out as well as he'd hoped.

At this point the door burst open, bunting the junior security guard out of the way. A fierce little woman, wearing black-rimmed spectacles and a navy blue, silk blouse tied at the neck with a pussycat bow, strode into the room. She had a name tag pinned above one pointed breast. It read: Ms. Jane Briggs. Manageress.

"Maxine on till 3, is worried that she might somehow have given the wrong impression about this gentleman," she said, without any preamble or apologies for invading what could have been regarded as security's personal space. "Apparently, he was not trying to steal anything."

"He stole a kitten," said the senior security guard indignantly.

"But not from us," pointed out Ms. Biggs. "Because we

don't stock them."

"Plus, he's supposed to be on medication," added the security guard. "Which he is not taking."

"Medication and kittens," said Ms. Biggs. "Not our department. However, in the interests of all round health and safety and by way of apology, I suggest that we call, and pay for, a taxi cab to take him home. Or, alternatively, to the nearest outpatient clinic. Whichever he would prefer." At this point, she finally looked at Arthur. "Are you known to social services at all?" He shook his head and gave her one of his big smiles. Jesus, she thought to herself, why is it that all the handsomest men have to be either emotionally stunted or complete tossers?

The taxi driver, having been paid generously and given a very large gratuity, was amenable to some adjustment in terms of destination. Soon, Arthur was standing outside of the chemist's shop that was in possession of his prescription. But it struck him, on the verge of becoming a medicated person, that mood enhancers might affect more than his mood during the day. They might affect his mood during the night. Consequently, it might be reasonable to assume that they would therefore affect his dreams. Jung had set some considerable store by dreams. He had written: 'Dreams give information about the secrets of inner life and reveal to the dreamer hidden factors of his personality. As long as these are undiscovered, they disturb his waking life and betray themselves only as symptoms.' He most emphatically did *not* believe, as Arthur had read with some optimism, that a dream is merely 'a meaningless conglomerate of memory fragments left over from the happenings of the day'. So, whilst dreams seemed a most convenient way to begin to connect with the true Self, the awkward question remained: would their validity be compromised by the consumption of pharmaceutical products? "We need to think more carefully about this," Arthur said.

Mike thought he had been thinking carefully. He had been thinking carefully about how a practised talisman would get Hansel and Gretel out of a gingerbread house. On the other hand, he hadn't come up with much of an answer, so he was naturally interested in how he could think more carefully still. So how are we going to do that?

"By eating," said Arthur. "Does Antonucci's Big Breakfasts ring any bad bells for you?"

No.

Antonucci's was relatively busy. It's surprising how many people want to eat fried egg and bacon with black pudding in the middle of the afternoon. Antonucci was a second-generation Italian immigrant so the crude culinary habits of the British populace did not offend him but made him a comfortable and, at least in terms of recipes, an undemanding living. Arthur found an empty booth and slid along one of the bench seats. He put Mike onto it between him and the wall and advised him to stay there. Antonucci was a man who, albeit accidentally, poisoned cats. It could be that he wouldn't be too thrilled to have one in his cafe.

When the waitress came, Arthur ordered a full English with tea and a glass of milk. Then he sat and thought about Jung and dreams. Jung had been emphatic that dreams could not be analysed using any universal language of symbols or word association methods or intellectually construed metaphor. They had to be interpreted in the light of the psychological state and the conscious mind of the dreamer. Something else that probably brokered against medication. "How much do we know about our psychological states and our conscious minds?" he asked Mike, thoughtfully.

Mike looked up at him. Less than we should, I think. Some of us.

The food arrived. "Do you want to try some black pudding?" Arthur mashed a piece with a fork and floated the result in a saucer of milk which he then balanced on the seat beside Mike. They were eating in silence, Arthur still thoughtful on the subject of chemically corrupted dreams, when somebody eased himself into the bench seat on the opposite side of the table.

"Damien?" Arthur swallowed a piece of bacon without having chewed it. "I didn't expect to see you in here."

Damien shrugged. "It's hard work outgrowing a culture. Impossible, in fact. Sometimes I just succumb."

Arthur nodded, trying not to choke in as subtle a fashion as he could manage.

"So what are you up to?" Damien asked him. "Still trying to find yourself?"

Arthur nodded again.

Damien took in the sweatshirt, the old overcoat and the stubble and said: "So how's that working out for you?"

Arthur shook his head.

"A few old books aren't going to change you, Arthur. Not really. Change is a charade. An act. If we try hard enough, we can get to play it out in better clothes and more affluent surroundings. That's all. People don't really change. We are who we are."

Being a busy man, Damien had ordered his food on the way in, so now a waitress slapped down a plate of toast and fried mushrooms in front of him.

"That's very sophisticated fare for in here," said Arthur. "You may have changed more than you think."

Damien picked up his fork with a smile. "What you got there anyway?" he asked after a few mouthfuls had gone down. He nodded in the direction of Mike, who was rustling about on the seat.

"He's a stray," Arthur replied, picking Mike up. "Apparently. From the back street behind here. I was giving him a bit of food"

Mike gave him a look.

It was true. Arthur's answer had carried an evasion. And one that was about to have consequences. Damien, however, gave Mike only the briefest of inspections. His interest in strays was non-existent. He'd grown up amongst strays of all species. Compassion fatigue had set in a long time ago. He redirected his attention to the mushrooms. But there were other people in the diner who were more easily touched. A girl in tight jeans and extremely high heels had caught, in passing, the word stray. And Mike was an extremely pretty kitten. With a cry of delight she leaned in to stroke him – finally taking him from Arthur's light grasp. "I'll have him," she said. "I'll give him a good home."

"No …" Arthur protested. But the girl was a quick walker.

"Excuse me …" Arthur said to Damien, "I really have to …" He scooted hastily out of the booth and hurried to the exit.

On the pavement immediately outside, the girl was stroking Mike's head and talking him up to her boyfriend – an intimidating person with a shaved head and prolific tattoos. He didn't present as an ailurophile, and his brow was deeply furrowed at the prospect of having to become one, but the minute that Arthur stepped towards him and claimed ownership of Mike his brow immediately cleared. He knew what he was now. He was a man whose girlfriend was about to lose something she had set her heart on having. And she was complaining rather heatedly at the prospect: "You said it was a stray. You said so. I heard you."

She was, of course, quite correct.

"I was speaking in the past tense," Arthur explained hastily. "As in, he *was* a stray or *had been* a stray but now he was mine."

"That's not what you said," insisted the girl.

Arthur sighed. He knew he had not been scrupulous with the truth. He had not wanted to reveal to Damien that his lunch date was a kitten. He had provided quite enough entertainment for Damien Price, one time and another.

"We'll take the kitten," said the boyfriend.

"Look," said Arthur, "I'm sorry for expressing myself badly before, but the kitten is already mine…" As he spoke he reached forward to lift Mike out of the girl's arms but found himself being peremptorily shoved in the chest. Staggering a little in surprise, he caught at a lamppost. "Forget it," said the boyfriend aggressively. "We are keeping it." And he pushed his face into Arthur's, in order to emphasise the point.

It was at this moment that Damien, delicately dabbing any trace of mushroom juice from his mouth with one of his spotted handkerchiefs, stepped forward from the doorway of Antonucci's. "Give back the kitten," he said conversationally to the boyfriend, as he carefully arranged the handkerchief back in his top pocket. There was no immediate response. "Now would be good," he shot his cuffs and picked a miniscule piece of fluff from his lapel.

"I don't think so." The boyfriend gave Damien's pinstriped self a dismissive glance.

"No," said Damien calmly, with a slow shake of the head.

"Don't do that. Don't make that mistake. Don't look at the suit. Look at me. Then I think we'll understand each other."

"Now," he went on in pleasant tones, "it was an honest mix-up between my friend and your girlfriend so the civil thing to do is to give back the kitten. There's a pet shop just down the road. I'm sure they'll find you another one equally as nice."

"I don't want any trouble," said the girl, and she handed Mike across to Arthur. The boyfriend made no effort to stop her.

"Thank you," said Damien. "Good decision."

"I'm sorry," said Arthur as the couple turned away. "I really am."

There was no acknowledgement.

"You can't apologise your way through life, Arthur," said Damien. "It only works to a degree. And only on reasonable people. Now, are you going to come to the office with me and say hi to everyone? Anastasia might be there. She was when I came out."

"No," said Arthur.

"Good decision," said Damien. And turning on his heel, he headed back to work.

Arthur, left clutching Mike, felt frankly choked. By many things. First, he now felt so strongly that he much preferred the kitten to the tablets that he felt obliged to apologise to Mike for ever having thought otherwise. Let alone having given voice to the idea. Secondly, he hated himself for not being able to walk fifty yards down the street to say hello to Anastasia. It was humiliating and unbelievably painful. It was even more painful to contemplate what Damien could now be telling her about him. Thirdly, he wondered if maybe Jung was wrong and Damien was right. People never really find anything different within themselves. There is no other Self. We are what we are.

At this point he realised that he had both forgotten to pay his bill and left the dream diary in the carrier bag in the booth. He turned back towards the diner. As he did so, an enormous jackdaw flew out of the open doorway holding a piece of bacon in its beak. As it whooshed past his head, he distinctly saw its pale beady eyes swivel mischievously in his direction. He knew it was laughing. Antonucci senior, in hot pursuit with a flapping tea towel, was not. "*Bloody rats, now bloody birds!*" he shouted. "We should have stayed in Sicily! We shot them there, we had guns, we had ..." he continued for awhile in spirited Italian.

"And so you do come back to pay your bill," he added to Arthur in English, without missing a beat. They walked into the diner together.

"Your friend paid it," said the Antonucci on the till.

"We could have had it twice," said old Mr. Antonucci with some expressive hand gestures. "We are from Sicily, after all."

Arthur laughed. "I had to come in, anyway," he said. "I left something in the booth. Has anybody handed in a carrier bag?"

Antonucci senior went round behind the counter and ferreted underneath. "What's in it, then?" he asked beadily, before agreeing to hand it over.

"A journal," said Arthur. "With a flying unicorn on the front. Covered in glitter."

"Correct," said the old man looking in the carrier. "And this is yours?"

Arthur nodded.

Antonucci's senior shook his head sadly. "I knew we should never have come to this country."

So, the career of the dream diary had, one way and another, begun in ignominy and it proceeded in much the same way. Arthur's hope that guiding light would emanate from his unconscious while he was asleep worked out about as well as Mike's plans for more impressive glitter in the dark. Except that the glitter was definitely there and Arthur was beginning to doubt that the guidance was.

Arthur soon realised that he was most unlikely to have a 'behold I bring you tidings of great joy' sort of dream. Even with the field narrowed down to a consideration of those dreams that disturbed him emotionally, or challenged his basic beliefs about who he thought he was, or which recurred with any degree of regularity, his contributions to the pages marked 'Arthur' pretty much conformed to the 'meaningless conglomerate of memory fragments left over from the happenings of the day' school of dreaming.

Even allowing for metaphor and parable and speaking in tongues Arthur could glean nothing from them. Even on those occasions when he awoke emotionally disturbed enough to satisfy the criteria for revelation, the sweat that frequently drenched him and the thumping of his heart were all that remained with him.

Mike's diary pages were even bleaker. They all had identical entries:

Dream: couldn't remember.

Analysis: oh dear!

So after an initial enthusiasm for the project, over and above the glitter aspect, Mike had begun to feel challenged by the entire enterprise. Not only because he slept too deeply, he claimed, to remember his dreams but because he couldn't write. Or, supposing he could write, he wouldn't be able to read it afterwards.

"Being able to read and write is not a given for kittens," Arthur had pointed out over another of those dispiriting breakfasts where he'd reported rubbish and Mike had looked blank. "Kittens are so rarely required to keep diaries, it probably wasn't worth kitting you up with a thumb on the off-chance."

The rather feeble joke had to be explained, so it didn't have the required mollifying effect. In the end, Arthur had realised that illiteracy in kittens was not a joking matter. He suggested that he read aloud, and Mike pay attention to the words on the page, and maybe the reading would come. Of course, he'd had to concede fairly rapidly that most people learning to read begin with: 'the cat sat on the mat' and not: 'No amount of scepticism and critical reserve has ever enabled me to regard dreams as negligible occurrences. Often, they appear senseless but it is obviously we who lack the sense and the ingenuity to read the enigmatical message from the nocturnal realms of the psyche.'

But, Mike wanted to know why the cat had to sit on the mat. Why didn't it get to sit on a cushion? Or on the bed? Or on someone's lap? Who was persecuting cats in this underhand fashion?

So, the learning to read enterprise had not gathered much momentum and, in the end, Arthur had read aloud but mostly alone, churning grimly through sections of Jung, paraphrasing and analysing, but continuing to project his voice so that it could reach all parts of the flat, including the area under the sink, where Mike was pursuing a new and pressing interest in vermin control.

"Mike, please come out from under there," Arthur said finally. "There is no mouse."

Mike stuck his head out. Are you sure? Somebody has

done something on the floor under here. Somebody is not following the litter tray rules.

"Well, if there is a mouse you're never going to catch it and, if you did catch it, you wouldn't know what to do with it."

I think I'm supposed to kill it and eat it.

"That's the way evolution would have it," conceded Arthur. "But, it seems to me that you are going to find yourself caught between that biological imperative and another one. You may not like it afterwards if you kill the mouse. It won't be a pretty business, what with your being so small, and it'll hang about in your consciousness. And we know where that sort of thing gets us."

Do we? Do we really? I think some of us are having a hard time grasping that.

Arthur didn't answer.

*****

So, this was the point they had reached towards the end of November. Mike wanting to read but being unable to resist the attraction of the mouse under the sink, Arthur wanting to dream but not being able to make sense of what he dreamt, both of them now eating tinned salmon for breakfast and neither of them opening the bank statement.

Financially speaking, Arthur had not planned for a sabbatical devoted to self-scrutiny. But, unpaid time spent looking for himself had to be catered for somehow. Hitherto, he'd always assumed that, barring death or long-term debility, neither of which the average thirty-year-old believes in anyway, he would always be able to scratch together living expenses on a hand to mouth basis.

"I think there's nothing for it but to open it," he said now, gingerly picking up the envelope stamped 'Barclays' between thumb and forefinger (and not entirely because it was sticky with fish oil).

Don't open it if it means we won't be able to have salmon any more. Mike checked the empty tin a shade anxiously. Maybe he shouldn't have shared it with Arthur. Maybe Arthur should have had cornflakes.

"It doesn't really work like that," said Arthur, opening the envelope as Mike watched him intently. In fact it had worked out rather well. Carruthers Sloan had professed extremely civilised views on redundancy payments and, in spite of Arthur's suspicions that these views would never be expressed in actual money, they had materialised on his bank statement. Had he not, during the complacency of full employment, spent some quite breathtaking sums at other people's prenuptial shenanigans, he would have been extremely flush. As it was, he had enough to keep the bailiffs from the door for a few months.

"After that, one of us will have to get a job," he said to Mike, "whether I've got a lead on my true Self or not."

I have a job. I'm a talisman.

"Seems to me that's more in the nature of work experience than a job," observed Arthur. But he felt better. Financial solvency can do that for people. Being hounded by security guards had made Arthur think that he ought to be recalibrating his ideas on sanity. His sanity. Reviewing the conversation that he had conducted in front of them, he could not be surprised that they had thought he was high. On the other hand, his talisman had failed to perform in any constructive way at all. Both of them had had to be rescued from a potentially disastrous situation by Damien Price. How could that do other but continue to rankle? "Aren't you supposed to do things?" he asked Mike. "As a talisman, I mean."

I was trying to catch a mouse for us but you discouraged me.

"Something relevant to the quest. Aren't you supposed to step in and turn things around?"

What things?

"Untoward events. You know this. You said it yourself. And I've also reminded you that you said it yourself."

Mike thought for a moment or two. Maybe I'm a different sort of talisman.

"I guess you must be." Arthur sighed. The emotional high brought about by the bank statement was starting to wear off.

*****

Using dreams as a starting point to the quest for Self was clearly not working out. Another rainy, depressing day went by. Arthur, lying on the lumpy, velvet sofa, contemplated the sitting room ceiling to clear his mind. It was the only uncluttered surface in the room. He focussed on what he had come to think of as the balanced Newtonian psyche - Jung's compensatory, homeostatic psyche. In analysing dreams, Jung had recommended repeatedly asking the question : "What conscious attitude could this dream be compensating for?"

Which meant that Arthur ought to be getting to grips with his conscious attitudes. The concept of analysing himself was not appealing. Under scientific scrutiny he had seemed to be largely characterised by noteworthy deficiencies. In a desultory fashion, and for want of some more pertinent and immediate plan, he consulted Jung on personality types.

Mike was not applying Jung in quite the same way. He listened vaguely to definitions of introverts and extroverts and thinking types with their logic, and feeling types with their emotional judgements and people who prioritise sensory input and have to smell everything, or see it, or touch it, before they can relate, and finally the intuitive types who run on unconscious perceptions. They all had their problems. As did he. He didn't even have the option of dreams to analyse, and using a catnip mouse to try and rebalance a personality was no picnic. Getting a piece of stuffed felt to show some sign of animation, for instance, involved a degree of self-deception that probably wasn't what he should be aspiring to. Altogether, a catnip mouse was proving a very poor substitute for the real thing, but he had been turning over the biological imperative business and decided that he didn't have to do everything cats did just because he was cat-shaped. He was, in fact, a talisman, a talisman with some work related problems to be sure, but a talisman that was embarked upon a huge spiritual task that cats normally never did, so, in the interests of prioritising what cats never did, he was trying to give up on the distracting business of doing what cats did do, i.e., stalk live mice. The catnip mouse was his way of weaning himself off it. The catnip mouse was Mike's nicotine gum. It would remove the imperative to hunt and make way for the more effective expression of his inner talisman.

"It says here", said Arthur glancing round, "that we have to remember the law of opposites. Which means that if one aspect of our personality is dominant enough to exclude its opposite from all expression, the suppressed side can suddenly pop out with surprising results … oh, yes … very funny!"

Mike had largely disappeared under the sofa during Arthur's ruminations but now he shot out covered in fluff. My mouse is stuck!

"Oh really! For a moment I actually thought you were listening." Arthur got onto the floor and poked helpfully at the catnip mouse with the handle of a feather duster which was, incidentally, the only action the duster had seen since its arrival courtesy of Arthur's mother. Mike watched him, thoughtfully. *What you were saying was boring. Jung never mentions cats at all.*

"Well, he wasn't a psychiatrist of cats."

Are there psychiatrists of cats?

"There are animal behaviourists. Even animal psychologists, but I doubt they are Jungians. We could go to one, if you insist, but I somehow suspect that you may be disappointed with a scientific opinion of you. It worked out that way for me and I wasn't even presenting myself as a talking kitten."

Then I won't bother. Mike fell to cleaning fluff from behind his ears. *Anyway, it's clear that I'm an extrovert - except on the days when I just want to sit under chairs. As for all the other stuff ... well ... obviously I'm a creature of the senses and powerfully intuitive, but on the whole I think I'm ...*" He stopped suddenly.

"Very small?" suggested Arthur after a few seconds of watching him wrestle ideas.

Not just that ... Mike looked around irritably for a moment or two.

"Underdeveloped?" supplied Arthur.

Undeveloped.

"That demonstrates a surprising grasp of nuance," said Arthur. "For a kitten."

I'm clearly going to be a very big cat one day. Mike looked pleased with himself.

"Yeah, yeah, yeah," said Arthur. "We all thought we'd be

big cats one day." And he went back to the book.

Mike made a piff-piff noise through his whiskers and decided to work some more with the catnip mouse. Getting to be a big cat, let alone a big cat talisman, never came easy to anyone.

Minutes passed and then Arthur said: "It says here, that a lot of scientists are extroverted thinking types. As a scientist manqué, I like to fancy that I was a thinker – until Carruthers Sloan made me stop – but I was never really what you could call an extrovert. Except I think Jung intended a slightly different meaning for the word." He paused for a moment to reflect upon the extroverted nature of scientists, then he said: "Introverts, on the other hand appear to be impractical and eccentric … well, that's hardly fair I must say … I can fix car engines. That's not impractical."

It is when the only car engines you can fix have to be fifty years old.

"Still practical," insisted Arthur. "What's worse, if I'm *impractical* and eccentric my suppressed opposite is an extroverted feeling type which could well surface in strange, unpredictable behaviour and childish naivety."

Mike looked up from killing his stuffed mouse with a slight air of self-consciousness. To re-establish aplomb, he fell to a consideration of what Arthur had been saying. You were a monkey scientist?

"Manqué. *Manqué!* It means failed."

So how did that come about then?

"Oh, I don't know." Arthur spoke quickly and dismissively. "It's not relevant. It was years ago."

And you think *I'm* the one not paying attention.

"Well, you aren't. Now is what matters and now I'm probably an introverted feeling type. Which looks rather good as it happens – a still waters running deep sort of guy. Very genuine. Not good at pretending to be what he isn't."

Arthur felt that this was the biggest psychological boost he'd received since some rich old lady he'd found one of those bijou residences for had announced: 'I think you're a very nice young man, and if I were even twenty years younger I'd be very tempted to seduce you'.

Mike gave him a look. And the suppressed side of the introverted feeling type?

Arthur scanned the page. "Oh, God. It looks like I'm liable to get caught up in primitive compulsions or mystical obsessions. I might even turn away from the world altogether."

He threw the book on the floor and looked at Mike despairingly. "Could talking to a kitten be classed as a mystical obsession?"

Mike gave the catnip mouse a final disgruntled flick. Depends on whether or not you're getting any response.

"Certainly nothing helpful," replied Arthur ungraciously. "This is hopeless, isn't it? None of this shows me exactly how I can get nearer to the finding of Self."

I want to hear about you being a monkey scientist.

"*It wasn't monkeys, for heaven's sake!*" Arthur snapped.

Mike stared at him with unflinching blue eyes. It was something I need to hear about.

"The trouble is," Arthur proceeded to ignore him. "Jung did not write his books for the purpose of do-it-yourself. He specifically avoids being prescriptive in any way. He won't even subscribe to any fixed meaning for relatively fixed symbols. Which makes dream analysis almost impossible for simpletons. Half a page on phallic symbols left me more confused than I was when I started it. He says here … listen

73

… 'I prefer to regard the symbol as the announcement of something unknown, hard to recognise and not to be fully determined.' In other words, human nature is complex and requires broad and multifarious approaches, none of which is going to be remotely within the grasp of Arthur Loveday of 29B, Acacia Avenue, London N3."

You seem upset.

"*I am upset*!"

Maybe we aren't being multifarious enough.

Arthur snorted.

What does multifarious mean, anyway?

"It means…," Arthur paused. For some reason the word was starting to ring a very loud bell in his head. "I think it means that it's time to go and see Madame Ibeg Boona."

Chapter Seven

Madame Ibeg Boona gave clients an appointed time and expected them to stick to it. So, at 3:30p.m. precisely on Friday 26th November Arthur, who had been accustomed to appointments and punctuality, turned up on her doorstep and rang the bell.

A noticeable fog was drawing the afternoon to a premature close. The traffic sounded muffled and the street lights were reduced to fuzzily haloed glows. From the eaves of Hampstead's imposing houses came tell-tale heavy drips that told of leaf-filled guttering.

Arthur pulled up the collar of his overcoat and eyed the brass monkey's head doorknocker with suspicion. He had avoided using it lest it metamorphose, Dickens-like, into something even less attractive and a great deal more startling. He was just deciding that the bell didn't work when the door was suddenly opened with a business-like flourish and Madame Ibeg Boona stepped dramatically into the frame, filling it from side to side, and almost from top to bottom. She was a particularly commanding shade of black, and wore a purple turban and long, flowing, flowery robes. Even to someone as tall as Arthur she looked immense. Unassailable. Totemic. She had sparkling eye whites and terrific teeth, but beauty didn't come into it. Majesty did. She was impossible to age. She could have been immortal. Death would have quailed before her.

Mike, who had insisted on wearing a purple collar to show respect for what he had decided would be a meeting with foreign royalty, was delighted to be colour-matched with her crown.

"It's a turban," Arthur hissed.

There's a jewel in it.

"I doubt it's a real jewel."

"It's a real jewel. Please come in." Her voice carried the resonance of ages.

The hallway was gracious in an English country house sort of way, but there were exotic carvings in ebony and ivory on the console tables and powerful landscapes of burning deserts and blood red skies on the walls. For the purpose, perhaps, of soothing those of a nervous disposition, there was also a prominent display of tastefully framed degrees and diplomas. But, in spite of such an extensive and mainstream education, Madame Ibeg Boona carried in her soul the flickering wildness of ancient beliefs and arcane methodologies. Contrary to Mike's conviction, she had never been an African queen but, long ago, in another land with fiercer sun and darker darkness, she had been a voodoo priestess.

The drawing room had oak floors, Knole sofas, and zebra skin rugs. There was a fire in the grate and, in spite of the dank stillness of the afternoon, the chimney sucked shrieking red flames up and over the cast-iron register plate with an implacable, hollow roar.

"So," said Madame Ibeg Boona, motioning them to sit down, "a white kitten. How very interesting."

There was a pause during which Mike felt that he'd

received a compliment and Arthur wondered how an impressive, not to say intimidating, woman like this would calibrate the word interesting.

"Tea?" she asked.

"Thank you." said Arthur. "He can hear. The kitten."

"Naturally."

There was a trolley laid out with china and cakes, and a spirit stove for the boiling of a silver tea kettle. Madame Ibeg Boona presided over this with the aplomb of a dowager duchess and a great deal more affability. While she involved with the tea-making process, Arthur thought it would be appropriate to acquaint her with his situation. She held up her hand to stop him. Apparently, Dr. Ibeg Boona had already done sufficient in this regard.

Nevertheless, Arthur felt obliged to keep up a level of theatre in order to draw attention away from the fact that Mike, excited by the compliments that he had been receiving, had upended a large bowl of potpourri onto a zebra skin rug. When Madame Ibeg Boona's back was turned, Arthur hastily occupied himself with surreptitious scooping and sweeping, and when she faced him he set up what he hoped was a riveting line in complaint about the uncooperative nature of his dreams, and the irritating vagueness of Dr. Jung's advice on how to deconstruct them.

Mike had nothing to say about dreams because he was convinced that his accident could be more effectively covered up by hiding the potpourri under the rug rather than putting it back in the bowl, and so he was busying himself to this end in a determined fashion.

"Lapsang Souchong?" asked Madame Ibeg Boona, "Or Earl Grey?"

"Could I have some sort of builders' tea?" asked Arthur,

who thought one tasted like smoke and the other like perfume.

"It may be," observed Madam Ibeg Boona, handling a Typhoo teabag with sugar tongs, "that you don't want too much recall of your dreams because you don't want to hear what they have to say."

"I doubt that," said Arthur. "Because there's not the remotest chance of my working out what they have to say. Dr. Jung was at least very clear on that point. He confused me for several pages precisely in order that I should get it."

"The whole point of a dream interpretation", said Madame Ibeg Boona, "is that it should be acceptable to the dreamer, and bring about a degree of realisation in him. He should accomplish this without a set of imposed guidelines. A therapist can suggest, of course. A person will only accept those suggestions with which he is secretly in accord. But, the greatest purpose is that the person should be brought, by a process of unconscious metaphysics, to a point where he begins to look at himself, or a situation, in a more illuminating way."

"You can stop that now," she added, handing Arthur a cup and saucer. "I do have a vacuum cleaner and that was a bowl of relaxing herbs which I'm sure the pair of you have already inhaled to a more than sufficient degree."

Mike sneezed.

"Bless you," said Madam Ibeg Boona. "Would you like some milk?" She reached for a china saucer.

"The oracular dream, Arthur," she said as she poured, "those that Jung also referred to as big dreams – that is, dreams that feel highly significant and prominently archetypal - only come when you are ready." She bent down and put the saucer of milk on the oak floor in front of Mike. Straightening up, she offered Arthur a plate of cakes. He selected a piece of Battenberg.

Madame Ibeg Boona watched him reflectively as he took a polite bite. Then she said: "It's quite fascinating really. A Masai warrior would have come with a white lion. A native American with a white buffalo, or maybe a white wolf. An Irishman with a white horse and a Scot with a white stag, perhaps. But an Englishman – well let's be frank – an Englishman would never have come at all in precisely this way but, now that one has finally managed it, he turns up carrying a white kitten. And they say that the powers-that-be have no sense of humour."

Arthur had no idea how he was supposed to react to this but Madame Ibeg Boona had already moved on. "So, tell me precisely, Arthur, why it is you have finally come to see me. Precisely, now."

But Arthur's anxieties were generalised as well as precise. 'I don't understand' was about as precise as he could get just at the moment.

"Understand what?"

Arthur cleared his mouth of cake. Damien Price's comments on change suddenly came to him. "Well, put it this way: I could have an oracular dream tomorrow. It could be analysed out to tell me that I've always had a deep and abiding need to be a carpenter. Fine. I could recognise and accept that. I could go and get myself a saw, and some pieces of wood, and make a table. But that wouldn't change me, would it? How does conscious recognition, even understanding, of anything actually *change* you? How do I become a better version of myself? Not a better employed version of myself, but this true, whole Self I keep hearing so much about? How does this actually happen?"

Madame Ibeg Boona poured out her Lady Grey tea using a tea strainer, added a carefully considered amount of milk and a raw cane sugar cube, then said: "Psychology, Arthur, has long recognised that to bring about change one has to get past the conscious mind. Talk and analysis frequently produce understanding but not any fundamental alteration. So, there are scientific approaches, neurolinguistics for example, hypnotism for another, that are designed to get at the unconscious mind. Dr. Jung, however, was a visionary. He took a step beyond provable science – though not beyond logical reasoned argument. His view of the unconscious moved into the realms of metaphysics. His was the psychology of the soul."

Madame Ibeg Boona took an experimental sip of her tea and nodded with satisfaction.

"I still can't see how changes within me are brought about," insisted Arthur. "Wouldn't I be better off with neuroliguistics?"

Madame Ibeg Boona took another sip of tea. "You make a fundamental mistake, Arthur. You miss the point of metaphysics. You think yours is the only energy, the only power, complicit in this. You, Arthur Loveday, the man, the ego, you don't produce a change. You *allow* a change. You create the space in which the change can happen. You grant the unconscious freedom of expression, you try to understand, you accept the proposition, as it were, and that which is beyond any of us to really understand, does the rest."

"The men with kingfishers' wings?"

"And horns apparently. The collective unconscious can express itself in extreme and disturbing ways. One has to be prepared for these things."

"Didn't Jung just imagine them?"

"Jung firmly believed that these things were not of his generating. He believed, as I do, that the psyche is an 'a priori' fact of nature."

"Which is?"

"A phenomenon irreducible to any factor other than itself."

"So, not just imagination then?"

"No. His process was an uncovering. A confrontation with what is in the cosmic abyss."

Arthur thought about this for a moment or two. "And you can't say anything more about how the change is wrought, other than it's metaphysical?"

"I can't explain metaphysics, Arthur. Metaphysics is considered speculation. It is theoretical philosophy as the ultimate science of Being or Knowing. I don't precisely know what it is that philosophy Ph.D.s and professors argue about. My job on this earth, one of them at least, is to get Being and Knowing to help us live better and more fulfilled lives. That was Jung's job too. Maybe, I have some methods that would have stretched even his open-mindedness, but, there we are. What I *can* tell you is that, in this business, intention is all. You do the inner work, the preparation for psychological adjustment, with an open mind and a hopeful heart and then the life force finds a way to work through and you change, and life becomes better, more manageable." She paused for a moment. "I would class the life force as divine. Maybe you wouldn't. Maybe you would prefer to think of some habitually trodden neural pathways somehow rerouting themselves and forming new connections. And maybe that happens too. It really doesn't matter. The question still remains. How and under what aegis? You know what I think. You know what Jung thought."

81

Arthur reviewed this silently for a few moments. So many leaps of faith. So much 'flying in the face of …'. Madame Ibeg Boona offered him the plate of cakes again. Absently, he took another piece of Battenberg.

"You can believe all of this," she replaced the cake plate on the trolley, "or, you can scoff at it. My pragmatic advice to you, at the moment, would be to believe it. Because the alternative …." She stopped suddenly and changed ground. "You've come early to this," she went on conversationally. "Normally, the emptiness doesn't come until you've passed forty. Young men are usually preoccupied with the biological and the financial. No time over for peering into the void. You weren't enraptured with the property business?"

"It wasn't enraptured with me."

Madame Ibeg Boona wasn't interested in any opinions that the property business might have held about Arthur. "Have you ever been enraptured with anything?"

"Nothing I could have."

"I agree that there is no use crying for the moon, but I get the feeling that you long ago stopped even reaching for a telescope."

Arthur chewed silently on the cake for a few moments, then took a careful drink of tea and said in level, neutral tones: "Jung is still much respected for his work, but the scientific opinion is that he just went a bit mad for awhile. Not full blown psychosis but … you know … maddish. That he had hallucinations generated by a stressed brain."

Madame Ibeg Boona nodded in satisfaction. "So, now we come to it, don't we, Arthur? Finally. You've been struggling to go along with things but now you are starting to panic."

"What things?"

Madame Ibeg Boona laughed. "Haven't we ignored the

elephant in the room for long enough?"

Having finished his milk, Mike had climbed up onto the sofa and had been rather drowsily studying the ocelot spots on the scatter cushions. An overdose of relaxing herbs had almost sent him to sleep but, at the word elephant, he came to with a little jerk and looked around with offended dignity. I'm a talisman not an elephant.

"It's just an expression," said Arthur automatically. "We know what you are."

"And there we have it," said Madame Ibeg Boona with deep satisfaction. "Don't you think that this is a little beyond the power of neurolinguistics to fix?"

Arthur caught his breath and looked at her with a burgeoning mixture of hope and anxiety.

"Let the kitten go back to sleep for a moment," she said. "He needs his little naps. He's very new, you understand."

"What did he say?" Arthur hardly dared ask the question. His heart was thumping. "You heard, didn't you?"

"He said: 'I'm a talisman not an elephant'."

Relief poured through Arthur like a high spring tide.

"But it's not given to everyone. This hearing. This opportunity to hear," continued Madame Ibeg Boona gravely. "You see, Arthur, your process of deep change has already begun. I should think it started when you lost your job. You felt drained. Done. Devoid of either rational thought or raging emotion. You were an empty vessel. And nature abhors a vacuum – the scientists taught us that. So, your emptiness made way for the doors of perception to swing open. And through them, Arthur, your inner being screamed for help. It cried out in despair - right into the void. And you got an answer."

There was a long silence, then Arthur's relief suddenly

gave way to a rather churlish surge of indignation. "I got a talking kitten! He's extremely loveable but, on occasions … Well, you saw him with the potpourri …" He paused and then gave a resigned sigh. "I guess he's just the sort of talisman I would get."

Madame Ibeg Boona laughed quietly, enjoying a moment of deep, private humour that was totally lost upon Arthur and then she said: "Long ago, in the deserts of Africa, there was an enduring belief that the god-hero was always made to look foolish. Foolishness, simplicity, naïveté almost to the point of idiocy was recognised as a divinely inspired state that had to be served as such."

Arthur declined to comment. After a moment or two he said :"Could you tell me what you know about the void?"

"Well … you are aware that we are mostly space? That an atom is almost entirely space?"

"Yes." It was a very cautious 'yes'. Hard to tell what would come next if Madame Ibeg Boona got into the cabbage patch of atomic physics.

"In that space, which is esoterically dubbed the void, is the quantum realm of our real consciousness. The universal mind. The collective unconscious. And ultimately, the All That Is. Or God. Depends upon your viewpoint. 'A rose by any other name …' to purloin Shakespeare. Awareness of this quantum entanglement is what we call enlightenment."

"So I'm either mad or enlightened?

"You are neither at this point. The gateway has opened, and you're on a journey. In many cultures, over many ages, individuals have gone through this sort of thing. Sometimes voluntarily, as would a shaman for instance, sometimes not. Does it always end well? I won't lie to you, Arthur …. The conscious mind has to bear this. It has to deal with it, integrate it and survive it. To use a Christian analogy, one could say that this is something in the nature of the forty days and forty nights. But, it's a long, hard trip through that desert for an ordinary man. Your job now, Arthur, is to weather and contain the process. You didn't need Jung to ignite it, but you do need him to get you through it. The attainment of Self, of finding out who you truly are, is never easy when you have been thrust into it in quite this extreme a way. But … given luck …"

"Tell me about this luck," said Arthur.

"Ah …" Madame Ibeg Boona spoke in gentle but serious tones. "Now, we come to the destiny of the white kitten. Let me explain …"

Mike woke up from his herbally induced sleep with a sudden feeling of immense portent. He knew at once that this was his time. That the defining moment of his brief career as a talisman was already upon him. Excited, as only the very young and very innocent can get, he sprang to his feet amongst the squashy cushions and gave a tremendous and exultant miaow. But, the effort of producing such a very big miaow from such a very small body, together with a certain haziness about the word sacrifice, meant that he missed the part where he had to die.

Arthur, considerably shaken, but determined to proceed with a degree of cross-cultural respect, said: "So, this is what? Some voodoo way of petitioning the gods? I get help, if I'm lucky, but I get a dead kitten for sure?"

Madame Ibeg Boona sighed patiently. "Look at it less like a sacrifice and more like a trade of energies."

"In which I get a dead body?"

"In which you get a relatively painless path to progress."

"How?"

"Psychic energy, like physical energy, can neither be created nor destroyed. It can be transformed into an alternate experience through death and rebirth."

Arthur didn't respond. What, within the realm of politeness, could he possibly say?

"Would it help if I drew a physics analogy for you?" Madame Ibeg Boona offered. "Have you any understanding of potential and kinetic energy?"

Arthur nodded.

"We have potential energy here, in the kitten, incredibly powerful but held. Trapped even. And we ask for it to be turned into kinetic energy. For you. So that you can move forward as a person and get on with life. Now. In the instant. We take a shortcut as it were."

"But we still have a dead kitten?"

"Possibly."

"You mean he could survive?"

"Not as such. Most likely, we'll have no kitten at all."

By this point, Arthur had been rendered incapable of constructive thought. Quite apart from the wildness of the premise, and the appalling price that had to be paid, it occurred to him that this relatively painless path to progress might be much like that panoramic view of the city promised in estate agents' brochures. You would have to keep climbing onto the roof to get it.

"I think," he said stiffly, "I'll have to decline your offer."

Mike looked confused. Madam Ibeg Boona was gracious. "A queasiness about killing kittens, eh?" she suggested gently.

"Bit of a national trait, I think you'll find," said Arthur.

Madame Ibeg Boona agreed wholeheartedly. "By and large," she said. "The English would rather drive round the kitten and kill the man. Is that what you would have me do?

Because this kitten could make everything so much easier for you. It has the potential to be a very effective sacrificial lamb. In the biblical sense. We could ensure that you become whole and not …" she paused, "… lost."

Arthur said nothing for a moment or two. He asked for no amplification of the word lost. He could feel its resonance all too clearly in the great, dark, empty cavern that lay within his chest. He stood up. "I bow to your knowledge of these things because I have no concept of them," he said rather formally. "All I know is that, in sacrificing Mike to make things easier for me, my motives would lack something that I strongly believe they ought to have. I just can't accept that a sacrifice made at the behest of the beneficiary can be the right thing to do."

Madame Ibeg Boona regarded him steadily. The jewel in her turban glowed with a disconcerting inner fire. "You may suffer a great deal for this choice, Arthur," she said, "and I'm not sure that the kitten agrees with it. It may be that he's not talking to you, just now."

"I doubt he had a full understanding of all the implications. Besides which, I don't think there was really a choice," said Arthur.

"Oh, indeed there was. Indeed there was. But, as my good cousin the doctor no doubt warned you, there are no free lunches. Not ultimately. Not anywhere. Not ever. So maybe you chose wisely."

"I doubt it," said Arthur. "Choosing wisely never seems to have been my strong point, so I prefer to regard this as no choice at all."

"Unfortunately," warned Madame Ibeg Boona, "talismans are very individual and they are difficult things to fully understand or predict. The kitten's greatest power may turn out to be the one you have just declined to use."

"But, not in my eyes," said Arthur. And he picked Mike up from the sofa and hugged him. Mike gave him a sulky, baffled look and turned his face away. Arthur sighed and turned back to Madame Ibeg Boona. "I'm very grateful for your time," he said. "You've helped my understanding, even though I was not prepared to take all of your advice."

"I expect that's how it was supposed to be," she said philosophically. "But allow me to give you a little more. And less equivocal. You have given up on too much in your life. Love. Aspiration. I cannot clearly see what the aspiration was but I know that you walked away from something that was very special to you. But this, Arthur, this that is happening to you now, there is no walking away. You have to get through it. Whatever it takes to do that, you have to find. Do you understand me?"

"I do."

They shook hands, and then Arthur set off into the foggy December night clutching a silently protesting Mike to his chest. Strangely enough, he took his leave with a sense of regret and loss. In spite of the jewelled knife and blood soaked altar that he felt sure she had in the basement, Madame Ibeg Boona had been undeniably appealing. And he'd found her apparent familiarity with the unnerving, the bizarre and the potentially horrific, oddly reassuring.

For her part, she watched him thoughtfully as he faded off into the fog, and then she nodded to herself and went back inside to make a fresh cup of Lady Grey tea.

Chapter Eight

"You'll have to come out sooner or later," said Arthur. "For one thing, my sister's here and wants to see you, and when Polly wants something it's a very brave kitten that defies her."

I don't want to come out. I was meant to be some sort of powerful lamb. Madame Ibeg Boona said so.

Mike was sitting under the bed, elaborately rigid amidst a littering of dustballs.

"*She was going to kill you,*" said Arthur. Up to now, he'd avoided bald statements like this, but the moment for plain speaking had arrived.

She was not! That's a horrid thing to say! Madame Ibeg Boona thought I was special.

"You *are* special," said Arthur with rising exasperation. "But the word used was *sacrificial*, a *sacrificial* lamb. And just because you were high on potpourri at the time and didn't quite get it ..."

"Who on earth is Madame Ibeg Boona, and what is all this talk of sacrifice?"

Polly Loveday (married but disinclined to be called Polly Parry and especially not Pauline Parry) was Arthur's twin sister, and she had all the forcefulness, exigency, resolution, aspiration, focus, etc., etc. that Arthur ostensibly lacked. Her inkblot test would have indicated that she could have run a country, a world, a complete universe - but not necessarily along democratic lines. Polly was that most contrary of things, the pro-active ice maiden. She managed to remain self-containedly calm and distant at the same time as prodding people to heights of accomplishment or fury (and occasionally both) with forensically sharp argument. Even the head of the board quaked before her - though he quaked even more at the prospect of losing her.

Polly was a troubleshooting lawyer in a huge company. Nobody wanted to lose her, especially not the shareholders, though it has to be said that her manner would have seriously condemned a less strikingly attractive woman. The arctic blond hair in its efficient chignon, the perfect nose with the black framed reading glasses half way down it, the 'on the knee' pencil slim skirts and four-inch heels meant that men, in particular, were willing to forgive in Polly a generous measure of what could be conservatively described as bossiness.

"I am in awe," she said now (without waiting for an answer to her question because conversation aimed at kittens did not really merit analysis) "in absolute awe of the amount of mess you can exist alongside. There are wheelie bins, provided by this very borough council, and there are cleaning fluids, produced by industrial chemists, then carefully marketed by highly paid smart alecs so as to be indispensable to the average consumer, and yet ..." she paused. "*Arthur, get up!* My urge to see this kitten is not so powerful that I require you to grovel under the bed in search of it."

"I'm coming," said Arthur, "in a minute."

"Too late," said Polly. "I have children to collect, rival companies to outwit and a life to live."

When Arthur finally went out into the living room, he

found she'd left him a note: 'I came, I saw, I went home sick.'
He pulled a face and then went on into the kitchen where he
put Mike on the table, amidst a scattering of cornflakes, and
began dusting him off. "I wouldn't lie to you," he said. "It
was an exceptional task that Madame Ibeg Boona wanted you
to perform but I couldn't agree to it. And, as you were to
undertake it on my behalf, I believe it was my choice to
make."

Mike looked mollified, though he didn't wholeheartedly
feel it. He'd been hoping that, somewhere in this lamb
business, there might have been some revealing subplot in
which he discovered what sex he was. It was a subject he felt
diffident about bringing up in the normal way of things.
Confusion over whether he was a male or a female could lead
critical observers to the conclusion that he was feeble-minded
when he wasn't. He was just a kitten, or maybe a failed lamb,
with a few biologically consistent, intellectual handicaps which
he fully intended to overcome. Of course, gender might have
been an irrelevancy in the world of lambs so there might have
been no revelation. No revelation, and he might never have
seen Arthur again. He looked up. I think I'd like something to
eat now, please.

Arthur was uneasily aware that very soon after becoming
incensed with his overflowing waste bins, and the fact that
her Jimmy Choos had stuck to the kitchen floor, his sister
would contact their parents and demand that something be
done about him. And, accordingly, within three hours he was
invited (commanded) to Sunday lunch for premedication with
roast beef, followed by deep and probing questions. As was
his lifelong habit, he took the line of least resistance and
agreed to go. Furthermore, in order not to provoke, he had a
shave and a shower and found a clean set of clothes. His

mother was not one of those who thought that because one had been made redundant one could go about the place dressed anyhow. He could not decide if all of this preparatory acquiescence made him craven or cooperative.

In the event, his mother's attention was seized by the fact that he turned up with Mike under his arm. He explained that Mike was a talisman, and so obviously could not be left at home.

"Mike is an odd name for a kitten," observed Mrs. Loveday, who would have unfailingly called him Snowy. She knew what a talisman was, broadly speaking, but she chose to regard this piece of information as inextricably linked to her son's current outbreak of oddness - which was something to be addressed presently, and not precipitately. It was obvious to her that a full frontal attack on the doorstep could serve no useful purpose.

Mrs. Loveday was visually subdued but mentally robust. She wore browns, fawns and creams and trousers with pleated fronts and sharp creases. Unlike her daughter, Polly, whose attractions were occasionally (and most improperly, of course) referred to as 'librarian porn', Mrs. Loveday had actually been a librarian. Family photographs, household paperwork and kitchen utensils were rigorously filed. She was not given to frivolity but now and then she broke out into discreet and tasteful earrings. Her one vanity was her hair, and it was noticeable that it held no trace of grey. On a monthly basis, she emerged from Mimi's salon with highly organised, rich brown curls.

Mr. Loveday had been something high-up in the post office in the days when the G.P.O. had been a revered and inviolate institution. Pained by its continual bowdlerisation, he had welcomed early retirement though he was not able to relax much beyond the exchanging of his smart, striped shirts for country style, Viyella checks. He wore these on a daily basis with virtually interchangeable, tweedy ties which he coerced and cajoled into the smallest knots to which they would submit. Somewhat in contrast, he had an upended shock of mad professor hair which had proceeded from a curious shade of buffy blonde to a curious shade of buffy grey. Unlike his wife, he was not prejudiced against grey, though he viewed men who wore grey shoes with a degree of suspicion.

After the preliminary greetings, Arthur sat on the sofa (regency stripes, maroon and cream, firmly stuffed to discourage overt relaxation) and listened to the pair of them rattling crockery and conversing in tragic whispers in the kitchen. It was not a large house. Twenty minutes drive to the west of the capital it had been chosen, on his parent's retirement, for its proximity to common land and its ease of upkeep. It was a place of fitted carpets, reproduction furniture and fully tiled, easily swabbed utility spaces. The Lovedays were walkers, not fixer-uppers, and they had never been drawn to the historical or the quaint, unless it was owned by the National Trust.

The table at the dining end of the room in which Arthur was sitting had a white cloth and placemats with pictures of roses stamped on them. Mr. Loveday grew roses in a 'must just keep the garden decent' sort of way. Presently, he came in and offered his son a glass of something that approximated (this being December) to Christmas punch. There was, at any rate, a pronounced smell of cloves about it. Mike, who had not yet become accustomed to car journeys at speed, complained that it had reawoken his queasiness.

"Does the kitten want something?" Mr. Loveday asked.

"I think he feels slightly sick," said Arthur. "It's the car trip. I built him a booster box so he could be safely confined and have a good view but he wouldn't stop watching the traffic whizz by on the M3. It'll pass."

Mike wasn't so sanguine. Are you sure?

"Yes. That's how car sickness works."

Are you sure?

"Trust me. It'll go off in a minute. A bit of food will help. Lunch won't be long."

Mr. Loveday kept opening his mouth as if to say something and then shutting it again. Arthur wondered if he was about to commence 'the talk'. The normal procedure in the Loveday household was to raise awkward topics at the table. This meant that people who didn't want to listen had to make a pronounced statement to that effect by leaving halfway through a meal. Arthur was rarely up to flagrant gestures of this kind. He pondered this while he sipped the punch and his father apparently aborted the urge to speak and began adjusting the fire with its pretend coals and real gas flames.

"Time to sit up, dears," Mrs. Loveday called from the kitchen. They took their places at the table. While the horseradish was circulating, Mr. Loveday, in response to significant glances, began clearing his throat. In an unprecedented pre-emptive move, Arthur decided to speak first. He had a plan, he said. Enormous relieved smiles greeted this. The assumption obviously was that there'd been some sudden and plucky career realignment. He had a plan, Arthur went on, to examine his unconscious mind and find his true Self. It was a quest that inevitably had whiskers and overflowing wastebins as occasional side-effects, but it came with full professional backing from his doctor, a counsellor with a Ph.D. and a big, black lady with an M.Sc. in esoteric psychology and a sideline in voodoo.

There was absolutely nothing else that he could even have imagined saying that would have stunned his parents more. The emotions that coursed through their normally placid brains could not be translated into speech.

Arthur took advantage of their paralysis to deliver some calm and balanced exposition, which he hoped would clarify his decision to embrace the Jungian theory that the purpose of life was individuation. The parental silence began to ring like a fire alarm as inflammatory words like psychiatrist, collective unconscious, visions, neuropsychic, numinous and self (qualified with a capital S) were regurgitated at them across their nicely laid out lunch table.

Mr. and Mrs. Loveday were pragmatists through and through. They did not have unconscious minds. They were always in full occupation of the mental forefront, ready to rationalise, rectify, remedy and, above all, *act*. Unconscious minds were for the mentally impaired and the physically idle. They were the route to hell in a handcart by way of drugs, cardboard boxes and sex acts too awful to mention. The Lovedays used the word hell merely for effect. There was, of course, no such place.

Just as there was no such thing as a vision. Mr. Loveday could not even recall a dream of any substance. For him the word vision equated to a plan for further employment, with solid saving, a sizeable pension and a commitment to an exhaustive medical with a recommended private physician. And not one of African extraction. Or Asian. Or Chinese. Or any extraction at all that was predisposed to the fanciful. And, since hearing about Jung, he was beginning to feel that there was more to be held against the Swiss than cuckoo clocks, dubious bankers, and their country's egregious neutrality.

Mike was shut in the kitchen, sitting disconsolately on cold Italian tiles. At the onset of lunch, he'd been confined to the realms of impermeable flooring by Mrs. Loveday who'd talked, rather rudely in his opinion, about casual potty habits. As the touted talisman on this trip, he'd expected better treatment. And better food. Some sort of ambrosial kitten chow. As it was, he was looking at a frothy, grey pile of mechanically pre-masticated Sunday roast. Not being a dog, he was not in favour of food that looked like it had been eaten once before. He was in possession of a feline fastidiousness that he felt was being disobligingly overlooked.

On the plus side, he could still hear everything that was being said. Mrs. Bunce at Cat Rescue would have been astonished at the acuity of his hearing. All he needed was for his understanding to catch up. In the meantime, he had to be alert for words he didn't quite get. Words like sacrificial. Surprisingly enough, the giant non-event that had been the reading lessons must have borne some sort of fruit. Most of what was being said, he got. And what he also got, even through the irritations of a closed door and a very cold bottom, was the significance of the silences. Arthur had made a definite start on the road to individuation by rendering his parents completely speechless. Mike twitched his whiskers and decided to try the roast beef purée after all.

Back in the dining room, the senior Lovedays were still dealing with feelings that were altogether less satisfying. If this was Arthur's true Self starting to emerge, then its further development could be an alarming prospect. So much worse than anything Polly's telephone call had conjured up. And it had conjured quite a lot: personal hygiene crises, dirty flat crises, long unemployment queues crises, rent crises, even 'nobody loves me' crises. Straightforward psychotherapy they could have coped with - though it would have been a foreign country to them - but the hallucinatory quality of what they'd just been told …! Mrs. Loveday had, in fact, dissociated herself from most of it after the word 'voodoo'.

Finally, the horseradish sauce boat in her hand began to twitch. The knowledge that the food had to be going cold returned her to earth. She congratulated herself on having heated the plates thoroughly. She busied herself with condiments. This was the real world in front of her – sliced and smartly served.

"I think the beef will be nice and tender," she said. "He's a good butcher we have here."

Mr. Loveday made some approving noises about the roast potatoes. Arthur, eating steadily and with evident appetite, agreed with him. He felt oddly optimistic – a state of mind that must have visited him entirely upon a whim, because there was no immediate vindication for it. Historically, parental silences had never proved auspicious. Pudding came and went without conversation branching away from the subject of custard. Afterwards, Arthur offered to help clear but the plates were taken from his hands.

"I think you must have more pressing things to do," his mother said.

"Like tablets to take?" suggested Mr. Loveday, as Arthur went to collect up Mike.

"Hush," Mrs. Loveday looked conspiratorial.

"Well, I think we have to say *something*." Mr. Loveday had finally recovered his wits but Mrs. Loveday's were slightly ahead.

. "He's obviously into some unfortunate phase," she whispered. "But I think we need time to consider our approach. We don't want to alienate him, or frighten him away. He could end up in some sort of hostel, living on charity soups."

"I still think we need to say something."

"Such as?"

As they gathered together at the front door for the departure, Arthur's father cleared his throat. "Son," he said, "I would just like to mention that I have some reservations about your relationship with that kitten."

Chapter Nine

The conviction with which Arthur had addressed his parents was not deep-rooted. His faith in Jung's ideas, in the process, in all manner of things including his ability to get through it all, began to waver as the image of Madame Ibeg Boona and her absolute belief, in all its unimpeachable vividness, no longer filled his mind. And the kitten, sitting on the rug washing its whiskers, started to look less and less like some powerful talisman, and more and more like a symptom of serious mental disfunction.

Mike looked up. Can't we do something? It doesn't seem like much of a quest just sitting here. Quest is a doing sort of word.

"That's a verb," said Arthur absently, running his hand through his hair. "A verb is a doing word."

Well, then we should go questing.

"In what way, exactly?"

Read the bit about creative play again. Didn't Jung get to understand the unconscious when he was out playing in the garden? Isn't that when the fairies turned up?

"They weren't fairies."

There was a beautiful woman called something or other. I remember that much. But anything will do. I'm not getting much of a shot at being a talisman just sitting here on the mat. Read. Read it again.

"I'm not really sure I got creative play," said Arthur. "I remember writing down a significant sentence or two about it." He opened his notebook listlessly. "Here it is. 'Fully aware as he is of the social unimportance of his creative activity, the patient looks upon it as a way of working out his own development.' I've also written and underlined 'to understand the meaning of his individual life the patient must learn to experience his inner being'. Old news, Dr. Jung. Old news." Arthur sighed.

Mike climbed up onto his knee. I remember this. This was about painting and drawing. But not to produce art because that involves the ego and is therefore counterproductive, Dr. Jung said. You have to just represent, as fully as possible, whatever's working within you. Dreams and fantasy and stuff. Read it. Read some more .

Obediently, Arthur read: "If the patient can come to an intellectual and emotional understanding of his work and consciously integrate it, discoveries like this can shift the centre of gravity of the personality."

But could we shift your personality about outside somehow? Does it say we can do that? I'm not really in a sitting and watching you paint sort of mood. They are the wrong verbs altogether for me today. I'm in a different sort of doing word mood. What does the garden look like?

"It's a moonscape full of random bits of appropriated public property,"

What's that?

"In this case it's traffic cones and road signs and the like. Anything that proved heistable on a Saturday night."

And the point?

"Obscure. It's just something that comes over young men when they drink too much alcohol. Police cones, for instance, become as catnip to them."

Odd.

"Very. And I never understood how they always ended up in the taxi with me. I know why, of course. It's because I was the only one who didn't live in a minimalist converted loft in a fashionable post-industrial building."

And the only one stupid enough to let it happen to him.

"I prefer to think of myself as innocent."

Well, let's go and look at this public property, then. Maybe you brought a beautiful young woman home with it and she is sitting there waiting for us.

Arthur had never brought a beautiful young woman home with him - they'd all ended up in those minimalist converted lofts in the post-industrial buildings. And he felt pretty sure that one wouldn't turn up now, even if it had been flaming June and his garden a festival of roses. Which was fine by him, because his failure to magic a general run of real-world beautiful women into 29B, Acacia Avenue hadn't weighed at all heavily upon him. Beyond the entertainment value it provided for Damien Price, that is. Damien's slick moves were not confined to the selling of houses, and he was very fond of trying to initiate Arthur into this alternate variety of slickness - largely, it has to be said, because in the setting of a bar or a nightclub, it was a great provider of pantomime. The fact that it never took at a level beyond this was, in Damien's opinion, solid testimony to something exasperating about Arthur. Arthur, himself, had never been exasperated by it. His requirement for non-specific female diversion of a Saturday night was minimal. Any progress that he might have made in the beautiful woman department (and there was more of it than he ever recognised) merely reminded him that this was not the beautiful woman of his dreams. And once he had that firmly in his head, why would he need to keep reminding himself?

Sighing heavily, he got up off the sofa. The flat was gloomy and he felt gloomy and Mike was insistent about going outside. Barring the disturbing arrival of some beautiful woman from the collective unconscious, what had they to lose except the circulation in their extremities?

The estate agent in Arthur had always queried the judgement of his landlord in attaching the garden of number 29 to the basement flat. But there it was, he had access and he had dominion. A state of affairs that he'd largely ignored up till now.

Mike had never been up the basement steps into the garden. He felt quite excited. He chose a lime green collar for the occasion and, when he finally viewed the messy moonscape from the vantage point of Arthur's arms, he was thoroughly stimulated by it. Struggling impatiently to be put down, he began an adventurous scrambling over a pile of broken flower pots and empty bottles. In no time at all, he'd caught two dead leaves and a worm. The worm, in its search for organic matter with which to replenish the exhausted earth, was halfway down its wormhole. Obviously, it did not like being diverted in its task and it set up an angry and self-righteous wriggling. It was busy restoring an ecosystem, improving the foundations for all life, all growth. What, pray, was this irritating kitten doing? Mike removed his paw. I'm a talisman. We're on a quest to find our true selves. The worm disappeared down its hole, crackling its leaf indignantly. Obviously, it did not approve of advanced consciousness for kittens.

After more encounters with invertebrates, none of them particularly encouraging, Mike sat in a sunbeam. Largely shaded by buildings and the desperate, reaching branches of starved lilac trees, the garden was a dank and unlovely place. Such sunbeams as managed to make their way down to a kitten on the ground were powerful and motivated sunbeams. Mike drew strength from them. Closing his eyes, he took a little nap.

In much the same way as he had done at Madame Ibeg Boona's, he awoke with a start and a strong presentiment. Maybe he'd had one of those dreams he was supposed to remember. He blinked. One blink brought him to full alertness. Another blink completely wiped away anything that had gone on in his head while he was asleep. But the presentiment was still there.

"Puss wussie."

Mike looked round. A white ball of wool was forcing its way through the larch lap fence. A white ball of wool that twinkled with a golden, siren glitter. He watched it for a moment or two while it danced and twirled, describing arabesques in the wintry air. He knew that he ought to be beyond unquenchable attractions to highly suspect balls of wool, but there was something inside him that responded helplessly to it. Maybe balls of wool were powerful symbols in feline folk memory. They were no longer common in the real world but, once upon a time, every kitten in the land had known how to map out its future with a ball of wool. Sometimes these turned out to be briefly uncomfortable futures – especially when the balls of wool came attached to half-knitted jumpers. Fortunately for kittens, half-knitted jumpers were also a thing of the past, so it seemed to Mike that the odds of there being one on the other side of the fence were pretty slim. He pondered these things as his whiskers began to curl and his tail began to twitch.

"Come on, little cat. This is what you need."

Mike's tail stopped twitching. A rolling eye appeared at a knothole in the fence. The eye disappeared and a boney finger worked its way through. The ball of wool became more active in its sparkly dance, attracting those powerful sunbeams to itself and incorporating them into its radiant allure. It was almost certainly charmed. Cursed even. Mike watched it intently. Then suddenly, it came arcing through the air towards him, tumbling over and over, throwing off golden glittering loops… He could contain himself no longer. He leapt. A huge leap for such a little cat. Tail, body and limbs at full stretch, front paws spread wide, he caught the ball in mid air and hit the ground with it fighting and biting. They tumbled over and over together, till Mike was completely lost in snaky loops of glistening, white, witch's wool.

Arthur had an altogether more disparate and less interactive selection of items with which to embark on his creative play. Viewing the booty of misspent Saturday nights, he could no longer recall the exact provenance of it all. There was, naturally, an extensive and still strangely satisfying collection of police cones; a litter bin with an advertisement for ice cream on the side; the top off a set of traffic lights that still glowed red, amber and green when pointed at the sun; a lot of signage, 'no parking', 'diversion', 'ngs garden', that sort of thing, plus one that must have taxed somebody greatly in the getting because it was in German: 'Umleitung'. Sounded like the Chinese minister of transport, Arthur thought. He picked up a metre-high, plastic garden gnome and reflected, with a pained sigh, that this is what he'd shared a taxi home with. This grinning piece of kitsch. Not Anastasia Poliakof .

He looked around. He ought to be embarking upon a creatively playful trip to the council tip but, somehow, this random collection of purloined property had begun nudging at his unconscious. An odd urge was seizing him. He wanted a dark tower in which to imprison his less worthy aspects and his mistakes. A folly built of follies. But follies thoroughly bound. Held for all time. He wanted mortar. Powerful mortar. And bricks. He looked around some more. There was a pile of old bricks at the bottom of the garden. Useful. But there was also the remains of other people's creative play - a washbasin, some piping and an exploded mattress. Those were certainly destined for the tip - the eternal repository for follies everywhere.

He stood for a moment or two, contemplating further the shards of his wasted youth then, suddenly overcome, he sat down on an upturned bucket. The gnome stared at him with bulging blue eyes. *Get up, Arthur. Try. If you don't try, it will always be me in the taxi with you. Me and only me. Forever.*

Mike, meanwhile, had finished coming to terms with the ball of wool. He was no longer in thrall to its siren glitter, and he had strewn it around the garden to his own satisfaction. He came to tell Arthur about his completed work.

"Oh." Arthur failed to summon the enthusiasm he ought to have done. "Looks like a woolly knot garden."

It's not just woolly knots. Mike was insistent about this so Arthur got up from the bucket in order to consider the work more thoroughly. For such a tiny kitten, Mike had fought an effective and wide-ranging battle with the wool. It was extensively draped in an attitude of grubby defeat over stones and half-bricks, the winter skeletons of wasted weeds and several years' worth of mixed-origin, green bottles.

"Roughly in a circle," Arthur spoke in carefully impressed

tones, "and circles, of course, quite apart from their ... Well ... *usually* pleasing geometry always have a certain profundity. They involve the magic number pi for instance, plus ... in arcane terms, they keep things in and they keep things out." He paused. "I suppose, in fact, it's actually a mandala. Jung was very keen on mandalas. He built his garden house in a shape that was sort of a mandala."

So what is a mandala? Have I made a good one?

"The word 'mandala' comes from a language called Sanskrit and it means a magic circle. Sometimes, the basic circle is embellished with a square in the middle or a cross - usually with four as the basis of the structure." Arthur waved a stick around to demonstrate. "Jung came to think that mandalas represent the way in which all paths in the psyche eventually lead to the middle, which is the essence of Self."

I don't seem to have made a middle.

"No, but there's an interesting embellishment at two o'clock there where you trail off into the bushes. Any idea what you were going for with that?"

I wasn't going for anything. I was being driven.

"By what?"

Mike looked slightly embarrassed. I don't know.

"Where did you find the wool?"

A witch poked it through the fence at me.

"Really? A witch? Not a neighbour at all?"

A witch.

Arthur considered the white woolly circle again. "Do you think she was a good witch?"

Well, she wasn't young. Or beautiful.

"You got a good look at her?"

I got a good look at one eye and a finger.

"So, an old finger and an old eye attached to some sort of

witch."

She could have been good. Mike took another look at his mandala.

"We can but hope." Arthur shook his head. His knowledge of witches was thin. He thought they'd grown in popularity of late but he'd never met one personally. He doubted there was a witch of any stature in the vicinity of Acacia Avenue. But then he'd never expected to find a talking kitten a few doors down from Carruthers Sloan. "She did you very well with the wool, anyway," he said. "I just wish we could analyse the symbology, then you could consciously assimilate it in order to produce one of those personality shifts."

What's the matter with my personality?

"Nothing drastic. I just thought that shifting personalities around was what we were supposed to do with creative effort that came from within. You did say that you felt you were being driven."

Mike thought about this for a few moments with no significant results.

"I need some cement," said Arthur presently. "Fancy a trip to the builders' merchant?"

Arthur had last parked the Morris just outside, on the street, and as he emerged from his driveway, something grabbed him. A set of gnarled, old fingers clamped over his forearm. Mike shot up onto his shoulder, hissing. It's the witch! She's got us!

Arthur tried to pull his arm away but the grip was astonishingly powerful. Though the old woman came barely up to his chest, she seemed possessed of supernatural strength. Moreover, it seemed that there was something she desperately wanted to communicate. Waving a bony hand in front of his face, she proceeded to intone apparent nonsense at him in tones of querulous doom.

Desperately, Arthur glanced up and down the street. Was nobody about to claim this mad old lady? But the street was deserted, and the old woman showed no signs of letting him go. It was all very well for people to talk glibly about venerating the elderly and listening to their wisdom, he thought, but it was quite another thing to have to do it in broad daylight, in the middle of the pavement, when you had no idea who they were or what they were talking about. And no obvious humane way of dislodging them. But, there it was, he'd been cornered by instinctive guile and obsessive purpose and he had little option but to allow the situation to unfold.

It was hard to get anything from the unfolding, but two doubtful possibilities eventually presented themselves: either she just wanted to stop him from going anywhere or, even more ridiculously, she wanted him to have some kind of birds and bees type talk with Mike. The second option did not strike him as at all appropriate. Mike was a magical kitten and Arthur was by no means certain how the magical kitten version ought to go.

In fact, never having been the recipient of a particularly successful version himself, he was at a loss to see how any variant could be a triumph. His father had started off on the odd occasion : "There are times between a man and a woman..." and declined repeatedly to evolve a significant follow-up. The biology master had progressed from earthworms to rabbits, with a quick and unattractive sortie into people somewhere along the line, but not even a hint as to the state of affairs with magical kittens.

Moreover, Mike was not a reliable construer of conversations. Arthur was still not certain that he understood the implications of the word sacrifice. If there was a wrong end to the sex stick – and there was – Mike stood a good chance of getting it. And he did not need to be frightened to death by hearing this old witch repeating, in spasmodically convulsed outrage, that he needed to know things. The word wool came through at one point, as did the word arrow, but by and large it was unintelligible nonsense.

Mike, hanging onto Arthur's shoulder for grim death, wasn't entirely at one with the conversation, but it did strike him that if he had been revealing himself in wool it might have been helpful to hear about it. Lately, he had been starting to think of himself, very definitely, as a 'he' and now, in a flash, he had a sudden and strange vision of being laid out in sacrificial drapes, while an angry man in a white coat poked about his innards for non-existent 'she' bits. He gave a tremendous shocked miaow and the old lady took her hand from Arthur's arm in order to reach out for him. But Arthur had been waiting for just such a moment. He had youth and elasticity and a convenient telegraph pole on his side. He shot to the car, unlocked it and squeezed himself and Mike into the passenger side, slamming the door against the old woman, who was faster than he'd expected but not an efficient squeezer.

As he scooted quickly across into the driver's seat and put the key in the ignition, he could see her in his peripheral vision, gesticulating gruesomely at him from the pavement. The old Morris started up at the third press of the starter, but now, horror of horrors, progress was blocked by a seemingly enormous jackdaw spread-eagled across the windscreen with a determined grip on the wiper blades. Mike fluffed himself out and spat, Arthur revved the engine, blew the horn and banged on the glass. The jackdaw flapped and squawked but refused to let go.

Suddenly, the old witch leapt forward with astonishing alacrity and fetched it one round the head with a half-clenched, bony fist. There was what sounded like a serious exchange of furious squawks between the pair of them, and then the jackdaw let go with a phenomenal flapping of feathers and flew off down the street. Arthur pulled away in the opposite direction with a scream of spinning tyres. In the rear-view mirror he could see the old witch shaking her fists in the air - a crabbed, angry figure from another age with a purple feather in her hat and a huge carpet bag.

Mike climbed into his booster box with a mixture of relief and regret. He felt that the old woman had had a message and that neither he nor Arthur had handled the situation at all well. It seemed a certain thing that if one of the archetypes had taken the trouble to become manifest, you were not supposed to either call her a mad old crone and threaten to take her to the police station in order to find out where she's escaped from or, and this was humiliating, run away.

At the end of the street Arthur stopped the car and looked in the rear-view mirror. "She's gone." He paused. "Was she real?"

Well, for something that wasn't real she was very impressive. *Of course she was real.*

"I mean *really* real."

It's all real. Jung said so. 'A priori' fact of nature, remember?

"You got that?"

Mike, feeling touchy at once again having failed to distinguish himself as a talisman, took this as an imputation on his intelligence that was positively offensive. *I did!*

"Well, I'm sorry, but you didn't do too well with the word

sacrifice, as I recall."

Mike looked out of the car window with a show of elaborate grievance. *It all depends on whether I'm myself or my Self.*

"Oh, very smart. So, in fact, when you're sounding smart you're channelling your self with a capital S?"

Possibly. Or, and you think about this, I could be channelling your Self with a capital S.

"I don't want to think about it," said Arthur. "And don't even mention the word psychosis."

Now, that I don't get.

"Nor me, exactly. But the word alone carries with it social death and a huge pharmacopoeia of stuff *nobody* wants to have to swallow every day before breakfast."

Alright, I won't mention it.

"And, maybe, this Self that comes through in your more professional or professorial moments could get itself digitalised because, most of the time, trying to get sense out of you is like searching for the shipping forecast on a crystal radio set."

I'm a kitten! You think you would do better with a stag or a buffalo? They'd never even fit in the car! And think of the litter trays! Mike sounded indignant, but in his heart he was wondering if, maybe, Madame Ibeg Boona had been right. Maybe, the only way he could fulfil his purpose as a talisman was by dying. Sacrificing himself. Would he know when the moment was right? Would he recognise it when it finally came? Should it have been last week? Should it have been now? Could his death have been the witch's real purpose? How could a kitten know these things?

Arthur thought that maybe he'd spoken too harshly. In truth, he was more shaken than he cared to admit. He was going to need steadier nerves than this to weather the process. "I'm sorry," he offered. "We are going to have to get used to this sort of stuff, do you think?"

She'll be back.

"The old woman?"

Oh, yes. And next time we'd better listen more carefully.

There was a thoughtful silence then, during which Mike perused the passing streets with every evidence of deep deliberation. Where are we now?

"This is the North circular. There's a builders' merchant just off to the side somewhere, I believe."

Is belief necessary?

"No. Just accurate memory and appropriate navigation."

And there'll be real cement?

"I sincerely hope so, after all of this!"

Chapter Ten

Building and masonry are crafts that have to be learned, and one of the things that has to be learned is that cement does not go off properly in freezing temperatures. Arthur, as a scientist manqué, probably did know that cement hydration is an exothermic reaction and the retention of the heat produced - unlikely in sub-zero temperatures - is necessary for the production of effective mortar. Knew it and disregarded it - driven by some inner compulsion to press on regardless of the frozen soil, the flurries of snow and the plummeting temperatures. So, maybe, he shouldn't have been quite so surprised when, leaning against his half-built tower to have a warming drink, he found himself on the ground, soaked in coffee and surrounded by rubble and police cones.

He sprang to his feet and kicked angrily at the debris. "This is the story of my life!" He banged the Chinese minister of transport furiously on the ground, knocking off cement and spraying snow over everything. "I get so far with something and then it falls apart!"

Mike appeared at the entrance to the gnome. He had a camp in there with cushions, a hot water bottle, a catnip mouse and some food. Arthur had prepared it for him, lying the hollow gnome on its side, providing its bottom with an advantageous view, and making it warm and comfortable. He called it a microenvironment and, though much impressed with the name, Mike hadn't wanted to use it. He'd wanted to climb on the bricks and spend time looking into cracks and under things generally. But the weather conditions got worse and, though the snowflakes were stunningly beautiful and draped themselves artistically around so that even the neglected garden looked magical, his paws were frozen. Soon, the inside of a gnome began to look surprisingly attractive.

He surveyed Arthur's pile of rubble with interest. *And what happens after it's fallen apart?*

"Nothing! It's fallen apart!"

Mike looked at him. *But now we are trying to put things together again, aren't we?*

"Well, we can't put this together," said Arthur. "It's too cold and there's more snow due. Cement is obviously out of the question."

Then find some other way. You told me you were a practical person. Think of something.

"Like what?"

Carpentry. You told Madame Ibeg Boona you wanted to be a carpenter.

"That was just illustrative. It's never occurred to me to be a carpenter."

Masonry, carpentry, why be picky?

*****

"Arthur! How lovely to see you!" Mrs. Loveday sounded ecstatic to see her son, but it had required some serious crashing of mental gears to produce this ecstasy in the face of his physical appearance. "Should you be driving in this snow?" She looked up at the sky which was an ominous, leaden grey. "Come in, for heaven sakes."

Arthur stamped snow from his boots and stepped into the hallway. "Have you still got that flat-packed shed?"

"Flat-packed shed, flat-packed shed," Mrs. Loveday found herself repeating the words like a wind-up doll, while she thought. What could be the down side of confessing to continued ownership of the flat-packed shed? Could it contribute in any way to her son's persistent descent into … whatever it was he was descending into? She'd almost selected the word madness, because it finished the sentence in a tidy way that appealed to an ex-librarian, but she couldn't bring herself to articulate it. Even mentally. And, if confirmed ownership of the flat-packed shed couldn't contribute to this non-specific descent, was there any way it could prejudice recovery? And, goodness me, how on earth did one develop a pressing need for such a thing in the middle of a snowstorm?

"Come and have a hot drink," she said, "while I ask your father about it."

Hastily, she made a pot of coffee, shut it and Arthur and Mike and a packet of biscuits in the sitting room, ran upstairs and banged on the bathroom door. "John! John! Come out of there at once!"

Mr. Loveday appeared, fastening his belt in fumbling haste, and carrying a newspaper. "Good God!" he exclaimed. "What on earth is the matter?"

Belatedly realising that she'd been a little loud, his wife led him stealthily into a bedroom. "That was Arthur at the door."

"Well, that's nice."

"Not really. You should see him. He's wearing tracksuit bottoms stuffed into the oddest boots with steel toe caps; some sort of navy blue jacket with leather across the shoulders like a road sweeper; and a ghastly hat with ear flaps hanging down. He's brought that kitten with him, again, and he's so pale, John. Like he hasn't eaten for days …. And he used to look so handsome in his suits." She paused, regret filling her voice. "But, worst of all, he looks completely absent and the only thing he said was: 'Have you still got that flat-packed shed?'"

"What flat-packed shed?"

"Oh, don't you start! You know. The one we bought to put up in the garden and never found time."

"Vaguely."

"Well, it's out there anyway."

"And?"

"And I think I could get it in the Morris with the hood down," said Arthur, putting his head unceremoniously round the bedroom door. "But only if you don't want it any more."

"I don't *think* we want it any more," began his father cautiously, "but …"

Arthur interrupted him. "Is it all right if I load it up, then?"

"Now? In the snow? With the hood down?"

"Yes".

"Son, I really don't think …."

"It's fine. I'll manage on my own." Arthur clattered downstairs and into the kitchen, heading for the back door. His boots on the tiled floor set the cutlery rattling. He'd bought them at the builders' merchant. They pulled on easily. They came halfway up his calves. They were made of real leather and when he was wearing them he could drop breeze blocks on his toes without noticing. He was extremely pleased with them.

"The kitten will freeze," his mother shouted after him, "in an open car. In the snow." It was a cunning ploy but it didn't work. Mrs. Loveday had to settle for watching - aghast and verging on tears - as her husband, in a hastily flung on overcoat, made ineffectual attempts to help manhandle the snow-covered sections of wood that Arthur was manoeuvring into the car with blind and disconcertingly brutal determination. The thanks and goodbyes were meticulous but mechanical. Arthur drove off into the gathering storm as if he were simply unaware of it. Mrs. Loveday clutched her husband's hand. "What on earth are we going to do?" People were being advised not to travel. Transporting sheds in the middle of snowstorms - Arthur had to be slipping further into ... whatever it was he was slipping into. Once again, Mrs. Loveday shied away from any attempt to define it. "What can we do for him, John?" she asked desperately, reduced to the helpless inanity of repeated appeal.

"We'll ring him," her husband replied. "When he's had time to get home. Frankly, I think that's about all he'll tolerate at the moment. He was quite savage with that shed."

"Why hasn't he got a wife to keep him in order?" asked Mrs. Loveday as they turned defeatedly into the house.

"Nobody seems to go in for wives much these days." Mr. Loveday's tone intimated no particular sympathy with this state of affairs, but the remark earned him a sharp look.

"Well, a partner then," said Mrs. Loveday, after a moment or two. "Even a girlfriend. Some sort of counterbalance – ballast if you like ..." She shot her husband another look. "Something to keep him anchored, stop him from slipping over into ..." She was incapable of finishing yet again, when inspiration suddenly struck: "Could he be gay? Could that account for all of this ... confusion? Is that what all this finding of Self is about?"

"Being gay is normal now, isn't it?" replied Mr. Loveday.

"It doesn't require psychiatrics. Or voodoo. I don't think." He reached for the kettle. Putting the kettle on was his standard displacement behaviour. "Anyway, Polly would have told us," he added. "She would know. Maybe he's just shy of women."

"Pshaw!" exclaimed Mrs. Loveday. "Shy is definitely irrelevant in this day and age. Women are upfront lobbyists now, and Arthur is so much better looking than he realises … any shyness would just get swept aside. So what is the matter with our son that women aren't sweeping him aside to get at him? Are we sure that he isn't gay?"

"Maybe, he's just particular."

"Well, he's going to have to stop that now, isn't he? Men who dress like beggars and carry kittens around all the time can't be choosy!" snapped Mrs. Loveday, her maternal despair suddenly ousted by angry frustration.

"It's a phase, dear." Mr. Loveday made soothing noises. "You called it that yourself. Being made redundant upsets people. We'll ring him in about …" he consulted his watch, "an hour."

The old Morris crawled and skidded its way onto the M3. The shed, fluttering red rags to warn passing vehicles and low flying aircraft that here was something that needed a wide berth, stuck up like a huge sail, collecting snow and becoming, together with the car, a strange slow travelling chimera - a thing less and less recognisable as belonging to this earth. Mike crouched in the igloo half-light of his snow-covered booster box. He couldn't remember Dr. Jung having been anything like this adventurous in his creative play. That had to be a good thing, didn't it?

*****

Arthur found useful items in skips. In north London people were having new kitchens for Christmas. Reject pieces of plywood and passé pine cladding travelled to Acacia Avenue in the long suffering Morris. In the strange, winter twilight Arthur swept aside snow, and in subzero temperatures hammered and banged and drilled with mindless determination. He did not think. He lived merely to fit one piece of the jigsaw against another. To top one folly with the next. He wanted no chinks, no cracks, for there was a terror that came with talking kittens, and it wanted in. *'I'm here. Can we discuss this? Will you listen? By any other viewpoint I am reason. You know this. You are sick. Go to the doctor. Tell him that you have a kitten that talks. See what happens. The black, voodoo priestess is just that. A black, voodoo priestess.'* But Arthur only drilled harder and hammered louder, bleeding from his own miscalculated blows. His fingers were blue, bruised and swollen, his face red and chapped and his feet, in spite of the fine boots, completely without feeling. Tears froze on his cheeks. He noticed none of it. And gradually, piece by bloody piece, his dark tower rose into the air – a monstrous patchwork of pain and futility.

And then it was finished. He and Mike crouched inside, surrounded by flickering hurricane lamps. Their shadows played over the inside walls. Snow blew in through the cracks because, however hard we try, there are always cracks. But Arthur felt calmer. Safer. Surrounded by a physical and emotional carapace of his own generating, he could think again. Mike got off the cold floor onto his leg. Are we going to live in here now?

"Jung felt he could only be himself when he was in the place he built at Bollingen," replied Arthur. "He did menial tasks and lived the simple life, allowing deep, buried thoughts to rise to the surface. It was the place where he best accessed his unconscious."

Do you think there was any tinned salmon there?

Arthur picked Mike up and put him in his jacket for warmth. "It had a tower too, in the end. Just like we do. The building of the whole went on over many years, the new bits representing the new parts of Jung's evolving psyche, his developing being. And, on a free standing stone, he carved a verse which referenced the alchemists' stone, the 'Lapis Philosophorum'. I can't recall the exact words, but they meant that spiritual insight was often rejected and despised by people because it was not understood."

*****

Mr. Loveday, wrapped in mufflers and sneezing into a fistful of paper towels, gazed at his son's handiwork with an air of puzzled unbelief. When he spoke, however, it was with careful circumspection. He complimented the size and scope of the project, querying only the nature of the building materials.

"It's a metaphor," explained Arthur. He'd tried the bit about understanding and integrating unconsciously produced creative effort, but that had seemed to be seriously straining the parental credulity - though he thought he'd detected some relief that he was still able to manage polysyllabic words. That he wasn't just babbling.

"I thought you said it was a folly."

"It represents my follies."

Mr. Loveday didn't really think that representing follies was the express purpose of garden buildings, especially when they could be seen by the neighbours, but he forbore to say so. Mrs. Loveday, clutching a large casserole and a bottle of vitamins, seemed rather in favour of the work. As it happened, she had been psychologically prepared for exactly this sort of thing by accidentally catching some television coverage of a famous flower show - where all sorts of odd edifices and metaphorical mishmashes had won gold medals for pushing the boundaries of horticultural design. In addition, she was so relieved that the journey into the snow with the shed had not killed her son outright, that she was prepared to extend a little leniency to the kaleidoscopic construction before her. Audibly at any rate.

"Is that what they call avant garde then?" asked Mr. Loveday. "Is it avant garde?"

In an effort to contribute further clarity to the discussion, Mike was hauling himself industriously up Mrs. Loveday's trouser leg. He looked up at her. It's about the process. We discover ourselves through the medium. My medium is wool.

"He cries a lot, this kitten," said Mrs. Loveday, picking him off and putting him back on the ground. "Never done howling for attention, is he?"

"I expect it's because he's covered in bits of ice and wood shavings," said Mr. Loveday. "Can't be comfortable."

After putting up what they considered to be a finely judged and well-improvised performance, Mr. and Mrs. Loveday sat in their car for a few moments before driving off. It was a fine car – finely judged, in fact, to be economical, easy to park, and suitable for long trips to B&Bs in the remoter reaches of the country. The perfect car for a couple technically pensioned-off, but full of vim for a walk or two up a Welsh hillside. It was no longer brand new, however, so it was past the point where they just wanted to sit in it and look round and make congratulatory noises to themselves. Mrs. Loveday finally asked her husband why he wasn't starting it up. In truth, he said, he felt a little peculiar.

"No wonder," said Mrs. Loveday. "Having to watch one's son build monstrosities out of council road signs is enough to make any father feel peculiar."

"I thought you seemed in favour of it. You said it would win prizes."

"Not exactly. And we had agreed that, in the face of psychoanalysis, we ought to be supportive. Encouraging, even. He'll get complaints, of course. From the neighbours. But he seemed normal to talk to, don't you think? Within the confines of the subject matter, at any rate."

"There was an artist talking on the radio the other day," said Mr. Loveday, apparently irrelevantly. "I'd have changed station but I was covered in glue. Anyway, he sounded normal and he explained that materials become, by an artist's use of them, almost sacramental. Invested, as it were, with mystical powers. In fact, he sounded so serious, that when I'd finished putting that shelf back together, I took a long, hard look at it before I hung the mugs back on."

"What?" Mrs. Loveday felt his brow. "I think you could be a little feverish. Here, let me drive."

"I think you're right," her husband agreed. And he got out of the car and walked round to the passenger side. "And the other thing," he said, as his wife shuffled across and he got in to replace her. "Has it ever struck you that there's something really weird about that kitten?"

"Sorry, dear, I didn't hear that. I was too busy shuffling."

"That kitten. Weird in some way."

"What way?" asked Mrs. Loveday.

"Well, it doesn't grow, does it?"

"He hasn't had it any time."

"Little animals grow quickly, though."

"What do you know about little animals?"

"Nothing, apparently," said Mr. Loveday.

"Still," his wife stared through the windscreen for a moment or two. "It would be typical of Arthur to get a kitten afflicted with some sort of arrested development." Then, with a shake of her head, she turned her attention to the adjustment of the seat and the rear-view mirror.

"Sometimes," said Mr. Loveday, "when it's miaowing, I get the feeling it's trying to talk." Fortunately, this sentence got lost in the clunk of the seat mechanism.

"When it's miaowing, what?"

Mr. Loveday took a moment to sneeze. It cleared his head. "Nothing, dear. Just mumbling to myself."

"Well, stop it. I've enough to worry about with Arthur."

*****

I like the brazier.

"Me too. Good find, eh?"

Makes it cosy. Even in the snow.

"Mmm."

But I'm pleased we don't have to live out here all the time.

"I couldn't get it quite big enough for that."

Do you think it's a good build?

"Well, not in the eyes of any craftsman who has eyes."

What about in the eyes of Dr. Jung?

"I thought we were doing what he suggested."

Did he suggest taking all the things you like least about yourself and building them into a monument?

"I thought I was getting rid of them in a creative way."

But, they're still there.

Arthur looked around for a moment or two. "Well, if they haven't been removed they've certainly been re-orientated.

'Please do not park in front of these gates' is upside down. I didn't notice that before."

Nor me. Mike's reading still lacked for something.

"Unlike Jung, I didn't have pristine stone," Arthur explained. "I had to recycle, reconfigure. In essence, I had to up-cycle myself out of what I had. And what I had was 'please do not park in front of these gates' and so on." He had not, he now decided, been binding his follies as he had previously imagined, but recognising them and recasting them as the building blocks of what he would become.

Mike was still doubtful. But they are still there.

"Yes, I suppose they are." Arthur decided that it was easier to concede. "Still, your old witch didn't come back, did she?"

Not yet.

They stared, thoughtful, into the sputtering flames provided by leftover wood and a few odd pieces of coal found in a half buried bucket.

Could we eat that casserole now, do you think?

Chapter Eleven

I want to go.

"Well, you can't."

I want to.

"No."

Yes.

Arthur put the invitation to one side. He had been considering it for days but he wished he hadn't read it aloud. Mike could obviously not grasp the hideousness attendant upon going to the office Christmas party of a firm from which you have been lately sacked. In fact, Arthur would have deemed the invitation a secretarial error had there not been a handwritten postscript: 'Arthur, do come'. Was this conciliation? Regret? The possibility of re-employment? He felt a disturbing compulsion to go. And this urge was insistent – rather surprising in view of his lack of satisfying responses to the inevitable questions. Being a seeker in the realms of the unconscious was not credible cocktail party currency in the world of corporate entertaining. He'd never been to anything where the conversational stock-in-trade had been snippets of psychological mysticism. When these people were suffering losses they seemed to prefer fighting their way up squash ladders, or pedalling furiously on bicycles that went nowhere.

Why can't I go?

"I'd rather not say."

That's rude.

"No it's not."

Yes, it is. It means you've thought of something nasty about me and don't want to speak it.

"There is nothing nasty about you."

What then? Why can't I go?

Arthur gave a final exasperated sigh. "Because you'll make me look silly."

How? How will I make you look silly?

"You'll *be* there."

Doing what?

"Nothing. Just being there will be enough."

Mike was deeply affronted. I've never made you look silly!

Arthur manfully refrained from bringing up the dream diary and the security guard incident, or the way he'd ended up having to face the woman he wanted to impress most in the entire world amongst the highly suspect leather goods of a shop called Of Human Bondage. "Well, I can't take you. 'Cocktails at 6:30', it says. 'No kittens.'"

You're telling fibs now. You shouldn't fib to me. It's not nice.

"You are absolutely right. It's not nice," said Arthur finally. "So, here is the truth. You will not make me look silly, but I will feel silly anyway. It's my defect that I haven't the self-confidence to enter a party, full of city financiers and movers and shakers generally, whilst carrying a kitten. It requires more aplomb than I can currently muster. Just walking in there, in the first place, will take everything I have."

Mike retired to his patchwork cushion to think this over.

It didn't seem fair that he was forced to sit for hours in dark towers but not allowed to go to parties.

*****

"So why go?" asked Polly.

Arthur had openly acknowledged that it was going to be hell, and his sister had been endeavouring to allay his anxieties by pointing out that it was, by all accounts, going to be a very large hell. Carruthers Sloan were not cutting back on the rubbing shoulders business. Obviously, they viewed the current economic doldrums as the moment to keep as many fingers on pulses as they possibly could. That way, any land and property that was getting unloaded in panic would not fall beyond their reach.

Arthur, however, had inwardly accepted his fate and so had moved on from the concept of corporate hells to the concept of haircuts. This new, and presently voiced, preoccupation with appearance struck his sister as encouraging, so she encouraged it – pointing out how good he looked in a suit. Recommending that he did not respond to this sudden impulse to have his hair cut because he looked better with it less efficiently barbered. Besides which, fresh haircuts made people look over anxious. Except, as always with Polly, the advice was much sharper than this and considerably wordier. Arthur considered it for a moment or two. His sister had undoubted skills when it came to appearance. On the other hand, her motives were often obscure and occasionally suspect. She had, for instance, actually used the word poetic somewhere in there. A chilling sort of compliment - Polly had never been the type to pine after poets. "Poetic hair," said Arthur thoughtfully. "Neglected hair. What's the difference?"

"It's subtle," Polly replied. "But specific. Broadly speaking however, you are neglected. It's beyond me why you haven't got a girlfriend. Physically speaking, you're considerably more than acceptable. You're athletic-looking, with great teeth and a good jawline – none of which you deserve in view of the bulk-buy Mars bars in the kitchen. Man cannot live by Mars bars alone, Arthur. He needs food with some level of nutrition in it. He needs a purpose. He needs a woman. He simply cannot survive as nothing more than a fleshed-out list of unfulfilled basic needs." Polly paused for breath. "Not that any sane female would tolerate you, the way you're behaving at the moment," she added.

"I'm working on myself", said Arthur.

It was a foolish defence.

"Then I have to say you are going a very odd way about it." Polly shook her head in desperation. She'd tried, not determinedly but with a gesture in the direction of goodwill, to work up a sympathetic perspective, but it had required too much flexibility of outlook. "Can't you get yourself another image consultant? This Jung person doesn't seem a particularly good one."

"*Doctor* Jung was not an image consultant. He was a very eminent psychiatrist."

"And that's another thing, Arthur. I wish you would stop using the word psychiatrist in front of Mummy. Couldn't you at least refer to the man as a psychologist? So much less evocative of padded rooms and electroconvulsive therapy!"

Arthur snorted. He loved his sister but there were times when he just wanted to stick her with a pin. Polly re-buttoned the jacket of her designer suit and prepared to leave. "And where's that kitten? Is he skulking under the bed again?"

"No. He's sulking on his cushion. He wants to go to the

party."

Polly paused in the doorway. "You see, Arthur, that's the problem. You say things like that as if you actually believe them."

Mike raised his head. Of course he believes it. He knows I want to go to the party.

Polly fired a final salvo at her brother before she left: "And when are you going to dismantle that monstrosity in your garden?"

"When it's done its job."

"Which is?"

"Helping me find myself. It's where we go to do inner work."

Polly found this ridiculous on so many levels that there was nothing more to be said. She left the front door open on her way out.

Arthur closed it with a sigh. He was grateful that his sister, on a precious half day, had gone out of her way to call and see him, but ... He had a suspicion that there was a family rota for 'checking on Arthur' and these checks were frequently discomforting. He looked at the clock. He had to have a shave and a shower and find a clean shirt. He had to get across London in rush hour on a Friday night.

*****

The location chosen for the party was not a convenient one for Arthur. Sacheverall Sloan was the current master of a London livery company. The Worshipful Company of Reivers was one of those well-heeled companies with a long purse that had its own premises with a grand hall in the city. Arthur began to wonder, as he bent his head against an icy gust outside the Old Lady of Threadneedle Street, what exactly was the point of this expedition. Was he proving anything to himself, or indeed to anybody that mattered, by this? Or was he - and this was the truth that he had been refusing to acknowledge - just trying to ease the deep-seated, low-grade ache that was his permanent in-dwelling need to see Anastasia. He shivered. He had forgotten to eat and, rather stupidly, he had not put on an overcoat. He walked quickly to keep warm. Tiny snowflakes danced before his eyes and coated the pavements.

By the time he reached the premises of the livery company, he was feeling slightly light-headed and, in the moment before he crossed the threshold, he was painfully aware that half-empty dream diaries and dark towers had not yet wrought any fundamental change in him. He was still uneasy when he trod the doorstep of power and privilege.

"Sir?" A doorman with a list held out his hand for the invitation. Arthur handed it over, wiping snowflakes from his eyes and shoulders.

"End of the corridor, sir, and on through the double doors."

Straightening his jacket, Arthur prepared to project a manufactured cheerfulness. The corridor was rather ghoulishly ornamented with grimacing, glassy-eyed, stuffed things. This was not a livery company that invested funds in contemporary works of art. What had been stuffed, had been stuffed many years ago - heraldic beasts: falcons, boars, bears. No sharks.

"Champagne, sir?" A waiter, got up in various crushed and quilted velvets to achieve a medieval picturesqueness, offered a tray and then, as Arthur shook his head, gestured him grandly into the great hall. It was possibly a question of perception but, as Arthur stepped forward, it seemed to him, in his undernourished, chilly and emotionally beleaguered state, that he was entering some corporate gathering of the netherworld. He felt seized by some pervasive, primal force. The magnificent vaulted space with its ancient timbers and grinning, puckish plaster works was heavily garlanded with fresh and powerfully aromatic evergreens – pine, spruce and darkly glowering yew; holly with blood red berries; ivy with its jet black hanging bunches; mistletoe in blanched ivory clusters. Pagan symbolism, hijacked for a Christian festival, but loaded with ambivalence. Arthur could almost feel the presiding patronage of more ancient gods.

He moved farther into the room. Silver candelabra cast flickering candlelight over tables replete with meats and fruits and candies in every hue. Conversation leapt like forked lightning between silk-tied men and bejewelled women. Laughter, equivocal and golden, floated up to the rafters.

He edged his way towards a table and found a plate. He knew he needed to eat.

"Arthur?"

He swung round.

"It's Lisa!"

"Of course. Sorry."

Lisa, from a different branch office but familiar enough, was another of those who had been made redundant. She looked radiant. "Wasn't that psychologist marvellous?"

"The inkblot man?"

For Lisa, the consequences of seeing rabbits, babies and profiles of William Shakespeare had been fortuitous and revolutionary. She was, it transpired, born to teach. A virtually, forgotten and somewhat indifferent, science degree had suddenly become as treasure trove. Future training and employment were assured. The country's schools were screaming out for people who knew that 02 was not just a big arena. In the meantime, she had a new husband to attend to. Life was good. In fact, her encounter with the psychologist had been such a positive affair, full of deep truths, that she was extremely disappointed to learn that Arthur's encounter with deep truth had been inconclusive. She gave him a great consoling bear hug (there was a well fed, healthy heft to Lisa) which overbalanced him into a platter of seafood, disrupting ranks of highly organised, pink things with extravagant whiskers.

"It'll be alright, Arthur", she said. "It'll be alright in the end, I'm sure of it. Now, you have a lovely evening. Try the pigeon breast. I never realised that people still ate pigeon. It's remarkably good." And she pushed her way into the crowd, bearing a heaped plate of food to share with her husband.

Arthur began heaping up a plate of his own - pigeon breast, of course, boar pâté, medallions of venison, devils on horseback, a tiny pot of syllabub and the desperate-looking crustacean that was still clinging to his sleeve. He did this without much thought but with overt industry - he knew it would be fatal to appear unoccupied. He would be buttonholed by some grand imp wearing an ancient order tie, and dragged down into that special circle of Hell that is reserved for those who have failed, their entire lives, to learn how to work a room. He would grow dimmer and dimmer before the relentless questioning and, eventually, the will to live would leave him altogether.

He looked round for floor space to move into. His casting eye was caught by a furiously semaphoring Damien Price. Damien wasn't a choice resting place but he was the devil Arthur knew. And, because hailing Arthur had enabled Damien to escape from the dowager Mrs. Sloan, he was grateful enough to say: "Didn't expect to see you here," in a semi-pleased tone.

"I was invited."

"That was Anastasia. She was tasked with organising this. But don't get excited. She used the fact that this is also serving as her leaving party to invite all the down-and-outs she's ever crossed paths with. Didn't think you'd have the nerve to come, actually."

Arthur acknowledged this agreeably. Damien flicked an eyebrow.

"So, Anastasia's leaving?" Arthur asked.

"I told you she would. She was just acquainting herself with the lie of the land for a few years."

"What land?"

"No specific land. Just the land and property business generally. Contacts, you know. That's what it was all about. In the meantime her family has got a huge charitable foundation up and running. Shockingly rich lot. Finally flogged off the Russian Crown Jewels. Or maybe it's fossil fuels in Siberia. Who knows? All we get is rumours. Anastasia doesn't respond well to direct questioning. Just shrugs and says: 'Family money. You know.' Actually, I don't, dear. My family, such as it was, didn't have two brass pennies to rub together. What I don't earn, I don't get. But there we are. She's off to indulge in the usual guilt assuagement exercises pursued by the obscenely rich ..." He broke off momentarily and adjusted his tone. "Oh, Anastasia! How are you this fine evening? Wonderful party you contrived for us all. I was just telling Arthur here, you remember Arthur, his hair's grown otherwise nothing significant has happened to him, that you are leaving us to pursue good works."

Anastasia nodded, "Damien." Then she leaned in and

kissed Arthur on the cheek. "I'm pleased you came."

"That doesn't count," Damien whispered to him. "Social kissing doesn't count. I can tell by the greenish hue of your skin that you have remained a frog."

"If you will both excuse me," he added aloud. "I'll leave the pair of you to catch up."

Arthur could still feel his cheek burning as if the light kiss had carried a scorching passion. Anastasia's upswept hair showed off the slim, ivory column of her neck and the delicacy of her collar bones. She was simply lovely. Arthur longed to reach out and take her face gently in his hands.

"Not sporting any of the leather goods, I see." she said with a smile.

"Turned out that they weren't really me, after all," said Arthur.

"And the kitten?"

"They weren't really him either."

"So, apart from training kittens to be discerning dressers, what are you doing?"

"Not much," said Arthur. "Trying to bring a little light out from under the bushel maybe." He ducked and looked round.

"What's wrong?"

"Nothing … I just thought …" He ducked again.

"Arthur?"

Arthur had developed the strangest feeling that he was being assailed by some unseen force. He could feel things swishing past his ears and catching at his hair. "Is there a bird in here?" he asked. "I keep feeling …" He ran a hand over his head.

"I doubt it," said Anastasia. "Although sometimes pigeons get in these places and roost in the rafters." She glanced around for a moment or two and then said, "They missed you at Carruthers Sloan, you know."

"Yes, no coffee and muffins any more."

"Not just that. It eventually began to occur to Harvey that no one else was quite as adept at telling frantic clients that their completion has been postponed yet again, but their buyers insist on going forward, so presently they will find themselves pounding the pavement for temporary accommodation accompanied by a furious wife and a pack of wailing children."

"I see."

"Actually, I don't think you do. Apart from anything else, you're still looking for that bird. There isn't one, Arthur. I assure you."

But Arthur could not rid himself of the discomforting feeling that something was trying to get into his head. He barely caught Anastasia's explanation of how no-one had realised, until he'd gone, just how much his soothing of the angry, and reassuring of the panicky, and being unfailingly courteous to those who were barely civil, had made doing business a much pleasanter affair. He just grasped the idea that he was one of those people who don't make you pay a big price for their presence, and so is never missed until the coffee doesn't appear on time.

Disturbing shadows were flickering in his peripheral vision. Something caught at his cheek. He put up a hand to the spot and his fingers came away with a faint streaking of blood. He turned quickly again but he saw nothing. Surreptitiously, he felt in his pocket for a handkerchief.

"Arthur? *Arthur!* "

"Sorry." Desperately Arthur tried to focus his attention upon the conversation. "Yes, Damien said you were working in the family foundation. What exactly is it that you do? "

"Housing associations, youth centres, special schools … that sort of thing. Wonderful ideas, of course, but the problem of trying to help the world is that you have to involve the world. And everybody from the Prime Minister down has an opinion and a demand. Which would be fine, if they all had similar opinions and demands." Anastasia paused for a moment or two. Then she said, "I take it you haven't got another job yet? So tell me, how important to you is this bushel business? …. *Arthur, there is no bird!*"

Arthur was painfully aware that twitching and ducking were not the adroitest ways of indicating to Anastasia that he counted every word he exchanged with her as the bliss of heaven, but he could neither control nor shake off the dark turbulence that was building round him.

"Arthur! Can you please pay attention? There is no bird! But there is something …. There is something I really need to …" she stopped suddenly and took a deep breath which, even to Arthur's distracted and struggling senses, sounded somehow decisive and hugely significant … He stood still. His heart stood still. Time stood still. And in that uncounted infinity, a fading and half-buried dream, stunted and desiccated thing that it had become, raised itself from deep within him and turned its poor face to the light ..Then an arm, princely and proprietal, snaked around Anastasia's waist. Arthur felt a painful, talon-like snatch at his heart and he knew that the world had moved on and his moment had been taken from him. Hope ebbed away in slow, sinking waves till his very soul seemed drained and empty.

Anastasia turned to face the prince. "You remember Arthur?"

"Not really. Are we supposed to have met?"

"Very briefly," said Arthur. There was real pain in his

chest and in the flicker of the candles he thought he caught a strange redness in the princely eyes. Discerned a little more length and a little less whiteness to the canine teeth. And where the princely parts blurred into the crowd and the half-light, Arthur almost expected to see wolf-like extensions appear where the human left off. He looked suspiciously at his plate. He'd taken a bite or two of pigeon during his conversation with Damien. Was that the bad taste in his mouth? He felt as if he had consumed Snow White's apple. He began taking some hasty and rather inappropriate spoonfuls of syllabub.

"Arthur?" Anastasia was looking at him with some irritation.

He apologised. "I'm sorry. I didn't like the taste of the pigeon. It made me feel weird."

"Something obviously has."

Arthur was trying desperately to pull his scattered senses back to the matter in hand. It was important. So important … "You were going to say something about my bushel," he offered.

The prince made an impatient gesture.

"It doesn't matter, Arthur," said Anastasia. "Maybe some other time. You're obviously not yourself. Have a good Christmas." And she turned away into the crowd. But after a couple of steps she swung back again and said in a low voice, "Arthur, I would like to talk to you. Do come and see me. And don't eat any pigeons on the way."

But she spoke too softly for Arthur, beleaguered as he was, to catch. "There was a pigeon after all?" he called hopefully after her. But Anastasia had disappeared into the crowd.

Arthur made his way in the opposite direction – pushing

towards the exit he felt claws once more rake his face. Emerging thankfully into the brightness of the stuffed beast corridor, he caught at a side table, put down his plate and leaned against the wall. As he stood, eyes closed, the turbulence that had been building up around him began to abate. A calmness settled over him. He took a deep, easy breath and opened his eyes in relief. In front of him a dramatic figure, in floor length flowing paisley and a feather trimmed turban, settled out into majestic familiarity.

"Madame Ibeg Boona?"

"Arthur Loveday! Fancy finding you here!"

"Of the two of us," said Arthur, "I should have thought that you were the more surprising. I come under the banner of employee. Albeit ex."

Madame Ibeg Boona nodded agreeably. "Me too. Except that I have the distinction of being current."

"You mean you sacrifice kittens for these people?" There was more of shock than diplomacy in Arthur's voice.

"Kittens?" Madame Ibeg Boona was hugely amused. "You have no idea of the sacrifices that get made in the pursuit of money and influence. Wives, children, business empires, small countries." She gave a great laugh at her own joke and Arthur's reflex shock, and then she looked carefully at him, taking in his paleness, his confusion – and his fear. "These people can cast enormous shadows," she said. "But you know that, don't you? You felt it. I can see. You felt the darkness. And you were afraid. And in that fear you felt it all - your self-persecution, your inability to reach out for success or happiness. Your failure to stand in the face of love."

Arthur shook his head vehemently. "No!"

"Don't lie, Arthur. You felt it. You felt that which keeps your life at a standstill."

Arthur, having become calm and secure at the moment of her arrival, began to inch away. Madam Ibeg Boona reached out at hand. "Arthur, Arthur," she said gently. "I am merely an instrument. I serve the greater purpose. I help to work out the dark side for all. These people here," she waved a hand, "they make the modern world go round. And they can bring so much benefit with their energy, their drive, their inventiveness and their determination. But these things, these attributes of theirs, these powerful motivators – they are not the prerogative of the light. You see, Arthur, the shadow must not be feared but dealt with, negotiated with, in order for it to facilitate all that can be. In order that our kindness, our generosity and our good intentions do not just cower in the corner, too helpless and afraid to come out. The darkness and the light, they need each other. They are two sides of the same coin. The darkness, Arthur, gives the light the guts, the strength and the sheer, damned determination to shine, and to refuse the darkness this outlet is to store up and accumulate a darkness that forgets how to live, how to love and how to forgive. All the visionaries knew this. Jung knew it. Blake knew it. And Blake expressed it beautifully: 'Go to heaven for form and hell for energy'. We all have a shadow side, Arthur, and to keep the balance, both cosmically and personally, we cannot deny the stranger."

Arthur felt sick. To say that his evening had been a disaster was gross understatement. He'd come because he'd had no other choice - driven by a blind, unspecified hope that lacked the wherewithal to help itself. And yet he could not understand what Madame Ibeg Boona was telling him. To hear is one thing, to fully comprehend and act accordingly is quite another.

"Start small, Arthur," she smiled reassuringly and, opening

her handbag, took out a roughly fashioned calico doll without a face and offered it to him. Arthur leapt back as if burned. Madame Ibeg Boona shook her head in exasperation. "Look upon it as a worry doll," she said. "They're everywhere now. It's a Mayan tradition. You are supposed to confide your worries to the doll, put it under your pillow and tomorrow they'll be gone. It's a symbolic act. And the unconscious mind is very susceptible to symbolism and ritual. It does not always differentiate between an outer act and an inner one. Contact your shadow side symbolically, Arthur, because it has to be dealt with, one way or another. Hold out your hand. Give a nod to the dark power. Honour the stranger. Because where the light and the dark come willingly to merge and reconcile - there is the brilliance of the infinite and the everlasting. The point where miracles occur. Come to the arrangement, Arthur. Take the doll."

"No," said Arthur and, pushing past her, he set off down the corridor.

"Where's the kitten?" She called after him.

"He's at home."

"Then you go carefully on your way back there. A talisman serves no purpose in the cupboard. That kitten could have saved you this. He could have moved you on. But you made the choice, and now all he can do is get you through it. A much harder task. And one upon which your sanity depends …." She gave up with a sigh, as Arthur disappeared round the corner into the lobby.

Out on the pavement, Arthur turned up his collar against the bitter December cold and set off at a brisk walk. He hurried with ringing footsteps down the draughty canyons between the city's towering monuments to Mammon. The wind, driven and bounced by the buildings, carried untraceable echoes and sent the finely falling snowflakes into gusty turbulences. Arthur was once again aware of things repeatedly brushing against his cheek. He noticed, with dissatisfaction and a level of self-contempt, that he had broken into a trot. He swiped at something above his head and felt an aggressive rush of feathers and the stinging catch of talons. He had no great knowledge of nature but he felt pretty certain that it was owls that came out at night, and maybe something civilised and sweet that sang in Berkeley Square. Not jackdaws. And yet, from the corner of his eye, he caught the sinister cowling of a grey hood and the unnatural whiteness of malevolent eyes. The trot became a run. It was with overwhelming relief that he gained the busy brightness of the tube station.

"Lucky holly? Sprig of lucky holly? Just a pound to keep the evil spirits away!"

"No, thank you." Arthur tried to brush past without looking, but this was not a brushable sales person. In front of him, an old gypsy woman was strongly planted. Brought to a halt by necessity, he put a hand in his pocket. As he fished for change his eyes roamed anxiously around, finally coming to rest, with something like relief, on his own feet. And then the gypsy's feet. And then the gypsy's large and disturbingly familiar carpetbag. He dropped the change in shock and, as it bounced and rolled, he ran.

"You cannot keep on running, Arthur! To reclaim your soul you must find the courage to stand and take whatever comes!"

But, in two bounds he had vaulted the barriers and was plunging down the escalators three steps at a time. Careering onto the platform just as the doors of a train were about to close, he flung himself inside and collapsed onto an empty seat. It was three stations before he noticed blood dripping from his clenched fist. Opening his fingers he found a sprig of holly.

*****

Barely able to fit the key in the lock, Arthur let himself into 29B and dropped onto the sofa fighting for breath. He had broken into a run the minute he'd left the tube at Finchley Central. The physical pain in his lungs and the stitch in his side were welcome reassurances of reality. Mike patted his face solicitously. What happened? Wasn't it a good party?

Arthur was still only able to gasp. Two minutes elapsed.

Now can you tell me?

Arthur sat up. "Oh, God! he said. "*Oh God.*"

So it was a bad party?

Arthur had to double up for a moment or two to ease the pain in his side. "I don't know. Something weird happened. It was okay at first … Then Anastasia came across …"

The lady we met in the leather shop?

"Yes … And it was … Oh, it was so good to see her but I couldn't … I felt as if there were things … things flapping around my head … Perhaps they were in my head?" He felt at his cheek. His fingers came away clean.

Mike watched him. What sort of things? What sort of things flap about like that at cocktail parties? I've never been to a cocktail party, you know, so I need to be told.

Arthur felt too drained and exhausted to rise to the bait of recrimination. "Madame Ibeg Boona said …"

Madame Ibeg Boona was there?

"Yes."

Did she mention me?

"She said you could serve no purpose left at home in the

cupboard."

You see? Some people know how a talisman should be treated. Mike felt vindicated. Tell me about the flapping things now.

"Well, she said it was the darkness ... everybody's darkness ... mine too. Self-persecution and failure and strangers needing to be talked to ... But maybe it was just the pigeon breast."

There was pigeon breast? You left me with tinned catfood – with ring pulls I can't pull, incidentally – and there was pigeon breast? I don't believe it! Mike was extremely put out.

"Never mind the pigeon breast! What about the darkness?"

Well, what else had Madame Ibeg Boona to say?

"She tried to give me some disgusting voodoo doll so that I could make a pact with the devil or something. I don't know what she was getting at."

Then maybe you ought to go and ask her, because frankly your story sounds a little garbled. Did you bring some of that pigeon breast away with you, by any chance?

"No. I didn't think. I'm sorry. It wasn't good, anyway. I'm sure there was something in it. Maybe. But, the worst part, almost, was that at one point something wonderful seemed about to happen ..."

Wonderful how?

"I don't know. It was just a feeling. But I couldn't ... I just couldn't ..."

Couldn't what?

"I don't know." Arthur laid his head back on the sofa. "Nothing made sense to me. It was like I was going ..." He stopped.

Going what?

Arthur didn't answer.

Mike tried again. Going what?

Arthur shook his head. "I don't know," he said quietly. "And I'm afraid ..." He closed his eyes, but the darkness was too dark and his fears grew larger there so he opened them again, and studied the geometry of the wallpaper, counting and multiplying and dividing. Counting, multiplying and dividing ...

Mike patted his face consolingly. I'm here. Don't be afraid. We'll be fine.

Arthur put up a hand and stroked him. "I hope you're right. Because I don't know what to do."

You will tomorrow. You'll see. And he laid his cheek against Arthur's, closed his eyes and willed it so.

Chapter Twelve

The following day Arthur awoke at first light, drenched in sweat and fighting for breath. He was in bed with no memory of having got there. But, one way or another, bed and sleep had claimed him, though he'd tossed and turned all night, having hideously disordered dreams in which strange and violent things had been happening to him.

Oddly enough, the dream that had woken him so shockingly, with his heart leaping from his chest, had begun rather well. He'd been on a beautiful three-masted galleon, under full sail, moving majestically across a blue and gently swelling sea. The dawn sun had just been clearing the horizon, and the light of the new day had borne with it such a feeling of promise that it had put a little song in his heart. But, suddenly the galleon had begun to stagger and roll. Its bows had come up and the billowing sails had started to snap and tug like terrified, tethered creatures. Within seconds, the main mast had splintered with a crack like gunshots. But, before it could topple, a huge serpent had risen from the bowels of the ship and wound its long, scaly body around the shattered wood. Why Arthur was alone on this ship he could not discern. Certainly there were no lifeboats, lifebelts or flotation devices of any sort - nothing designed to preserve him from being sucked into the giant whirlpool that the sinking galleon would create. The serpent had bought him time, but it was beginning to fail, so he sought desperately to improvise – an empty barrel, a wooden box, a discarded trunk, anything. And then something hard hit him in the stomach and he fell backwards with such force that the breath was knocked from his body. The sea was already beginning to sluice across the deck, but now a great weight, bearing down on his chest, was preventing him from getting to his feet. He flailed his arms desperately and beat at the thing with panicky fists, but it couldn't be moved. As his rib cage was slowly crushed and his breath became shorter and shorter, the thing began to take ghoulish shape and drag towards it a large, and horribly familiar, carpet bag. Arthur's eyes fixed on the bag with helpless horror as the creature slowly opened it and drew forth – Arthur could hardly bear to look – a Wheatstone bridge.

What's a Wheatstone bridge? Mike was hugely disappointed. This had been such a promising tale: galleons, serpents, ghouls. He'd been expecting a climax of epic proportions – but now, some sort of bridge? What kind of lame finish was that?

He was sitting on Arthur's chest, where he had taken up residence after Arthur had woken up. He'd had a fairly disrupted night himself - wanting to share body heat, but having to scramble here and there with alarming haste in order to avoid being squashed. This interesting dream story had been some compensation but now this disgraceful, pricked balloon of an ending … well …

"A Wheatstone bridge," said Arthur, picking him up, easing into a sitting position and putting him back, "is a device for measuring electrical resistance."

Mike thought about this for a moment or two. Now, that is interesting.

"Not interesting," said Arthur. "Ridiculous. It just goes to show what unfettered nonsense the unconscious flings together during the night. Who could you intimidate with a Wheatstone bridge, for heaven's sake?"

A monkey scientist?

"*There were no monkeys*," said Arthur, in exasperated tones. "How many more times do I have to tell you that!"

Not too many, I hope. Mike gave his whiskers an enigmatic curl. Can we have bacon for breakfast? I think it's a bacon sort of day.

It was obvious from the eerie light in the room that it had snowed again.

"I'll have to walk to the shop and get some," said Arthur.

We won't have to eat it out in the dark tower, will we?

The dark tower had become a slightly contentious issue. Mike was still of the opinion – especially when the temperature fell well below freezing – that it was an enshrinement of Arthur's failings, not a sublimation. Except he didn't use those words, Arthur had supplied those words. But, in fact, Arthur preferred to believe that the construction of the tower had been a necessary part of his 'becoming' process and, to further this process, he had erected a huge easel in there and set about the business of painting what came from within. This method of inner engagement, as a means of bringing about resolutions in his psyche, had never struck him as a particularly likely path to progress but he'd been doing it anyway. And, as the rules were that there had to be absolutely no kind of artistic endeavour, he'd found it quite liberating to commit raw splurges of stifled need, caged emotion and screaming soul to large pieces of hardboard salvaged from skips. Using reject cans of emulsion, he had created huge swirls and sweeps in oranges and reds, purples and black.

So what are these paintings telling you about yourself? Mike, sitting upon an upturned bucket, had watched dutifully.

Arthur had paused, dripping brush half-way to yet another giant sheet of hardboard, which had once formed the back of someone's kitchen cupboards.

Mike rearranged himself on the bucket (which wasn't anything like as accommodating as his patchwork cushion). You have to think about these paintings, you know. They are like dreams. If you just make them, and don't think about them, they can't help to take you forward. You might just as well go in and paint the kitchen ceiling which, incidentally, is badly in need of it.

"They're a purging process," said Arthur, slapping the brush onto the hardboard and squirling it around.

Mike considered this. Well, I don't think they are. Because they are all basically the same. You keep throwing up the same thing again and again. It's not getting flushed away, or even modified to any extent. A man who is painting the same thing again and again has to be in serious trouble.

"Great artists always painted things again and again. One of them painted the same mountain eighty times."

Yes, but they were artists. They were probably practising. Anyway, nobody ever accused them of being sane. I think your stuff looks like Van Gogh's skies. You either have a thing about Van Gogh, or a thing about skies.

Arthur didn't comment.

Hmm … Mike put his head on one side. Not skies. Space. Now what is the connection between monkey scientists and space? Didn't somebody send monkeys into space? He watched Arthur carefully. No, that's not it.

Arthur had flung the brush down. "You're talking rubbish," he said.

Not about Van Gogh's skies. You're just baffled as to how I know about them.

"Yes, I am baffled," snapped Arthur. "I'm baffled as to why you aren't looking at your own handiwork and getting the implications of it!"

Mike hadn't been sitting on the upturned bucket the whole time. When he had despaired of divining anything about the inner Arthur from swirly skies, he had acquired a blob of red on his head, and four socks of mixed muddied colour, from dabbing at discarded paint pot lids and marching around on the recumbent sheets of cardboard that formed the floor. In this way he had produced some interesting dot paintings, after the manner of Damien Hirst. And he had, in fact, peered at them for revelations about his inner self. Evidently, he had deeply held fantasies about going round in ever decreasing circles - which was what he and Arthur could actually be doing. Or, more hopefully, it was the tower's fault for being basically round. And that had brought him back, once again, to the fact that he had some problems with the tower - over and above its ability, in the coldest December for decades, to visit great physical discomfort upon him.

In short, this morning's heavy snowfall was silently welcomed. Mike felt that the galleon dream needed to be dealt with in the relative comfort of the kitchen, not sublimated onto sheets of hardboard then thrown onto the fantasy reject heap. He half-jumped and half-fell from the bed onto the floor. I like the smell of frying bacon, do you? He picked himself up cheerfully.

"Everybody does." Arthur stepped into his jeans, pulled

on a sweater and ran a hand through his hair.

I expect it helps with analysing dreams.

"No, it doesn't. And it was a senseless dream." Arthur slammed the door on his way out.

Either way, the smell of frying bacon finally filled the kitchen and Mike inhaled it luxuriously from his new vantage point on the formica table.

"You really need more effective teeth for this sort of fodder." Arthur sliced meticulously at a cooked rasher to get it as small as possible. "Here, try this little bit."

Mike chewed away, head on one side, blissfully and energetically manoeuvring the fibres of bacon between his miniscule molars. Arthur began on a bacon sandwich and a large mug of coffee. Mike paused to give his jaws a rest.

What's that?

"What's what?"

That coloured thing sticking out of the carrier bag.

Arthur reached out and picked up a packet. "It's plasticine."

What does it do?

"It's more a matter of what we are going to do with it."

Are we going to make it into a Wheatstone bridge?

"No. We are going to make manikins."

Something of Madame Ibeg Boona's dissertation on worry dolls had taken root in Arthur. He had worries in ample supply and the idea of voicing them to a manikin held some appeal - if only in the same way that making a 'to do' list was an improvement on having to waste time mentally rerunning and prioritising life. Moreover, since Jung had made himself a manikin at one point, which apparently served as some sort of confessor, it seemed a vaguely valid thing to do on a snowbound morning when the dark tower was more inhospitable than usual.

That a manikin could actually take away worries or expiate sins was, of course, not the case. The figure would not be imbued, voodoo-like, with some unwholesome power. It would merely serve a turn as a rather flimsy psychological tool. Like a journal. Only man-shaped. At least, that's how it started out.

Mike didn't want to make a manikin for himself. He didn't like the smell of the plasticine. Or the fact that he could only have the brown piece or the grey piece. Moreover, in the morning chill of the flat, the stuff was undentable by the average kitten paw, and so the enterprise promised little other than a review of the evolutionary relevance of thumbs. Suffice it to say that he was never going to produce anything approaching a five centimetre model of a kitten. And all of this was quite apart from his philosophical objections.

The first objection being to the word manikin. What was the feline equivalent? What on earth sort of hybrid would a kitten manikin be? Secondly, and most profoundly, why couldn't he serve as a confessor for Arthur? His express purpose on this quest was to help and, unlike a piece of plasticine, a talisman was supposed to have powers. True, since his failure to become a lamb, he hadn't seen very much evidence of powers. In crisis situations his contributions had been … well … mostly contributory. A fact that he was secretly beginning to concede. Plus, in physical terms, he was still falling off the bed and getting stuck in the cat-flap. However, and in his mind he could see the word highlighted in glowing colours, he felt that he was starting to have significantly helpful thoughts. And didn't a confessor's job have to be largely in the thinking line?

He looked in disgust at the shapeless, grey, foetal blob in

front of him and flicked at it crossly with a paw. A couple more millennia of evolution and maybe it would be able to wriggle. His mind drifted to the mouse under the sink. Maybe it could be lured out with a piece of bacon. There was no harm in looking, was there?

Arthur, meanwhile, even with two thumbs and hands bigger than Mike's entire body, was making no better fist at the job. Originally, he had envisaged something in the nature of the garden gnome – at least as far as the blue jacket and the red trousers went – but there had been repeated reworkings due to poor craftsmanship, and now he was holding a disgusting lumpen effigy with the unpleasant mixed-up colouring of raw streaky bacon. It certainly wasn't the sort of creature you'd want to be sharing your innermost workings with. Had it come to life, or even twitched a little, there would have been an unmanly scramble for the door.

In response to Arthur's snorts, Mike abandoned his mouse fantasies and gave the effigy the benefit of some serious consideration. Presently, he began to feel pleased. Not because Arthur had failed, but because he had succeeded.

"How so?" asked Arthur, with a degree of irritation. "Go ahead, surprise me."

You made your shadow side. This is the evil stranger.

"This represents my shadow side?" Arthur held up the manikin.

That's what your unconscious wanted you to produce, because that's what you need to look at. It was surrendered creativity.

"Well, you have surprised me," said Arthur. "How come you've started thinking these thoughts?"

I don't know. They think themselves. One moment I'm wondering about the mouse under the sink and the next moment I'm thinking thoughts. With clever words in there.

"Well, it's very disconcerting," said Arthur.

Why? Madame Ibeg Boona thinks clever thoughts.

"Well, she's disconcerting," said Arthur with feeling. He hadn't at all enjoyed being trapped in the carcass corridor with her. "But at least she is … human."

That's speciesism.

"There you go again."

Maybe, like I said before, I'm thinking your thoughts. Or … maybe, I'm thinking what you ought to be thinking. That would be the most helpful, wouldn't it? Except now I'm back on the mouse again. Are you on the mouse too?

"No, I am not," said Arthur firmly. "The mouse definitely does not intrude upon me."

I think Polly thinks it ought to. Maybe I have a mixture of your thoughts and Polly's thoughts and kitten thoughts and …

"Stop!" said Arthur. "Just stop."

Why? I thought you wanted to know.

"Because I don't want to think about Polly, or mice."

Why not?

"Because I want to think about lust."

Oh, interesting. Very interesting. Let's think about that …

There was silence for a good minute. Which is a much longer time than most people imagine. Or need, in fact, when it comes to lust.

Mike's little chest suddenly heaved in disappointment. I can't think of anything. I think better about mice than I do about lust.

"Oddly enough," said Arthur, "so do I. And therein, my little furry friend … therein lies an insight for the day."

Mike hoped it wasn't going to be as anti-climactic as the

dream.

"According to Jung," began Arthur slowly, "the shadow contains all of the personality traits that are not acceptable to society. Right? We suppress them and dissociate ourselves from them until, in effect, we create a part of ourselves that we do not wish to know. That we may even fear. We may even project it onto other people as the evil stranger. That's the gist. That's what we read, isn't it?"

Yes. Then you made it. Mike studied the effigy.

"Nevertheless," Arthur went on, "the dark side of human nature remains part of us and, in order to become whole, we have to come to terms with it – not least because it contains a great deal of instinctive energy and creativity. That's what Madame Ibeg Boona was holding forth about last night - and in very scary tones I might add. In cosmic terms it's the reconciliation of heaven and hell."

The reconciling of heaven and hell struck Mike as too distant a concept to become embroiled in. This could go the way of the galleon dream if he gave Arthur too much verbal leeway. When am I going to hear about the lust business?

"Lust," said Arthur ,"is one of the seven deadly sins. And I haven't kept enough of it handy for occasional and temperate usage." He shook the effigy thoughtfully. "The shadow here has it all bottled up. In fact, I probably need a bit more of all of them. All seven."

Not sloth.

"True. At the moment sloth is figuring prominently with me. Hence the mouse." Arthur took a visual inventory of the kitchen, reviewing his 'last dish' approach to washing up, and his 'not until collection day' attitude to household waste. "But, think about it. Sloth is akin to relaxation and, without a sensible helping of it, we could all work ourselves up to heart attacks."

Like Polly's probably doing.

"Exactly. It's all about balance. The Newtonian psyche - you know, for every force, there is an equal and opposite one."

So, tell me about lust now.

"Well, lust is slightly more complicated for me than sloth, so are you sitting comfortably?"

Yes!

"Not preoccupied with the mouse?"

No!

"Right then."

And so Arthur began. All his life, he explained, apart from a few lacklustre episodes (the effort at a pun went unnoticed) he'd tended to be a torch bearer. He had, to use Polly's words, carried candles for women instead of dating them. It had begun at school, with Serena Watson – clever, thrillingly sporty in lycra shorts, and eventually head girl. He'd spoken to her exactly twice, and both times she'd responded with an air of patronising and callous indifference. Oddly undeterred, he had proceeded through life in a series of devotional fits and starts, until he'd finally come face to face with the woman whose very name could deprive him of rational thought. Anastasia Poliakof.

And all of these women, Arthur now realised, conformed to a pattern. All of them, in common parlance, were out of his league. And the reason for that, apart from the fact that realistically they probably were out of his league, was that he was projecting his anima – the feminine side of his personality – onto these women.

Mike shook his head. A shadow person *and* an anima. Must be getting crowded in there.

"It's starting to feel like it, actually," said Arthur reflectively. "No wonder there are schizophrenics."

Mike made disapproving noises. Nature seems very wasteful. It makes one person out of what appears to be the material for a lot more.

Arthur looked quickly at him. "It's funny that you should say that."

I thought it was a little more than funny. A little bit smart maybe.

"It was. Especially when you think that you were actually paraphrasing Goethe."

Paraphrasing a goatherd?

"Goethe. An eighteenth century German writer. Oddly enough, he wrote a play about pacts with the devil. Those didn't work out so well, as I recall."

I should listen to Madam Ibeg Boona when it comes to the devil. I'm quite sure that she has more of a grasp on him than a German goatherd. Mike was insistent about this. Arthur had to agree.

But tell me about the paraphrasing, anyway. Mike was curious. Why did it strike you so?

Arthur looked out of the window for a moment or two. Mike decided that he was going to avoid answering, but eventually he said: "I had an extremely clever friend, once, called Jono, who was always getting drunk."

Is that extremely clever?

"He was academically clever. That's different. And there was another clever friend, who didn't get quite so drunk. Quite so frequently. And when the drunken one was drunk, the less drunken one would quote Goethe at him. In the German. The same bit. Maybe it was the only bit he knew, but it always sounded impressive. The barmaids were impressed, anyway, which was probably the point of the exercise."

So what did he say?

"Schade dass die Natur nur einen Mensch aus dir schuf, Denn zum wurdigen Mann war und zum Schelmen der Stoff."

In English ?

"Nature, alas, made only one being out of you, although there was material for a good man and a rogue." Arthur looked out of the window again. "I don't know why I should remember that so clearly now. It feels as if it were just yesterday, and yet I haven't seen either of those friends … well, in a long, long time."

Tell me about them. Tell me about then. Mike felt somewhat disappointed at having to put the lust business to one side, but this seemed more important.

"No."

Why not?

"That was then and this is now."

Mike sighed. If only it were so simple.

Arthur remained silent.

Mike studied him carefully for a moment or two. Fine. We won't go there, but to backtrack to the matter in hand - we have it from the mouths of dead psychiatrists, voodoo psychologists and German goatherds that people have a lot of aspects. So, we'll take that as read, not get diverted into schizophrenia or old friends, and get back to the lust business. He patted the mannikin encouragingly. We can't have a fine example of surrendered creativity going to waste. You've obviously been very well acquainted with how to chat up a barmaid and yet, apparently, never have. So let's find out why not.

"Alright," Arthur rested his chin on his hands and stared thoughtfully at the streaky piece of plasticine. "All men have a feminine side, right? It's the balance thing again: good/evil, masculine/feminine. It all regulates behaviour. And, according to Jung, the feminine side – or anima – of a man contains the qualities that the male persona lacks. So, bearing in mind my inkblot test, this means that my anima got all the exigency, resolution, aspiration, focus, etc., etc. that I apparently lack. In other words, she has to be a pretty formidable creature."

Mike twitched his whiskers. Exciting. I'd call her exciting.

"Fine," said Arthur, "you do that. But now comes the bad part. For me, at any rate." And he went on to explain that if, as Jung believed, the process of falling in love consisted of projecting the anima onto a real live woman, then the object, of his, Arthur's, affections automatically became an embodiment of attributes that put her far, far out of his reach. He created, in effect, some goddess for whom he could do little but sacrifice his life. And the practical upshot of this was that he had sacrificed his life. He had become a piner. He had pined his way through birthday parties, dinner parties, bachelor parties, innumerable Saturday nights on the town and vast tracts of daily life in between. It had been an undemanding, if depressing, role. An incalculable number of maudlin moments spent gazing into a pint of bitter.

However, and this was the point, had there been a dash of lust in his approach – lust being, arguably, a more powerful force than wistful worship – he might actually have been able to turn votive candles into something you had on the table in a restaurant on a real date.

Mike jumped around on the table. Yes, a date! I like that idea! But best of all I like this fierce, frightening female you've got set up inside yourself. I can see her now. A big amber-eyed fighting cat with a long, swishy tail and spots. Or maybe stripes. Yes, stripes I think. Except, some days she's a goddess cat – lithe and slinky and black all over, except with green jewel eyes. Enigmatic. Haughty ... He stood still and stared off into space for a moment or two.

Arthur gave him a poke. "Haughty? *Haughty*?"

Mike blinked a couple of times. Yes. It's a good word, isn't it?

"So is lust, and I think I'm beginning to see a bit of it. And I should tell you that all of this amber-eyed, hot cat stuff has not come out of my head."

Mike looked airily around. I expect I took a trip into the collective unconscious. Because, being a back street, orphan kitten, I didn't get to grow up with a giant warrior female in my life. In fact, there's been nothing that would encourage me to constellate such an archetype and give myself a huge complex.

"Constellate? Constellate? You might *look* like an orphan kitten but it's becoming increasingly obvious that it's not at all the same thing as *being* an orphan kitten," Arthur said.

Well, I am. You, on the other hand, grew up alongside an extremely haughty, spotty cat with a very effective swishy tail.

"We never had a cat!" exclaimed Arthur triumphantly, as if this actually clinched something.

Mike looked at him with an exaggerated air of weary tolerance.

"You mean Polly?" Arthur asked eventually. "*Polly*? You mean to say that my fearsome anima and barren love life have been all Polly's fault?"

Not at all. I'm quite sure it's all your fault. For letting it happen. It must have suited you in other ways to sit in the corner at every party. But we have to deal with these things as they come up, and right now it's Polly. But that's your inner work, as Jung calls it. I've suddenly got this big, black goddess cat to cope with.

"Good luck with that," said Arthur. "If she's even remotely like Polly you're in deep trouble." He turned this theory about his twin sister over in his mind for a minute or two, and then he said: "I feel as if we're confusing things. Animas, complexes, twin sisters ... I'm sure Dr. Jung wouldn't be mixing up his theories like this."

I don't think he'd care as long as the patient was heading towards some degree of deep understanding. Which I think you are.

"Well, let me get to the end of my deadly sin train of thought. Now ... pride, you see, is akin to self-respect. I could do with more of that. Greed has got to be a good motivator, if it comes out as healthy competitiveness and business acumen. I've got a minus quantity of those. Point is, how do you get stuff back out of here?" He gave the plasticine manikin a speculative shake. Its chest caved in and its head flopped back, but it released not so much as a spark.

I don't think that's a problem.

"You don't?

Not the immediate problem.

"So, what's the immediate problem?"

The reason they're shut up in there.

"I explained that. The shadow is the repository for antisocial character traits ..."

But, you would have a bit of self-respect and competitiveness, and a healthy amount of lust, if you hadn't shut them up so thoroughly. So, you're naturally self-effacing, and there's Polly on top, but we can't blame Polly for all of it, dominating though she is. Not at this point in time - we're supposed to be outgrowing family stuff by the age of thirty.

"So, why have I done it?"

Well, that's where the galleon comes in.

"What galleon?"

The galleon in the dream you're so determined not to analyse. The galleon, the Wheatstone bridge and the monkey scientist. That's what you have to deal with.

"I thought I had to deal with Polly?"

You'll do that.

"How?"

Recognition starts repair.

"Oh, very trite." Arthur sat back in his chair and folded his arms with a snort.

It's a process. Remember. And conscious power is not the only one involved in it. It's what you don't want to deal with that means all of this is going to keep following you about like a sick puppy.

"A sick puppy ?" Arthur snapped. "Or a small orphan kitten?"

Chapter Thirteen

It had occurred to Arthur - largely because his mother was prone to comment on the matter - that Polly had pulled off quite a performance in contriving a brilliant career, a husband and two children by the age of thirty. Indeed, by current standards - at least in terms of children - it seemed unnecessarily premature. But what now struck Arthur with force was how, exactly, Huw Parry, his brother-in-law, had got Polly to do it. Getting Polly to do things that she didn't want to do was next to impossible, and Arthur had never once heard, during his sister's constant teenage recital of her goals and ambitions, the word husband, or children, or anything of rough equivalence. So how a bulky, stolid prop forward, whose ears and nose had been unbecomingly processed by hours of semi-professional rugby, had scored so early and so effectively with such a difficult catch on such a determined trajectory was a mystery to Arthur. It was also one of those questions that you just can't ask. Which was a pity, because in reflecting upon one's own effectiveness – or lack of it – this sort of thing is of indisputable interest. But then, family gatherings, particularly on Christmas day, naturally give rise to questions like this. Every cooked turkey in the land probably had a veritable thundercloud of them hanging above it. How on earth did you end up married to my sister? Why on earth did she settle for you? Getting them answered in any amicable way is, of course, quite another matter.

In fact, Arthur really liked Huw. He just wanted to know, in explicit technicolour, how Polly had come to like him quite so much. Maybe, what had worked on Polly could work on Anastasia. But, speaking of work on Polly, Arthur had some of his own to do. Since Mike's unflattering view of their prevailing sibling dynamic, Arthur had felt oddly disposed towards her.

How do you feel about Polly now? Mike's face appeared inquisitorially above the pile of presents in Arthur's arms. So the questions had begun on the doorstep – long before the turkey was even fully cooked.

"Oddly disposed."

Well that has to be progress.

"No. That's probably just how it's always been. My sister has always had the capacity to stir up an exasperating mixture of moods in anybody and everybody."

But you've built your moods into a complex.

"*Well, I had to share a double baby buggy with her!*"

Huw opened the front door with a beaming smile. He had a fresh chip off a front tooth. Arthur's original question immediately reasserted itself. How on earth did this man catch Polly? How many helpings of deadly sin did it take?

Huw and Polly's four-storey Georgian in Notting Hill was as big a miracle of light and space as a very healthy, but not indecent, amount of money could buy. It was all whiteness and natural wood, plantation shutters and toys in a giant playroom in the basement alongside independent living for a nanny. In the main reception room, the chairs and sofas were covered in pale blue and white striped linen. Arthur put Mike, who had not been explicitly invited, on the floor and advised him to stay there. Mike was happy to comply because the floor was obviously an exciting space loaded with discarded wrapping paper, tangled ribbon, and teetering piles of presents. Its potential was exceeded only by that of the Christmas tree, which was ten feet tall and dressed entirely in shimmering, dangling clear glass ornaments and tiny white doves – all of which he was promptly forbidden to touch. Arthur folded himself up and sat on a pouffe in order to keep an eye on him.

"So, Arthur," Huw handed down a cup of gluhwein. "How is life according to Carl Gustav?"

There was no implied criticism or suspicious subtext to the question. Huw was an exceedingly amiable man. Loading and subtext were Polly's department. Huw asked simple and genuine questions. As a solicitor, he did conveyancing and probate. That was as uncomplicated as he could make a career in law that had always run second to the game of rugby. Polly, however, had never run second to anything in Huw Parry's life. And therein, possibly, lay his secret, Arthur thought now.

Huw's inherited funds, though they had no doubt initially lessened the pressures in many ways - allowing him, for instance, to be home early enough to share the children's tea - would never have weighed with Polly, whose confidence in her own power to plough a straight and highly productive furrow was absolute. And, even though there was no financial imperative, Huw respected her continuing need to do so because it was deep-rooted and implacable. And he loved her.

"Come on, Arthur. What's been happening to you?" He gave Arthur an encouraging nudge. Arthur almost felt like responding with a touch of the heartfelt outpouring business, because Huw was always remarkably unperturbed by things that perturbed other people (Polly for example). But even so, Arthur felt he couldn't be honestly forthcoming. He could not, much as he felt inclined, discuss things that no sane man could dignify with the credit of having actually happened.

"It's been a bit weird," he said finally.

"Weird how?"

Arthur thought for a moment or two, and then said: "Weird enough to make me fear for my sanity on occasions. Side-effects, including visuals, that can't be attributed to tablets, for instance."

Huw stared thoughtfully into the fire. It was real logs. Arthur was surprised that Polly had a tolerance for wood ash drifting out onto her floors and floating up onto the Adam mantelpiece.

"I spent a lot of my childhood with my grandparents, as you probably know," said Hugh finally, and apparently apropos of nothing. "Because father was away playing rugby and mother was ... well ... dead. And, as you probably also know, my grandparents made their money on the stock exchange. What you don't know is how they were so successful at it." He paused for a moment, as if not entirely committed to going on, then he said: "Grandma Edith had a spirit guide. A spirit guide that was, apparently, fiscally attuned. She called him Amos, which choice of name frequently incited non-PC comment by the way. Anyway most people, non-PC or otherwise, were of the opinion that she invented the spirit guide because my grandfather was the sort of man who might not have taken a woman's financial opinions over his own."

"He would prefer the word of a disembodied spirit?" asked Arthur incredulously.

"People obviously thought so," said Huw. "But the thing

is, I was virtually tied to my grandmother's apron strings. Not literally, because there was a maid who wore the aprons, but grandmother, having lost her only child, my mother, kept me obsessively close. And I know that, as far as Grandma was concerned, Amos actually existed.

"And do you believe that he existed?"

"The thing is, Arthur, I believe that there are things that would never be dreamed of in Polly's philosophy."

"Does that help any?" he asked after a pause.

"It could certainly allay the panic somewhat," said Arthur. "Because there are times …" He stopped. "She was sane, was she? Your Grandma?"

"She died at ninety-two years old, as sane as you or I. Or maybe just I." Huw gave a great chipped-toothed grin.

At this point Huw and Polly's daughter, six-year-old Sophie, came across and pressed a pink plastic pony into Arthur's hands. Sophie had inherited her mother's looks but coupled them with an earnestly concerned disposition, which made her a hugely appealing child. Arthur was her biggest fan. He was a willing babysitter and an inventive playmate. He gave his niece a hug and smoothed the pony's mane obligingly.

"Mike's playing with the ribbons," Sophie said.

Mike was deeply impressed by Christmas. He wasn't precisely clear as to its purpose or its origins, but its association with some very powerful energies he understood from the joyous surge that lately coursed through every fibre of his being. Christmas was brighter, sparklier and better-smelling than anything he'd hitherto encountered. People brought trees indoors, cooked food on glowing embers, and dressed up in red suits and white beards. If that wasn't a manifestation of something extraordinary, then Mike didn't know what was. And today, viewing things from beneath a canopy of discarded wrapping paper and ribbon, he found the world as full of sweetness and light as it had ever been. Until, that is, Polly came and perched herself portentously on the arm of her husband's chair, stretched out a shapely leg, studied the Manola Blanco on the end of it for a moment or two, then said to Arthur: "I met a friend of yours, the other day."

Arthur felt the icy breath of imminent persecution sweeping over him. "Which friend?"

"Damien Price."

"Oh, dear."

"Don't you like him? I thought he was charming."

"Was he trying to sell you a property?"

"Yes."

"Well then, he would have been."

"Have you been looking at houses by the river again?" Huw asked.

"I have. But that's not the issue I wanted to raise. Damien was telling me about Arthur's love life. Or rather, the lack of it."

"Does Arthur want this raised?" Huw sounded profoundly sceptical.

"Arthur never wants anything raised," said Polly. "He thinks it's an admirable character trait to remain tight-lipped about absolutely everything – except the disturbing discourses of long-dead psychiatrists – when actually it's enormously worrying for mother and father, and totally tedious for the rest of us. Also, and this is the pertinent point, it doesn't get him any dates."

"I expect Arthur could get dates if he wanted them," said Huw, in emollient tones. "He's just waiting for the right woman."

"He already knows the right woman," retorted Polly. "He worked in the same company, out of the same office, for three years and couldn't contrive to ask her to dinner, or otherwise betray his feelings in any effective way. You would have thought he could have got something in, somehow, on a slow day when the conversation was flagging, but no. Overall, I suppose, it rates as quite an accomplishment. Not a lot of men could have managed it."

"Damien told you this?" asked Arthur with a sharp intake of breath.

"He most certainly did," said Polly. "He was very forthcoming. He said he'd tried to make you see sense."

"See sense ... see sense!" Arthur wrestled with an oddly violent, 'back to the baby buggy' urge to bang his sister over the head with the pink plastic pony. "What sort of sense?"

"The sense to ask her out before she took up seriously with someone else. He said it was obvious that she just got sick of waiting."

"The devious bas... toad," Arthur corrected himself swiftly.

"What's a bass toad, Uncle Arthur?" asked Sophie.

"It's an especially malevolent type of toad," said Arthur, "that speaks with a forked tongue."

"Do toads have tongues?"

"Of course they do."

"Did someone stick a fork in the tongue?"

"Why don't you go and see what Granny and Grandpa have got for you?" suggested Huw, taking his daughter by the shoulders and pointing her encouragingly in the right direction. The grandparents Loveday had, of necessity, colonised the kitchen. Polly was hosting lunch but she was a shade absent-minded about the cooking of it.

"Do you want to tell us about this woman, Arthur?" Huw asked, after his daughter had dutifully but doubtfully trotted off.

"Damien has already done so," interrupted Polly. "She's called Anastasia Poliakof, Russian descent, family came here when the Bolsheviks got rowdy. She's well connected, and I think the expression Damien used was 'passing rich'. Also a little miffed that Arthur let opportunity after opportunity slide past."

"She could have made the first move," pointed out Huw.

"You've seen Putin," said Polly. "Maybe women of Russian descent are genetically programmed to prefer men with a level of enterprise. I expect she needed to see some evidence of it."

"Damien persistently told me that she was out of my league," protested Arthur furiously. "In fact, his last definitive words on the subject were: 'You're a frog, Arthur, and you will remain a frog. The princess is never going to kiss you!'"

"What princess? What princess?" clamoured his niece, who had come back to play with her pony. The kitchen had proved unproductive. Red-faced, irritable grandparents steering her away from hot pans.

"A very beautiful Russian one who loved Uncle Arthur, and Uncle Arthur did nothing about it," said Polly.

"Didn't he love the princess? Didn't you love the princess, Uncle Arthur? Could you not see that she loved you?"

Arthur cast about in his mind. Had there been anything to see? Had his instincts been entirely dormant? This was all ridiculous, surely?

"Uncle Arthur did nothing because he was a frog," said Polly.

"Not a swineherd?" asked her daughter doubtfully. "He couldn't have been a swineherd?"

"Much too enterprising," said Polly firmly.

Sophie took the point with a degree of anxiety. There were too many amphibians in this story. Nobody was going to get anywhere like this. Being a frog prince was a chancy business, and being uncle Arthur in the first place seemed chancy enough. Though, from the point of view of a six-year-old girl, not entirely understandable. Uncle Arthur had charm. He made a fine pirate in fishing waders when he handled princesses rather well, with brilliant smiles and astonishing leaps and bounds around the furniture. Why her uncle should fail so spectacularly to manage leaps and bounds in real life was quite beyond his niece.

Arthur was starting to feel oddly breathless. The thought that Anastasia might have been silently begging him to take her to dinner … He moved on from breathless to whoozy. Though he'd heard of out-of-body experiences, they hadn't had an in-depth Jungian treatment so he didn't know quite how to handle the feeling that he was floating somewhere in the vicinity of the chandelier, looking down on the poor, gasping fool crouched defensively on the pouffe. The sensation was nowhere near as full of soothing white light and the knowledge that all would be well, as near-death survivors had claimed.

Noticing his expression, Huw stood up and pulled his wife to her feet. "Polly, we really ought to give your mother just a little help. She is supposed to be a guest, after all. And Sophie, you come and play with your brother."

As Huw was speaking, Mike emerged in a rush from a bright pink carrier bag covered in iridescent stars, launched himself onto Arthur's lap and boxed him on the chin. Arthur blinked. Mike boxed him again, more energetically. Having Arthur jump out of his skin, just because he *might* have failed to notice that a princess *might* have been in love with him, was not encouraging. It did not look like promising quest behaviour to Mike. *Come down from the ceiling at once!*

That's a very unusual sort of kitten, thought Arthur vaguely from behind the chandelier.

Come down now!!

"What?" Suddenly back on the pouffe, Arthur drew back his head to focus the better on the insistent furry face pushing into his.

The jackdaw will get you!

"Jackdaw?" Arthur struggled for alignment.

Mike biffed him again to help with the grounding. He was wearing a red collar with a jingle bell on it which he'd selected specially for himself in the pets department at Harrods. He'd been there with Arthur, to pick up Christmas puddings for Polly, who'd started developing ploys to enmesh her brother in what she considered to be normalising activities. Mike was beginning to think she had a point. So, although Arthur was still looking glassy-eyed and short of oxygen, he felt obliged to forcibly acquaint him with the principle that floating up to the ceiling on account of a woman was not at all a good idea. Even a woman such as Anastasia Poliakof.

Plus, it was doubtful that this was the correct interpretation of the theory that love was essentially a process of projection.

"I suppose it is because I am so in love with her," acknowledged Arthur weakly.

Mike studied him anxiously. I love you. It doesn't make me jump out of my skin. And it doesn't make me miserable. Worried at times. Like right now.

"Different love," said Arthur. "Plus, you're a kitten. This type of love is a peculiarly human affliction and it doesn't always bring out the best in us."

Then you need to be very, *very* careful. You allow yourself to become too absent and the jackdaw will have your eyes. Then you'll never see the truth of anything.

Arthur treated this dramatic point to a level of fuzzy consideration. "From human love to jackdaws pecking out eyes," he said finally. "It's a conceptual leap that I am entirely failing to make."

You've seen the jackdaw. We have to be careful. Mike looked around.

Arthur gave an involuntary shudder. "So, what does he signify? Given that I am choosing to regard the eye business as a metaphor."

He's the trickster. He fools us and he gets us to fool ourselves.

"I see." Fully back in his body, Arthur rested his head for a moment on the arm of a nearby chair. Scraps of conversation came to him from the kitchen.

"Maybe he's got blood sugar problems. We should speed up lunch."

"Has anybody put the apple sauce to warm?"

"Petit mal epilepsy.' (This was definitely Polly.) 'That involves staring off into space. One of our directors has it. It's not remotely convenient."

"Is anybody stirring the gravy?"

"He should see a doctor."

"He's seen a doctor."

"Which doctor?"

"Exactly. A witch doctor!"

"I don't know why you always insist on Brussels sprouts.

Nobody likes them."

Arthur raised his head from the chair arm. "Hubble, bubble, toil and trouble." he said. Mike gave him another biff on the nose as a cure for talking nonsense.

"I'm quoting Shakespeare."

Who?

"The greatest poet and playwright ever. And an incidental psychologist of some talent."

Better than Jung?

"Apples and potatoes," said Arthur. "But, Shakespeare certainly understood the trickster archetype. *'Macduff was not of woman born, but from his mother's womb untimely ripped.'*"

It took some time to fully explain this to Mike, starting with apples and potatoes, but he got it: So, Damien said, 'she is never going to kiss you'. He never said, 'you're never going to kiss her.'

"Precisely," said Arthur. "The trickster energy is very strong with Damien."

He meant proper kissing, didn't he? Not these mercy kisses she gives people in shops, because I was wondering how exactly ...

"Don't," said Arthur.

A silence, interrupted only by the banging of cooking utensils, had been prevailing in the kitchen, then somebody said: "He's explaining Shakespeare to that kitten now. Can that be healthy?"

"Which play had a Damien in it ?" asked Mr. Loveday.

*****

There was an unspoken agreement that the family tactic of broaching awkward topics at mealtimes would not be employed over Christmas lunch.

"Do you think the kitten should actually be on the table, Arthur?" asked his mother, who didn't consider the behaviour of pets an awkward topic. "It doesn't seem entirely hygienic."

Arthur picked Mike up and sat him on a table mat. "Don't move," he said. "The rest of us aren't allowed to go wandering round while we eat."

"Of course you realise that's ridiculous." Mrs Loveday, still red-faced from the inferno that the kitchen had rapidly become and cross that she had forsaken her usual beige for a flamboyantly festive shade of crimson, was understandably anxious that nothing should detract from the meal. The huge turkey had been purchased at a frightening cost, which supposedly guaranteed that it had been humanely reared in the fresh air and fed upon nothing that resembled antibiotics or hormones, or the ground-up remains of other turkeys. The vegetables however, being organic, may well have been fed upon quite a variety of ground-up remains, thus ensuring a combination meal that provided the best of all worlds. Especially when accompanied by chilled champagne. What it didn't need was a side dish of kitten.

"For heaven's sake, Arthur, he's an animal. He'll be into the turkey and the sausages, the minute you let go of him!" Mrs. Loveday was in no mood to be amused by the tablemat ploy.

Mike fixed her with an extremely indignant look. That's not at all respectful!

Arthur's nephew, Charlie, who was barely four years old and had his father's brown curls and rather prominent teddy bear ears, burst into delighted laughter.

"Mother's right," said Polly. "The kitten could go down on the floor."

"He wants to enjoy the meal with the rest of us." said

Arthur. "He has a pronounced companionable streak."

"He's Uncle Arthur's mascot," said Sophie.

Mike didn't like having his status progressively impeached in this casual fashion. Companion, mascot ... I'm a talisman, Arthur! He demanded that this be explained. Charlie pointed with his fork and laughed delightedly. Arthur bent his head towards Mike. "Not now," he said sotto voce. "Explanations like that come under the banner of awkward topics. Eat your turkey liver. It was poached specially for you."

"Arthur, stop it! Whispering in company is rude, and whispering about us to an animal that is sitting in the middle of everyone's Christmas lunch is positively infuriating. I'm trying to teach Charlie table manners and he can't even concentrate on the food on his plate." Polly was coming to the conclusion that the best approach to Arthur's outbreaks of oddness was zero tolerance.

"It's Christmas," said Huw soothingly. "So, in the spirit of the lowly cattle shed, let's allow the kitten a seat at the feast as long as he stays ... well ... in the vague vicinity of the tablemat. He's no size, how dirty can he possibly be?"

"Why does he never grow?" asked Mr. Loveday, who had not yet received a satisfactory answer to this.

"Growing is not always about growing in body," said Charlie.

There was a surprised pause. "Where did you get that from?" asked Huw.

Charlie was small for his age and Huw thought that this sounded a very nice way for somebody to have explained to him why he was failing to keep pace with his friend Jack. "Did Mummy tell you that?"

"No way," said Arthur with undiplomatic conviction. His sister gave him a dark look.

"An old lady," said Charlie.

"You mean Grandma?" asked Polly. Now it was her turn to be in receipt of a dark look.

"Another old lady that was here."

"When?" asked Polly. "When have we been hosting old ladies? Huw?"

"No, my love," said Huw with a grin. "I do not bring old ladies home behind your back."

"She was just here. Before." Charlie looked round vaguely.

"Before what?"

"When I was playing."

"So she was a pretend old lady?" suggested Huw.

"No. But she had a big bag. Made of carpets."

"Did she have a purple feather in her hat?" asked Arthur with a feeling of dread.

"Yes. She was a very nice old lady with a feather in her hat."

"Stop it, Arthur." said Polly. "He's making it all up and this sort of thing won't play well at school. Plus, we don't need him ending up like you."

"Or Great Grandma Edith," said Arthur quietly.

Huw, who was near, caught it and pulled a face. "Let's just enjoy the food, and not get overwrought about old ladies, real or imagined," he said firmly. "This meal took a lot of cooking and it deserves our full attention."

No one was feeling quite churlish enough to dispute this.

*****

Arthur volunteered to wash the towering heaps of pans and bowls that would never make it into the dishwasher until Boxing Day, at the earliest. He knew that by doing this, he ran the risk of being trapped in the kitchen with someone who had been tacitly delegated to further enlighten him on more and better ways to improve his life. As it turned out it was his mother. The minute she said 'Arthur' he knew what was coming. He let her get through the preamble and then the bit about only wanting what was best for him and then he said: "I know you do, but the trouble is that your ideas of what is best for me and mine don't always coincide."

"Well, the thing is, Arthur," his mother replied, with some asperity, "the way you've been behaving lately, I'm not sure that you're actually much of a judge."

Arthur put down the scrubbing pad and turned to face her. "I can see that it must look that way," he said levelly. "And I concede that, in the past, I made some bad choices that I will just have to live with. But, this thing that I'm doing now …" he paused "… that is happening to me now … It has to be gone through. I can't explain it satisfactorily to you, because it isn't explainable in normal terms. But I will get through it, and I will be alright. Trust me."

His mother took a long hard look at him. "Fine," she said, after a few seconds. "Now be careful with that big ceramic dish because it's Polly's latest, and if you drop it on this tiled floor it will explode like a bomb."

Turning back to the sink Arthur let out a long held breath. He had spoken evenly enough, and earnestly enough, to reassure his mother. He had not, however, reassured himself. He was trying to treat his experiences as Jung had treated his own – observationally and analytically. But he was painfully aware that he did not possess Jung's education and experience. Or his absolute conviction. He was striving for pragmatic acceptance coupled with a light-hearted open-mindedness but, inside him, growing as implacably as any malignancy, there was a twisting black knot of fear. It hung between his heart and his stomach, maintained in a state of suspended animation by sheer force of will. The line between finding himself and living a life, or disappearing into the void forever, was the line between the sane and the insane. And all he had to help him police it was a pile of old books, a voodoo psychologist and a very small white kitten. The ceramic casserole slipped from his grasp and smashed on the floor.

Chapter Fourteen

Polly came rushing into the kitchen and stared aghast at the exploded remains.

"It was just an accident," said her mother, soothingly. "I'll clean it up."

Arthur turned to face his sister. "There's a theory," he said, "to which I am sure you would never subscribe, that there are no accidents. That everything we do is unconsciously motivated to serve a purpose."

"Are you trying to say that you did this on purpose? My favourite casserole?"

"It's not your favourite casserole, Polly. It's just your latest casserole. You have a kitchen here kitted out for the Roux brothers and you never cook!" Arthur gestured sweepingly around at the larder cupboards, the Aga, the huge American style fridge, the granite working surfaces, the endless gadgetry …

"So, you broke my new casserole out of spite because I never cook?"

"I'm a lot of things," said Arthur evenly." Or rather, the popular view is that I lack a lot of things, but I'm not particularly spiteful. What I would say is that, maybe, I was working out my shadow side. Paying out the dark symbolically, as Madame Ibeg Boona might put it. Now, I'm sorry about the casserole and I'll clean it up but I won't offer to pay for it because I'm quite sure that you forked out an awful lot more than it's worth. We all square it with the dark taxmen in our own way."

"What *is* he talking about?" Polly appealed to their mother in dramatic tones.

"I've no idea," said Mrs. Loveday. "But I feel oddly encouraged by the way he said it."

*****

Arthur swore to himself that he would avoid gatherings of any sort on New Year's Eve. It was a decision that he was able to stick to without any effort at all, because no-one asked him to go anywhere. His parents were attending some frugal bring-a-dish supper with friends who, like them, walked for fun. Polly and Huw and the children had gone to renew their appreciation of the various ways one could slide down a snowy mountain. The multi-headed beast that was Carruthers Sloan had cast none of its myriad eyes in his direction since the Christmas party. It was just Mike and he, squatting in the ever-increasing squalor that was number 29B. He had no intention of even answering the telephone. And yet: "Is that Arthur Loveday?"

Arthur did not recognise the voice – male, polite, cultured even – so he hesitated for a long moment. He did not, for instance, intend to be Arthur Loveday if the Death Incorporated insurance company was merely trying to sell him a policy that would enable him to pay for his own funeral. This seemed unlikely at nine o'clock on New Year's Eve, but Arthur understood very well that sales persons have a flair for catching people at their most vulnerable. They knew that there were times when the fragility of life was a concept that struck people more powerfully than usual and December 31st, with the looming prospect of another year, full of broken resolutions and unfulfilled expectations, could appear to a dedicated sales team to be just such a time. So, for whom, then, was Arthur prepared to be Arthur?

"Is Arthur Loveday at this number?"

The voice was starting to sound strangely familiar. It carried just that stir of echoes that made Arthur determined to say 'No'. "Yes," he said.

A breezy sense of jubilation came to him across the ether. "It's Ptolemy. Ptolemy De'ath from Balliol. Remember?"

Up to this point in the evening, Arthur had been slumped in front of the television, watching the kind of stuff that should have been an inducement to anybody with any brain activity at all to get up and go somewhere. But, going somewhere is not an option for the self-incarcerated, so Arthur had sat on, and on, time shuffling by so slowly that, as Death Incorporated would have rightly surmised, he had begun to wonder how he could get through his three score years and ten. Even when he closed his eyes and sought the brief oblivion of sleep, his tired and jarred senses imbued perfectly innocuous sounds with hideous portent and jerked him into wakefulness with overwrought inner shrieks.

And now, in spite of his protective isolation, there had arisen out of his long-dead past the one thing he least wanted to face. For ten years he had banished Oxford to a mental wasteland that he visited only under the pressure of direct and determined questioning from people whose curiosity far exceeded their sensitivity:

'You went to Oxford, didn't you?'

'No.'

'Somebody told me you did. Somebody who would have known.'

No answer.

'Come on. Why are you being so cagey about this? Did you get sent down?'

'No.'

'So what happened? You fail the exams?'

'No.'

'So what then?'

'I just left.'

'Why?'

'I just did.'

'For no reason?'

'For no reason.'

'Well, you must regret that.'

'Not at all.'

It's just that my soul drips blood whenever I think about it. It's not so much regret as psychological evisceration. I feel as if something irreplaceable has died. I feel as if I have died. And nobody will ever be able to bring me back.

But, unfortunately, even after ten years of attempting to mentally obliterate Oxford from his consciousness, Arthur still remembered Ptolemy De'ath. For one thing, the guy had a spectacularly memorable name. Spelt like death, written De'ath, pronounced dee ath and preceded by Ptolemy. How could one forget? At Oxford, the Ptolemy part had become corrupted to Tony by people called Dave and anybody in a hurry. Obviously, it had reasserted itself since.

"Friday afternoons, Arthur," said Ptolemy now. "We used to do practicals together when Jono took it into his head not to turn up."

Jono, Arthur's lab partner, had had a facility for the

physics business that was nothing short of infuriating. In fact, he'd found it that way himself, becoming so bored by the obviousness of it all that he'd regularly failed to put in an appearance. He'd go off and do some afternoon drinking instead. He got a first, anyway.

"Did you ever hear from him?" asked Ptolemy.

"No."

"What are *you* doing now?"

"Nothing," said Arthur. There seemed little point in elaborating.

"I mean *now*, not in general."

"Still nothing," said Arthur, determined not to be drawn.

"How are you going to let the new year in?" Ptolemy asked.

Mentally, Arthur acknowledged his memorable and peculiar persistence. "In my sleep."

"But it's such a lovely night."

"It's snowing."

"That makes it all the more beautiful."

Arthur half turned to look out of the window. On the street above him snow was falling gently through the golden halo of a street light. It was beautiful.

"Do you know Mary Jacob Park?" Ptolemy asked. "It's about a mile from you, as the crow flies."

"No."

"Very few people do. Victorian park. Several acres. Been shut up for years – some legal wrangle over ownership and development possibilities. Big walls, big gates, big threatening notices, you know the sort of place. But a sweet party venue for those in the know."

"Must be full of vagrants," said Arthur.

"Maybe some, but there'll be a crowd of us. It's a reunion

of sorts. Ten years on. Give or take. You know. The gates don't open, and they have spikes on the top, so a degree of athleticism is a necessary prerequisite for entry. Shouldn't be a problem for you, as I recall." Some directions followed this - street names that Arthur knew, others unfamiliar, the odd one unlikely. "I'm expecting you," finished Ptolemy, and then the phone went dead.

Arthur had no intention of going. It would be unendurable. Infinitely worse than the Carruthers Sloan Christmas party, without the consolation of a glimpse of Anastasia. So infinitely, infinitely worse that, in truth, he just couldn't go. His legs simply wouldn't get him there.

Mike had scrambled onto his knee. Can I come? Did he say I could go?

Arthur stared numbly at the telephone. "He didn't mention you."

Mike looked disconsolate. Madam Ibeg Boona said I wasn't to be left behind in cupboards.

"You aren't being left behind, because we aren't going."

Why not?

"You have no idea who that was on the phone."

I think I do, then. It was one of those monkey scientists.

"It wasn't monkeys," said Arthur dangerously. "And Ptolemy wasn't monkey. Oh, for God's sake you've got me at it now, manqué, *manqué*! He isn't manqué … he didn't fail …" Arthur's voice suddenly gave way.

I see. Mike considered this for a moment or two. You have to face these things, you know. You have to face your fears.

"I hate that," snapped Arthur. "Why does everybody trot it out when it's so obviously not true? Fear is fear, and it's there to serve a purpose. It stops us from getting killed by woolly mammoths."

There'll be woolly mammoths?

"You just don't get 'illustrative', do you?" Arthur was getting angry. "You never have ."

So there won't be woolly mammoths, then. There'll be no fears that you can't actually face.

"Facing fears … "Arthur found himself having to fight to remain civil, "… facing this kind of fear, reopening old wounds is … is … like opening a can of worms. They'll crawl everywhere, and you'll never get them back in again."

Mike looked at him. They're not in now. They're eating you alive. They've been at it for years.

Arthur didn't respond, merely stared off into space. Mike patted his face. What can possibly be worse than what you've been feeling lately?

Arthur looked at him in desperation. "Irreversible psychosis," he said.

And this will be brought on by seeing Ptolemy De'ath?

"It won't be helped by seeing him."

Are you sure of that?

Arthur didn't reply. A wretched silence prevailed for a while, then Mike gave him an encouraging poke. There is a very fine scarf in the bottom of the wardrobe. I could wear it when we go. It's snowing, you know.

"What scarf?" asked Arthur.

A Hertford college scarf.

It had probably been half a century or more since anyone had considered a college scarf any sort of badge of honour worth wearing. But the minute Arthur had been officially accepted for Oxford his mother had bought one. Somehow, it had survived and found its way into the wardrobe at 29B. If it got an outing on a kitten, it would be the first one it had ever had. The sudden memory of his mother's pride in him made Arthur feel sick.

It's got very nice stripes, that scarf. I really like stripes. I used to prefer spots but now I'm beginning to think ….

Arthur exploded. "*You are ridiculous! You must be the worst talisman ever!* It's impossible to compute your constant leaps between inconsequential drivel and what could be profound insights. Unfortunately, the drivel is the only bit I can vouchsafe as accurate. So yes, I'll concede that the scarf has nice stripes, however, as to whether or not you are right to insist on this excruciating expedition …" He stopped.

Mike was looking hugely upset. I can't be pronouncing all the time. I'm just a kitten.

"Excuses, excuses," snorted Arthur. "I can't write, I can't read, I'm just a kitten …"

Now that's just hurtful. How many talismans do you know of that can read and write? I ask you. King Arthur's sword, for instance? Could it read and write or make plasticine manikins? I don't think so! Mike's feelings were deeply hurt. Arthur was being angry and unkind and so unlike himself. But he was hurting too. And he was afraid. The world of talking kittens and trickster jackdaws and waylaying witches was swallowing him up, and on top of this some highly unpalatable aspect of his past had just reintroduced itself. Mike understood all of this, and so he forgave him. He looked kindly at Arthur. Let's just go and see Ptolemy and whoever else is there. It's important. I know it is.

"I don't want to see Ptolemy and whoever else is there."

I know. And that is why we have to go.

"And that's valid?"

It is in Dr. Jung's world. And that, whether you like it or not, is pretty much where we are.

So, finally, Arthur got up off the sofa and went into the bedroom in search of a coat. Then he helped Mike to retrieve the Hertford college scarf from the floor of the wardrobe. "I'm sorry about before," he said, holding it up and picking off fluff. "About your talking drivel and so on. It was harsh and I was being unkind, and that's not how I want us to start a new year."

I know. You love me. And I love you. That's right, isn't it?

"Exactly." Arthur picked him up. "You're determined to wear this, then? You don't think it's too big at all?"

It was past eleven o'clock and the streets were unusually quiet. The occasional car, the odd taxi slipped past leaving black wheel marks on the steadily whitening road. The taxis had no interest in being flagged down so Arthur walked on. Snowflakes fell silently through the technicolour glow of Christmas lights, a ripple of laughter floated in from somewhere, and a dog nipped round a corner on a mission of its own. Arthur continued to walk, feeling wretched, and nursing an uncomfortable residue of defensive anger. But, as he followed the somewhat rapid fire directions he'd been given, both of these feelings got gradually nudged aside by a growing sense of disbelief. He had a good grasp of London's layout, a fine memory for street names and a useful sense of direction. He could not imagine where this park could lie. He found it hard to believe that a large chunk of green real estate, apparently awaiting development for many years, had never so much as had its name whispered at Carruthers Sloan. The more he thought, and the farther he walked, the more the directions he'd been given felt like 'first star on the right and straight on till morning'. "This place doesn't exist," he said to Mike. "I feel as if I've been walking for hours and yet …" He stopped and looked up and down the road.

Mike stuck his head out of the scarf. It's just round the corner.

"How can you possibly know that?"

But it was. Two short streets of nondescript brick houses formed a cul-de-sac at the end of which was an enormous pair of heavily ornate iron gates. As the park had been billed as a party venue, albeit a clandestine one, with chains and heavy padlocks to keep you out, Arthur had expected the distant sound, if not the immediate spectacle, of people having fun. But as he dropped down from the wall, his only impression was one of crushing stillness and desolation. He had landed in a patch of brambles and fighting clear of their prickly, clinging arms he came upon what looked like the outline of a path. Scuffling aside the snow with his boot, he exposed stone slabs, their joints invaded by grass and moss. Apart from his own scuff marks, the path was untrodden. He looked around.

The place bore all the hallmarks of long dead aspiration and grandeur. Arthur recognised it in the type and careful placement of the trees: a magnificent, spreading cedar of Lebanon, a sentinel stand of Wellingtonias; and in the ivy-covered classical statuary - gods and goddesses, beheaded and limbless - a massacred Greek chorus around a huge, tiered, wedding cake fountain which decades of winter frost had attacked and crumbled. There could have been a touching beauty in these worn-down glories, but their collapse and decay felt stealthily linked to the threat of unseen and unpleasant things.

Mike fought himself clear of the scarf which Arthur had unceremoniously bundled into his overcoat before the ascent of the wall. He raised himself up on one paw and looked around. I like this place, do you?

"Not entirely," said Arthur. "There are a lot of things about it I don't understand." He paused, "Hear that silence?"

Yes.

"Well, where is the party? Where are the footprints?"

Maybe everybody came in another way.

"Maybe. But, this place has to be the holy grail of every property developer and land agent in the city, not to mention every vagrant and every drug dealer, yet it looks as if no one has been here for years. Enormous metal gates chained shut, and the only notice on them an ancient and broken 'Trespassers will…'? Not even any graffiti? Or any fingerprints left by Damien Price and his enterprising ilk? No planning notices…no *anything*?"

Well, that isn't the park's fault.

"Maybe not, but it's nothing short of astonishing."

That there is something right there and you've refused to register it for years? Disturbing, maybe. Not astonishing.

Arthur shook his head, "Which way on this path, then?"

That way. I can hear the hiss of gaslight.

"Gaslight? Impossible."

Cats have the greatest hearing range of any mammal.

"It's not the hearing, it's the idea of gaslight."

You'll see.

After walking a hundred yards or so, they did see. They came to the remains of a bandstand. And there were gaslights. *Gaslights!* Unbelievable! The bandstand had once been rather grand. A roofed and raised pentangle of intricate brickwork and fancy wrought iron, built for the purpose of adding musical entertainment to a walk in the park. There was a figure standing on the bandstand steps. It gave a whistle and hailed them cheerfully as they approached. A familiar voice carried crisply to them on the freezing air. "Hello, Arthur."

"Ptolemy?"

Ptolemy had changed. Grown taller. Significantly so. Lost his tendency to what could generously be referred to as puppy fat, and the cherubic physiognomy that had gone with it. He'd also lost his glasses. Now he looked easeful and almost Byronic in a long black overcoat, an equally long grey woollen scarf and some rather expensive looking biker boots with prominent buckles. Arthur couldn't believe his eyes. The difficulty of whether the pair of them should shake hands or hug was overcome by the expediency of doing neither.

"Are there others?" Arthur asked, glancing round.

Ptolemy smiled. He had a charming smile and an impressive arcade of teeth - commendably white and even. He leaned casually on the iron balustrading, evidently pleased with himself and the world around him. How on earth had he grown to look like this? Arthur wondered.

"So, how has life been treating you, Arthur?" Ptolemy asked.

"Up and down," said Arthur, with as casual a shrug as he could produce. "You know how it is."

"Not really."

"Your life is all up, is it?" Arthur's tone was carefully light.

"Went straight from Oxford to Harvard," said Ptolemy. "Did my Ph.D. there. Went with an American team to Cern. That was tremendous fun, of course. What travels faster than light, eh? These days, I'm at University College here in London working in the field of dark matter. Most of the mass of the Universe and we can't even find it! It's the new frontier, Arthur. Gran Sasso's starting in 2013. It's going to take place one and a half kilometres under the mountain, to avoid the radiation that comes in from space and the measuring device will be a flask of argon. Think of it!"

"Yes," said Arthur, because he had no other words. The knowledge that his private dream had been taken from him by Ptolemy De'ath and put to work in such a purposeful and successful fashion had deprived him of … well … anything.

When Arthur had given up on Oxford, halfway through his second year, it had been amidst a fearful emotional storm. His mother's tears, his father's pleadings, his own despair. Physics had been his magic, his love, the reason he got up in the morning. The very idea of something like the Hadron Collider had filled him with excitement. Extravagant theories delighted him, even the maths. He'd had a facility with mathematics well above the school norm. But at Oxford that had turned out to be no great accomplishment. There, he had been surrounded by self-confident brilliance and he'd allowed it to create in him a profound sense of personal and intellectual inferiority.

"So, what are you doing now, Arthur? Exactly?" Ptolemy asked.

"Nothing," said Arthur.

"Exactly nothing." Ptolemy looked him up and down in considered assessment. "It's a shame you left Oxford," he said finally. "We did miss you."

Arthur felt ridiculously grateful for this, and he was embarrassingly aware that this pathetic gratitude was probably showing in his face.

"Of course, it was inevitable," Ptolemy went on in casual, conversational tones. "You just weren't good enough. And you recognised that. It was a commendable piece of self-assessment." He paused, thoughtful. "Then again, with a different attitude, guts I think it's called, you might have stuck it out and maybe you'd have accomplished what you thought you never could. But your sister got all the guts, didn't she?

The incredible Polly. We were all very much taken with her that time she visited. Astonished, of course, that she took to that rugby fellow from Christ Church. Also astonished that she was your twin. Or, maybe it isn't so astonishing when you think about it. She took everything, didn't she? Nothing left over for poor little Arthur. In terms of character, poor little Arthur was the runt of the litter, wasn't he? And yet, still he wanted to shoot for the stars. Remember Annie Chung, the mathematician from L.M.H.? Never did dare ask her for a date, did you?"

Pain shot through Arthur like cracks through glass. He couldn't believe that Ptolemy had spoken to him like that. Couldn't believe that he'd be so cruel - and so accurate.

Mike was feeling extremely uneasy. He was starting to have severe reservations about the way things were working out. He could feel Arthur mentally buckling. Arthur. Arthur! *Arthur!! You've seen him now. It's done. It's time to go.*

But Arthur couldn't leave. The weight of his failure bore down upon him and held him fast. Mike wriggled furiously in the scarf.

"Good God," exclaimed Ptolemy. "Is that a kitten you brought along? What on earth is wrong with you?"

Arthur looked despairingly down at Mike. And when he looked up again, Ptolemy had gone. From the rest of the park came nothing but an ominous silence. He had a sudden and uncomfortable presentiment that something was seriously amiss. Even on the brink of irretrievable. "Ptolemy?" he called.

And louder: "*Ptolemy?*"

A thousand Babel voices answered him. They whispered and hissed and echoed in a myriad occult vaultings. Whirling snowflakes began to perform icy feats of prestidigitation -

vortices, tunnels, portals, came and went. Shapes and shadows slipped on by. Arthur felt the strengthening grip of some horrid and unwholesome power. And, in his rapidly tightening chest, improbability spawned a bastard brood of screaming fear. His terrified mind could form only one coherent idea: RUN.

But to run was not to entirely escape. Scenes that he would never have chosen to revisit, even in his mind, rose before him as vividly as if he were there again: a paper unfinished before him on the desk … Staring at it in fear and panic … I can't do this, I can't do this … A drip of sweat, teased out by terror and the early summer sun, landing on the page … His tutor railing at him with a mixture of disappointment and disgust … gesturing dismissively, washing his hands of him … Himself, white faced and mute with pain, loading his possessions into the old Morris; Jono simultaneously helping and pleading; Ptolemy standing by, silently appalled … His mother sobbing helplessly at the kitchen table, his father gazing at him in horror, as if he had been cast out for rape or murder …

He slipped and almost went down on the icy path. Desperately close to hysteria, he righted himself …To stay down was to stay here. Reliving the most painful moments of his life … Forever.

Chapter Fifteen

Arthur arrived home in a state of gasping extremis. He'd slipped endless times on snowy pavements, fallen twice and almost crushed Mike. Each time he'd scrambled desperately to his feet with that same terrifying sense that to stay down was to be lost. Once inside the flat, he collapsed onto the sofa, shaking. His clothes were sodden with melted snow and the sweat of fear and exertion. He thought he was going to vomit.

When at last he began to shake with nothing more than the icy reality of cold, he got up and lit the gas fire. Mike, who had been crouching silently on his chest, sat thankfully in front of it and stared fixedly into the flames. Neither of them spoke for a considerable time. They were well into January 1st, 2011 when Mike finally got up and went to a strewn pile of mail under the coffee table. The pile was predominantly composed of unopened Christmas cards. Systematically, Mike patted his way through them until he came to a smart cream envelope that had been opened and sent it skimming across to Arthur. Almost absently, Arthur bent down and picked it up. He took out a piece of card and read :

Reunion of 2001 Oxford Physics Graduates
December 31st, 9:30pm
St. James Park, London
Food and Fun followed by fireworks over the Thames.

There was a personalised and encouraging postscript signed by Ptolemy De'ath with his more casual name - Tony - in brackets.

Arthur stared at this for quite a while and then asked wearily: "Did I read this when it arrived?"

Read it and blotted it out.

"It says St. James Park, not Mary Jacob Park."

Yes.

"But there is a Mary Jacob Park? I mean, we went there, didn't we?"

Well, we're very wet and your coat is still torn from where you climbed over the spiky wall.

"And Ptolemy?"

I suppose Ptolemy was in St. James Park, where he was meant to be.

"Yes, he would be," said Arthur bitterly. At Oxford, he had found Ptolemy extremely irritating, and for one outstanding but petty reason. In spite of the fact that he'd stood only a few inches over five feet, was indisputably overweight and wore unflattering spectacles, Ptolemy seemed permanently and extraordinarily thrilled with himself. That's not to say that he was always joyously outgoing – there were occasions when he was downright disagreeable - but through every mood there had shone the unaltered consciousness of his self-belief. Ptolemy might not always have known exactly where he was going but, in spite of his myopia and the excess baggage of his weight, he was totally confident in his ability to get there.

It was a gift that Arthur had envied from the very depths of his soul. Not the bumptious aspect of it which was, he admitted now, primarily in his own mind and the means by which he could defuse his envy – but the sheer, undentable implacability of it. A calculation came out incorrectly and Arthur felt that he was an inferior student without innate ability. A calculation came out wrong and Ptolemy had merely made a mistake somewhere in the process. He would methodically backtrack and correct. An inaccurate calculation was a reflection of the care he'd taken, not of his potential or his innermost self.

"So, who did we meet in Mary Jacob Park?" Arthur asked.

You didn't recognise him?

"No."

You didn't see your biggest wish, your greatest fantasy, your wildest dream? You didn't see you?

Arthur sat silent for a few moments. "But why as Ptolemy? Why believe it was Ptolemy?"

Because you don't believe in yourself.

"I see …" Arthur said, though he wasn't entirely sure that he did. "So real, wasn't it?"

As real as the witch. A real place, Arthur. A real archetype. The unconscious reacts explosively when things badly need restoring. And it takes us there. Where we need to go.

"But I fail to see how this … this rubbing salt in the wound can possibly help. Dr. Jung met a beautiful woman who was wise and told him stuff. Constructive dialogue was had. Not carefully delivered insult. I mean, what purpose could this possibly have served?"

Nobody ever said that everything you encountered in the unconscious worlds was going to be nice. Or serve a purpose

196

that you could presently understand. As it happens, I think this - let's call him a modern archetype, the current hero as the successful man …

"What on earth sort of hero is that?"

It's what everybody wants to be, isn't it? Successful.

"But he was horrible to me."

And successful men are never horrible?

"But what about the hero part?"

I expect heroes do what they have to do. Whatever it is. If a hero always does what is the best thing in the long run then, by that definition, this archetype did exactly what he had to do.

"And what was that, for heaven's sake?"

He created a nice open wound.

"What?"

A way in.

"A way into what?"

A way into you, Arthur. Which, frankly, you weren't offering before. And, as long as we refuse to bring our suppressed miseries and memories into consciousness, we will continue to dream the same bad dreams, repeat the same old mistakes.

Arthur put his head in his hands. He couldn't do this anymore. He wasn't Jung. He wasn't, as Ptolemy that wasn't Ptolemy had so heartlessly pointed out, anybody with any backbone whatsoever. He was having a mental breakdown that would most likely … He looked at Mike and said: "There's a world in which I never come back from this, isn't there? A world in which I never get the genie back in the bottle. How do I stop it? How in God's name do I stop it?"

It's a process, Arthur, I'm not sure we're meant to stop it.

"But I won't survive it. Not in any useful form."

Mike looked at him. You must. So we'll go and see the only person who might know how.

*****

Do you think I'll need to be sacrificed? Mike was just the teeniest bit afraid. Afraid that it might hurt. Afraid that he might never see Arthur again because Arthurs didn't go to the same everafters as sacrificed kittens.

"Sacrificed? Goodness no!" Arthur exclaimed. "No … no …no …"

People in his immediate vicinity shuffled imperceptibly farther away. The tube train was crowded so it wasn't easy, but they tried. Nobody wanted to be near the wild-eyed, unshaven vagrant in the torn overcoat, who was talking to a kitten in a series of rather alarming non-sequiturs. He was far too big, and obviously far from sane.

Arthur was shocked. Not at the general and concerted effort to squeeze away from him, but at Mike: "Whatever gave you that idea?"

Madame Ibeg Boona said it would be hard for you if I wasn't. Maybe, harder than you could deal with. I think she's right. I think I should be sacrificed, if it's not too late.

"No," said Arthur sharply. "That's not an option! If anybody's going to be laid open on an altar, it's going to be me. At this point, frankly, I don't care."

The tube pulled into a station, the doors opened and a pile of people got off. Half of them got back on again a few carriages farther down.

*****

"So, Arthur," said Madam Ibeg Boona, looking him up and

198

down in some dismay. "Where do we start?"

"Not by sacrificing Mike," said Arthur. "I want that to be absolutely clear. Nor do we finish that way."

Madame Ibeg Boona seemed relieved that he had some fight left in him. She nodded, and the peacock feathers round her scarlet turban, iridescent in the glow of the fire, danced their approval. Mike marked them down as something that needed watching. Like balls of wool.

Madame Ibeg Boona handed Arthur a mug of builders' tea. "I don't really want to risk the china," she explained. "The cup handles come off so easily when people get overwrought. I've lost a lot lately. I think it's the time of year. So, now," she settled back with her cup of Lady Grey. "Tell me how it's been. How far back do you need to go?"

Mike, slightly on his guard in spite of all assurances, and keeping well away from the pot pourri and anything else that looked anaesthetising - or sharp - had, nevertheless, a firm opinion: With the galleon, the serpent, the bridge and the monkey scientist.

"Monkeys," repeated Madame Ibeg Boona in surprise. "*Monkeys?*"

"It was a dream," explained Arthur.

Mike gave him an accusing stare. And if he'd looked at it harder, the rest might not have happened. But he's stubborn.

"He is," agreed Madame Ibeg Boona. "But he's going to stop that now, isn't he? Tell me about the dream, Arthur."

So Arthur described the beautiful sea, the full-sailed galleon, the unforeseen sinking, the rising sea serpent, the ghoul and the Wheatstone bridge.

"What's a Wheatstone bridge?" asked Madam Ibeg Boona.

Basically, it's an electrical circuit used to measure an unknown electrical resistance by balancing two legs of a bridge circuit, one leg of which includes the unknown component. Mike looked pleased with himself.

"Goodness," exclaimed Madam Ibeg Boona. "This is a well-informed talisman. Such a shame one can't slit him open and send him to the gods. They would be thrilled with him." She burst out into a series of gleeful chuckles.

Mike climbed hastily onto Arthur's knee. I don't think that's funny.

Madame Ibeg Boona re-established an air of gravity. "Then I sincerely apologise." But her irreverence had proven relaxing. There was about her, as there had always been, a comforting air of being at ease with any situation and totally unthreatened by whatever it could bring. She shifted her gaze to Arthur. "No doubt you know the significance of this Wheatstone Bridge apparatus?"

"I know what it represented," said Arthur. And he told Madame Ibeg Boona about Oxford and his failed and self-sabotaged ambitions.

"So, when you think about it, Arthur," she said, after he had finished, "you were told pretty clearly in this dream what was taking you down."

And if he'd listened to me the next part might not have happened. Mike needed to establish that he had been trying.

"Possibly not," agreed Madam Ibeg Boona. "But, before we get on to that, I just want to draw attention to the serpent in the dream … It's one of those symbols that we can take a look at with some level of consistent understanding. Remember that a snake is coiled around the caduceus – the Hippocratic badge of healing of the medical profession. Though the snake, or serpent, has had its image badly besmirched in mythology, the creature has its compensations. It moves very close to the earth and, as such, it can represent the healing of rifts at the very deepest levels. So, it's possibly a good sign. And a healing sign - in spite of all appearances to the contrary." She paused . "So, that's the serpent then. But where were the monkeys?"

"It was manqué," sighed Arthur. "I used the expression 'a scientist manqué', meaning failed. It was very foolish of me. I should have known better." He gave Mike a weary look. "The word failed is perfectly adequate."

"I hardly think so," observed Madam Ibeg Boona. "Considering the consequences, I should say that the word 'failed' doesn't even begin to cover it. Tell me what happened next."

Mike was determined to tell a methodical tale, so he wanted to include how Arthur had floated up to the ceiling on Christmas Day, simply because he might have missed the fact that a woman called Anastasia might have been in love with him.

"Have you ever seen this Anastasia, Mike?" asked Madam Ibeg Boona.

Once.

"Is she beautiful?"

Arthur thinks so. I think he's right.

"And is she good?" asked Madame Ibeg Boona. "It's only in fairy stories that princesses are both beautiful and good."

"She's the most beautiful woman in the world," said Arthur. "And the nicest."

Mike looked anxious. You see the problem?

"Don't worry about it," said Madame Ibeg Boona. "The out-of-body business is relatively easy to counteract, and the idea of the sacred feminine can only help at this point. It was the thought of a woman that got Dante out of the Inferno. It was the memory of the beautiful Penelope that got Odysseus back from his odyssey. The sacred feminine is powerful, though at times her role may be somewhat abstract."

She studied the pair of them for a moment or two, and then she said quietly: "So, what's next?"

"Ptolemy De'ath."

"Now, there's a name to conjure with."

"You have no idea," said Arthur, and then he began.

When he had finished Madam Ibeg Boona remained silent for quite a while. Then she said: "You've got yourselves into deep water here, the pair of you. And uncharted water. The archetype, Arthur, gives form to the energy of the unconscious. But manifesting archetypes are …" She paused as if to arrange her thoughts. She had put down her cup of tea and taken to slow circuits of the room. "The modern interpretation of Jung," she went on, "would arguably be that archetypes are merely innate species-specific behaviour patterns that can become behavioural problems – or complexes – under certain circumstances. There is no current truck with ideas of archetypes that actually have an independent desire to be realised - even just in the mind. And there is no tolerance of talk about unconscious worlds being 'a priori' facts of nature. And the very mention of manifestations, of any sort, would be a heresy that would get you burned at the intellectual stake. In the modern world, people - sick, mentally compromised people - merely hallucinate. But, and it's a big but, regardless of what the biological scientists tell us, the truth of this world is that consciousness creates matter, matter does not create consciousness. And this anthropic universe was recognised by mystics long before it was speculated upon by physicists." She paused and studied Arthur for a moment or two before proceeding. "Creation, however, is not normally experienced by an individual consciousness in this way. But, once you step into the unconscious and through the gateway … Well … frankly, it's the part of the map that gets blurry and has 'Here be dragons' scribbled across the middle of it."

Mike looked at Arthur with some anxiety. Dragons?

"Illustrative," whispered Arthur.

Mike nodded. Got it.

Finally, Madame Ibeg Boona came to a decisive halt in front of them. "We learn from failed dreams, Arthur," she said severely. "We don't haul them around with us until their burden becomes so great that we finally conjure them from an imperishable past, and make them manifest out of heaven knows what material."

"One would have thought it quite a talent," said Arthur meekly. Mike gave him a reproving poke.

"I rather got the impression you weren't keen on it," Madame Ibeg Boona was evidently not in the mood for throwaway remarks. "Most people just settle for breaking down their physical bodies with their mental anguish." She looked at Mike. "Now, as you said, Ptolemy did us a backhanded service in the manner of some self-regarding anti-hero but that accepted, he is, from another viewpoint, failure incarnate. Arthur's feelings of failure have to be so powerful that they are virtually without peer. So, it is with them that we must begin."

"Ptolemy isn't anything to do with the shadow?" Arthur asked.

"The shadow is yet to come."

Arthur merely looked at her with weary resignation but Mike felt that their recent interpretation of the shadow needed an airing. We made our shadows, you know. At least Arthur did. I couldn't work the plasticine. Neither of us had any lust, as it turned out. I was worried that that meant I wasn't a boy kitten. I don't know what sort of kitten it made Arthur. Anyway, it seems that all the lust, apart from a little bit involving spots and stripes and so on, was in the manikin. Along with the rest of the seven deadly sins. And Arthur needs some of this stuff. Some fire to drive him. To get him through this. Not to make him a bad man. Arthur would never be a bad man, but he needs to be a good man with a dash of bad man. Don't you think?

Madame Ibeg Boona looked at Mike in surprise. "Spots and stripes?"

"Don't start him off," warned Arthur.

"Very well. I will confine comment to an expression of unbounded relief that your dealings with the shadow might not be destined for irretrievable disaster. Finally you appear to understand. I do believe that, in your own funny little way, the pair of you have actually got yourselves prepared." She shook her head with something of amused relief.

"The shadow will always be with you, Arthur," she went on, in more serious tones. "That's what it is to be human. To be anything, in fact. We have to learn to use its energies and defuse its excesses. It is the orchestration of harmony between the dark and light sides of our natures that gives us the balance that leads to victory over ourselves. And, as the saying goes, those who know this victory can never know defeat. But, for you, that is a challenge that has yet to be dealt with and, in order that you can cope with it fully, we must release the stranglehold that this Ptolemy, this perverted dream, has upon you. You cannot allow failure to make you less able to live."

Madame Ibeg Boona got up then and busied herself with her tea kettle. Arthur and Mike sat on in silence, accepting fresh drinks with somewhat distracted thanks.

"One more thing, Arthur," said Madame Ibeg Boona with deceptive casualness. "Is there any way that you could go back to University and reclaim this dream?"

"No."

"You're absolutely sure about that?"

"Yes."

"Then we must begin by removing the paralysing effect that this failure has upon you. You will always remember, of course, but the memory will be without power. And, when the memory is merely a memory, new energies and feelings can begin to take its place. Are you in agreement with this?"

"Yes."

"Good. Now, I am going downstairs to prepare the space. And it is a sacred space, so I would ask you both to treat it as such."

Mike shuffled uneasily on Arthur's knee. You're sure I'm not going to be sacrificed?

Chapter Sixteen

Madame Ibeg Boona's basement was a place of mystic and elaborate ceremonial. It smelt vaguely of some elusive and exotic smoke. The walls and ceiling were draped and tented in purple and deep red velvets encrusted with silver stars and moons. There were crystals and copper pyramids and more peacock feathers. There were slate shelves laden with huge jars of herbs, pestles and mortars and a set of scales with brass weights. At one end of the room there was what appeared to be a stone altar - one giant oblong of rough-hewn, dark stone containing a high proportion of magnetite. It had a smooth, well-used top surface into which had been carved two circles of identical radius, overlapping in such a way that the centre of each circle lay on the perimeter of the other. In the non-overlapping part of one of the circles there was a curved knife with a bone handle and in the other a vase of lilies.

On the wall above the altar there hung various mandalas and symbols. There was, at least to Arthur, no recognisable iconography from the mainstream religions. Madame Ibeg Boona was not inclined to constraint in her concept of God. She believed in the divinity and power of the universe, and she dealt with it in whatever manner it came, in whatever form, on whosoever's behalf.

"Is this where you turn base metals into gold?" asked Arthur, and then apologised.

"You'd better hope so," replied Madame Ibeg Boona, matter-of-factly. She walked across to the altar, put both hands on it and gazed up at the mandalas.

Arthur spoke reflectively to her back. "If I'd been referred to a psychiatrist, I'd probably be undergoing a spell as an in-patient now."

"Quite probably," agreed Madame Ibeg Boona. "And the psychiatrist would be listening to your litany of woes, if he had time, and making hasty notes and lacing said notes with wonderful words like delusions, hallucinations, paranoia, psychosis and schizophrenia. And there'd be a corresponding list of powerful pharmaceutical products with the side-effects conveniently disregarded, and he'd be fixing up brain scans and EEGs and all manner of neurological testing, and you'd be in and out of MRI machines and have wires stuck to your head for hours and, in the end, you'd be a poor zombie of a creature on permanent medication, constantly visited by social workers who would be endeavouring, in your very best interests, to find a company that would give you paid employment that didn't involve sharp objects."

"I've never been violent," protested Arthur.

"You may be moved to it, eventually."

"Oh, God!" Arthur put his head in his hands.

Madame Ibeg Boona turned round and beamed at him. "But not today. Today we remove what you could have been but weren't, and we replace it with a world of possibility. The past is another country, as they say, and we no longer want our experiences there to determine who or what we can become."

And she left the altar and crossed the room, coming to a halt beside a simple oak table and chair. She pulled out the chair and indicated to Arthur that he should sit. On the table there was an old-fashioned pot of ink, a quill pen and a pile of stiff, cream, parchment-type paper. Beside the chair, she placed a velvet cushion on which she requested that Mike make himself comfortable.

"This is ritual, Arthur," she said. "This is how we get at the unconscious mind. At least, this is how I get at the unconscious mind. Remember that it does not always distinguish between a real act and a symbolic one."

Arthur fidgeted at his table, crossing and uncrossing his legs. Madam Ibeg Boona watched him for a moment or two, and then she said: "Are you uncomfortable?"

"It's a small table."

"Let me rephrase. You *are* uncomfortable. You feel self-conscious sat at something like a school desk with an inkwell and a quill. Not to mention the velvet cushion and the talking kitten."

Arthur didn't answer.

"Even after all that has happened, you still can't repress the sneaking suspicion that you ought to have had another go at taking your troubles to Dr. Robinson. Am I right?"

"Or, it could actually be *on account* of all that has happened," suggested Arthur quietly. The urge for modern medicine was a deep programming. Especially when … He looked around.

Madame Ibeg Boona looked around with him, the peacock feathers in her turban waving gently, as if caught in some eldritch breeze. "I like it," she said. "If you are going to do unbelievable things, then it behoves one to have unbelievable décor, don't you think?"

Arthur certainly did think. Yes. The decor was unbelievable. As for the altar …

"Like any mythos, Arthur," said Madame Ibeg Boona, "what we are about to do requires a ritualised setting. It cannot work with mere intellectual assent. The great religions of the world are not run by fools, you know. They know that to find an enhancement of being, you have to step out of the norm and out of your accustomed mode of thought. People can't bring about change or deep understanding in themselves just by thinking it would be nice to bring about change or deep understanding in themselves. Psychology and religion - not the bizarre bedfellows you might imagine."

Arthur nodded.

"And if you did go to see Dr. Robinson at this point," Madam Ibeg Boona added casually, "do you think he would be there, or do you think that you would merely run into my good cousin again?"

"Would I?" It was a question without conviction. Somehow, Arthur knew he would. This was a never-ending circle. A snake with its tail in its mouth. He would not escape until Fate took the snake by the head and said: "You can let go now."

"Yes. That's right, Arthur," Madam Ibeg Boona nodded. "A path has been laid out for you and you have to walk it - whether you want to or not. So, shouldn't we just get on?"

Arthur nodded.

"I ask you this, then - and I assure you that a psychiatrist would also ask you this: Can you imagine that your failure could be serving some perverse but convenient purpose for you?"

"No. God, no! How could that possibly be?" Arthur was taken aback.

"You'd be surprised how convoluted the human psyche can be." Madame Ibeg Boona studied him for long thoughtful moments. "Very well then, let us proceed. For this to work, Arthur, you have to relive your pain. Experience one more time, and in full, your sense of failure. Every pain. Every type of pain. Every failure. Every type of failure. They must all be revisited mentally, and their reverberations felt physically. To do this in consultation with a counsellor or an analyst, however much of a quiet facilitator or silent reflector they purport to be, is to modify. Feelings put up for external consumption get subtly commercialised. Slightly recast. And you know the old adage : only the truth can set you free. Your personal truth. Enshrined in words that only you will ever read."

For Madame Ibeg Boona, the written word was not just marks on paper, a cumbersome communicant, misspelled and badly conjugated. She knew that words wrung from a consciousness by the power of violent and unedited emotion carried within them the energy of that consciousness. They were inhabited, ensouled - and transcendent.

"So," she said, "I want you to write. Everything you feel and ever have felt about the Oxford episode. All the calculations that you couldn't do. All the practicals that wouldn't come out. All the theories that you couldn't grasp. All your pain, all your fears and insecurities, all your jealousies and your social and romantic disasters. Each and every disappointment. Distilled from screams, written in tears and signed in blood. Got it?"

Arthur nodded.

"And then," she said, "and this is critical, I want you, as a final process, to address the deepest disappointment of all - the disappointment you feel with yourself. Do this in a direct question and answer fashion: Why am I hanging on to this failure? Why did I create it in the first place? What prompted it? What was it really about? And, at this point, I want you to write the answers quickly and thoughtlessly, in whatever words come to you - however abstruse, inappropriate or apparently meaningless. Do you understand?"

"Yes."

Her only interest, she told him, the only part of his writings that she wanted to see, was the answers to the final questions that he would ask of himself. And then she offered him a carafe of water because, she warned, he could be at this for a surprising length of time. Finally, she turned to Mike. "This may be a long sojourn for you, little cat. I'm sorry, but having you here is …," she paused, "necessary."

Then Madame Ibeg Boona nodded to them both, bowed her head before the altar, and left.

*****

It was four hours later when Arthur finally put down the quill. His cheeks were wet and his hand was cramped and painful. Mike was still sitting on his cushion, tiny body erect, eyes glued to the altar.

"Mike?"

Mike looked round and blinked. Have you finished? That seems very quick. Are you sure you've done it all?

Arthur picked him up and hugged him, and tears dripped on to his fur.

"So," said Madame Ibeg Boona, appearing with disconcerting promptitude. "We are all done at last. I feel it went well." She looked into Arthur's wet eyes and nodded. "That's how it has to be, Arthur. These things are never easy." Then she held out her hand. "Would you be prepared to give me the sheets whereon you asked yourself the questions?"

Wordlessly, Arthur sorted the papers and handed over three sheets. He felt completely drained but there was, along with the emptiness, a certain feeling of relief. Madame Ibeg Boona glanced at the self-imposed questions and the array of answers. Seemingly diverse and yet so similar. "And so we meet again," she observed quietly to herself. "The oldest of adversaries. When will we come to terms? When will you learn your place?" Shaking her head sadly, she placed the sheets in a large copper crucible. Then she indicated that Arthur should put the rest of his writings on top of them, and stand the crucible in the middle of the altar.

"This is the point at which the scientific community totally excommunicates me," she said with a somewhat weary sigh. "But, I am an unrepentant apostate. Psychiatry and psychology are determined to be fully paid-up sciences, so they will run from people like Jung, with his mysticism and his metaphysics, and they will embrace the more recent and more concrete pronouncements of the neuroscientists. But the mind is not the brain, Arthur, in the way that a computer programme is not the hardware that runs it. The job of psychology should be to describe and deal with the programme. And what a monumental task. But now," she paused and rubbed her pudgy hands together, suddenly mischievous, "we must proceed with that task and deal with that programme in the way I know it can be dealt with. The wisdom of ages knows little of neuroscience, and needs it even less. So," she gave a great laugh, "are we going to do some black magic, or what?"

She then explained to Arthur that the purpose of the etched overlapping circles on the altar was to divide it into three delineated areas, each having a different use. On the left was always something dark and forbidding and, for her current purpose, she removed the bone-handled knife and replaced it with rusted iron shackles. On the right would be something that represented the light and now she removed the lilies and, with a quiet by-your-leave, picked up Mike and sat him on the altar.

"Talismans," she said conversationally, "were traditionally used to ward off evil spirits, bring luck and facilitate ancient rituals." And, as she spoke, she gently stroked Mike's head, and he understood that he was sat upon the altar of change. His purpose was finite - a small kitten cannot live forever. That was the downside of his destiny. But, he also understood that his end, whenever and however it would come, was not to be faced today. So he waited, quietly unafraid, prepared to play his part.

The centre of the altar, where the crucible sat and where the two circles overlapped, was the place where good and evil meet and acknowledge each other in the divine paradox. It was, Madam Ibeg Boona said, the place of healing, the place of transformation, the place where miracles occur. "You could look at it," she said, "if you want to be smart, as an example of what scholars and philosophers call the 'coincidentia oppositorum' which is Latin for the coincidence, or coming together, of opposites. Jung himself used it in reference to opposing forces within the psyche. Mystically, it could be defined as a point at which, during a heightened encounter with the sacred, things that normally seem opposed coincide to reveal their underlying unity. The sublime cannot be sublime without its darkness."

"And now," she went on, "comes real ritual. And I suspect that Jung, old mystic that he was, would have loved it." And she handed Arthur a lighted white candle to hold. "Now, I act as your intermediary in this ceremony, so the words will be mine, but it is from your heart that they must come. Intention is all, remember. At times, I will ask for affirmations and then you must repeat what I have just said. If you find yourself with an objection at any point you must speak out, for you cannot adjust hereafter. Do you understand?"

Arthur nodded and the candle burned brighter and Madam Ibeg Boona began to intone. And it was part mass, part incantation and part supplication. And her voice was low, but it filled the space with a resonance that made the candle flame tremble. And she spoke of Arthur's intention to disarm and dismantle those parts of his psyche that were no longer appropriate. She spoke of disserving memories and worn out dreams and the hidebound thought forms of helpless habit. She spoke of freedom and transformation and the power of progress. And then she invited into Arthur's consciousness those disowned parts of him that could now serve him well and, as she did this, he felt something stir – within or without, he wasn't sure. There was much, as he stood there, that made him feel unsure. What was the true nature of what was being done? What exactly was the power inherent in this? Where and with whom did it really lie? Was Madame Ibeg Boona simply plumbing the depths of his psyche using smoke and mirrors, or could holy wafers, for example, be genuinely imbued with the energy of the divine? "You make a fundamental mistake, Arthur," she'd said to him during their first meeting. "You miss the point of Jung's metaphysics. You think yours is the only energy, the only power complicit in this …"

But now, she was suddenly urgent, speaking directly to

him, demanding hasty compliance: "Light the contents of the crucible. Quickly. Use the candle and repeat after me …" So Arthur leapt to touch the candle to his writings and began to repeat words of release and evocation that seemed to come to him, somehow, not from Madame Ibeg Boona but out of the mesmerising and dazzling bonfire of his own writings. The parchment burned with a powerful and brilliant flame, the combustion time seeming far, far longer than was necessary for a dozen or so sheets. The flames changed colour, flickered and danced, flaring up now and then into a blinding column that made them step back. And Arthur began to feel light-headed, as if dosed with more of Mr. Krishna's potent coffee, and the vortex thrummed violently in his chest and he had to put out a hand and grip the cold, hard edge of the altar in order to steady himself. For a mind-searing moment he felt held in the flames, part of the blazing and then, suddenly, there was only ash in the crucible and Madame Ibeg Boona was handing him a mug of builders' tea and a piece of Battenberg cake. "I got it specially," she said. "Sit and eat while I get something for Mike."

So, Arthur sat back down on the oak chair, legs trembling, mind now curiously empty and ate the cake. Mike watched as Madame Ibeg Boona went back up the basement stairs. Do you think there's a chance of some salmon?

"No sooner said …" Madame Ibeg Boona put a saucer of freshly poached salmon fillet in front of him. "Now," she turned to Arthur, "let us consider what we have done." She paused for a moment and watched him finish the cake. "We have, hopefully, tapped deeply into your unconscious and removed the paralysing effect that your failure had upon you. We have not, however, removed the reason for it. The reason that you never gave your dream its chance. Why you never give any of your dreams a chance." She took a turn or two around the room and then came to a halt in front of Arthur. "Fear," she said. "Fear was in the answer to every question you asked yourself. It is, when one really gets down to it, the most pervasive and destructive of forces, and it lurks behind so much of what we do. Or don't do. Fear, Arthur, is the main driver of the psychological self."

She pulled up another chair and sat down beside him, shaking her head in exasperation. "Fear has forgotten that it is there to serve us. To preserve. Not to rule. And so it has become the great unbalancer of the psyche with both the good and the bad amongst us at its behest. It can cause us to rise up and slaughter anything that in our ignorance we perceive to be an enemy, or it can sentence us to a life spent in a corner, going nowhere, doing nothing, dying of futility. And the cleverer and more ambitious we become, the more sophisticated its approach. You fear failure so you don't try. And in this fear you are not only afraid of what other people will think, but of what you will think of yourself. You are afraid that you will be revealed to yourself as less than you thought you were. And now, though you have the self-hatred that comes from having given up on the dream, you have the bizarre comfort of thinking: 'Well, I could've done it if I'd tried'. So fear takes away what you could have had and offers you the foolishness of an empty solace. And, unfortunately Arthur, in some form or other, fear will get between you and everything you want to do. There is only one way to live free of it and that is to live without hope, without change and without growth."

She stopped and watched, unseeingly, as Mike finished off his salmon. Then she turned back to Arthur and put a hand on his shoulder. "Fear will always come to you on its terms, but it has to be dealt with on yours. You have to find the courage to fail and not count yourself a failure. The self-belief to think you can succeed without the hubris to assume that success is your right. You need to be able to ask a woman for a date and take a refusal with grace in the knowledge that the sun will rise again the next morning, and so will you. A spiritual quest, Arthur is not about what you are, but who you are." She paused. "Unfortunately, in this cut-throat, practical world, the two get inextricably linked."

Arthur didn't immediately respond. He felt, in Madame Ibeg Boona's words, the spineless thing that he had allowed himself to become. "You said to me once, when I asked how I could change myself, that if I did the work the metaphysics would do the rest."

"This is the work, Arthur. This, and what you have been doing for yourself, is the work."

"And the metaphysics?"

"The metaphysics!" repeated Madame Ibeg Boona incredulously. "I would say that the metaphysics is outdoing itself, wouldn't you?"

"But I don't feel any different. In fact I feel a lot worse."

"I know," Madame Ibeg Boona touched his arm sympathetically. "But that is so frequently the way of it. Sometimes, Arthur, it is only possible to move forward if you have experienced a sinking back - into either nothingness or the primordial chaos of the beginning. That was actually the psychological premise upon which primitive initiation ceremonies were based - a regressive disorganisation of the personality. And ritualisation of the process was the key to the outcome. Through surviving unbelievable but guided stress, a boy was pushed from deliberately created mental chaos into a new state of consciousness. He became a man, quick time.

Which meant that he stood a better chance of survival. But he had to keep going. Remember? You were warned. You have to keep going. Today, we have closed a gate that needed closing and opened a gate that needed opening. Something will step through the open gate, and you will have to deal with it. Alone. As the boys did. It's the only way."

"And the guidance?"

Mike looked up from his saucer with salmon-covered whiskers, and Madame Ibeg Boona smiled down at him and nodded.

"Him?" asked Arthur with a sinking heart. "*Only him?*"

Chapter Seventeen

Polly Loveday had passed beyond the stage of indignation and barbed comment and started to worry. She realised that her brother was in a place where sisterly exhortations could no longer reach him. Arthur had not left his flat in two weeks. Or changed his clothes. He lay on the sofa, grey-faced under an old blanket. The flat felt as cold and as dank as a tomb. There was no evidence of anything fit for a man to eat.

"You're ill, Arthur," Polly said desperately. "You must realise this. If you have no faith in Dr. Robinson we'll pay for private treatment. Whatever you want, whatever it takes."

But Arthur didn't want anything. He was, in truth, no longer solidly tied to this earth and this existence. Madame Ibeg Boona's elaborate ritual seemed to have removed not only Ptolemy De'ath but everything else as well. The effort for Arthur to bring his senses to bear on opening a sachet of cat food or a packet of cereal was enormous and draining. When he slept he saw only Mary Jacob Park. In it he saw only two things: Mike's death and his own. Variety came only in the way they died. And, with each dreamed death, Arthur grew weaker. Yet, if he stayed awake he still saw Mary Jacob Park. It filled his mind's eye while he fought to keep his imagination focused on something pleasant. Something pleasant was invariably Anastasia. He had only one abiding image of her left, and it was the one from Carruthers Sloan's Christmas party - the upswept hair, the beautiful curve of her neck, and that curious expression in her eyes, part irritation, part need, part promise. And when he could conjure this image in sufficiently powerful measure, Arthur got again the feeling that something wonderful could happen – if only he could bring his mind to bear.

"Arthur!" Polly shook him. "Don't drift off while I'm speaking. I told father not to let mother come and see you like this. It would break her heart. As if you hadn't broken it already. For God's sake Arthur, you look as if you're dying."

Arthur didn't answer.

"Twenty-four hours," warned Polly grimly, setting a mug of coffee and a chicken sandwich down beside him. "Twenty-four hours and, if you haven't taken matters into your own hands by then, I'm bringing a doctor to you. I'll have you sectioned, if I have to."

And she left.

Mike climbed up onto the sofa and patted Arthur's face. Arthur. Arthur! *Arthur!!* We must get it done. You're getting weaker. I'm getting weaker. I can feel it. We must go. *Now!*

"Go where?"

To Mary Jacob Park. The same way we did on New Year's Eve. Take the same route. Climb the same wall. Face what has to be faced before …" Mike stopped.

"Before what?" asked Arthur.

Just before, that's all. Now get up.

"I can't."

You have no other choice. Remember what Madame Ibeg Boona said?

"She said a lot of things."

About giving up not being an option? That this has to be seen through to the end?

"Vaguely," said Arthur. "I can barely remember what Polly said fifteen minutes ago."

You see? You're in the last chance saloon, Arthur.

Arthur raised his head and propped it on one elbow. "Where on earth did you get that expression?"

I heard it on TV while you were asleep.

"You're such a funny little cat," said Arthur fondly but absently. He laid his head down again.

Up, Arthur. *Get up.*

"It has to be now?"

Yes. Death or glory. Today. *Now.*

"Chrissakes, what have you been watching?" But Arthur got his legs off the sofa.

I don't know.

"Well, I hope you're right about the death or glory thing because I couldn't stand it if it was death or forty more years of fucking misery."

Mike was scandalised. *Arthur!*

"God, my legs feel as if they don't belong to me."

You have to make them work. You have to get us there. Now, find a coat.

*****

"I can't remember the way." They stood on the street amidst melting snow and a freezing January wind while Arthur looked vaguely around. He never forgot the way anywhere. At Carruthers Sloan that had been his only acknowledged accomplishment.

Mike looked resolutely up the road. I remember it.

"Couldn't we take a taxi?" Arthur asked.

221

Taxis don't stop there.

"Taxis stop wherever you ask them to stop."

Don't you understand about Mary Jacob Park, Arthur?

"No. I said I didn't. I don't understand why it's there. Empty, decaying and undeveloped. A wasteland. London has some of the most expensive real estate in the world and ..."

That's an old conversation, Arthur.

"I know. I can't think of a new one."

It doesn't matter. Nothing matters except that we press on ...

So Arthur walked and Mike directed and nameless streets came and went and Arthur wished that his legs didn't feel like lead and his head like cotton wool, but most of all he wished that it was over. All that he had left – such as it was – had turned to ash on Madame Ibeg Boona's altar. He stumbled and almost fell.

Nearly there. Can you climb the wall, Arthur?

Three times Arthur fell back. "I can't."

You have to and you have to do it now.

"I seem to have lost my strength," said Arthur wearily. "And I'm afraid," he added in a whisper.

I know. But you must climb this wall and get into that park. Afraid or not. You're not alone in this. I'm here.

"And can you get us over this wall?"

Physically no. Mentally yes. And physically *you* can. It's just mentally you can't. But, Arthur, and this is rather the point ...

"*Alright!*" And Arthur began to climb.

The park was a wasteland. The elusive beauty conferred by the snow had melted with it, and there were only skeletal trees and rank grass and the steady drip-drip of what seemed like tears of melancholy from the broken statues and the fractured fountain. The bandstand was empty. No Ptolemy. No anything.

"I feel as if I've come here to die," said Arthur. "The place feels like a burial ground. A plague pit." He sighed and the sound had a sob in it. "Why are we here, Mike? I saw enough of this place when I was asleep. In those hideous, endless dreams."

That was different. You have to be here because you want to be here.

"But I don't want to be here."

You wanted to do as I asked. That's enough. Mike looked around. Let's go that way. Maybe that tunnel leads somewhere …

But Arthur had the urban dweller's aversion to anything that resembled an underpass or a tunnel. The very notion of going into the thing filled him with horror. He wondered why it was there. What had gone over it in times gone by? A road? A carriageway? Some long forgotten railway branch line? Nothing about this place had ever made any sense to him. But, as he stood there, filled with a paralysing mixture of confusion and dread, something shot out of the nearby bushes and flung itself upon them with silent and savage intent. Arthur felt teeth sink into his forearm and pain shot through him. It was all so quick, he barely had time to grasp what sort of dog this was. His only sense was of size and darkness. As he crashed to the ground under the sudden force of the impact, the weight of the beast bearing down upon him, his thoughts were predominantly for Mike. He'd tried desperately not to fall on him, wondering if the dog had registered the kitten or merely launched itself at him. As he reached for its collar with his free hand in some vague hopes of strangling it into submission, Mike leapt free and ran for the shelter of the underpass.

The dog caught sight of him and released its grip on Arthur. But Arthur had got its collar and he was not prepared to let go. Mike with his little legs needed a start - and a good one - and Arthur was determined to hang on for as long as he could.

The dog twisted and turned, snarling and snapping. More blood spurted from Arthur's hands and forearms as long, canine teeth caught him again and again. The protection afforded by his coat sleeves seemed virtually nil. But still he hung on. Then the dog's collar came off over its head and now it was impossible to control the thing. Arthur grabbed at loose skin and fur, clutching desperately for a grip, but he could not keep hold. The dog took a fierce snap at his face and then with yelping barks shot away after Mike. A screaming jackdaw flew down from a tree and swooped excitedly after it, harassing and dive-bombing, until the pair of them disappeared from view. Arthur scrambled to his feet and plunged after them.

He stumbled over broken bricks and splashed in puddles of snowmelt, struggling for his feet in the slime that was the mouth of the underpass. Only a few yards in and he could barely see. Then something, somebody, struck him in the chest with the effectiveness of a slamming door. It wasn't the dog. He slithered to an overbalancing halt and sought the side wall for support. Clutching his badly bitten right arm to his body, he squinted uncertainly into the darkness. Somewhere before him, no doubt, lay whoever it was that peopled this desolate place. The vagrants, the addicts, the dealers, the extremes of society who had chosen, or been driven by circumstance, to live that which is barely liveable. Beyond comfort, beyond consideration and probably, as Arthur acknowledged to himself with a sinking heart, beyond conscience. There was, he immediately understood, no way past this. Equally, there was no running away. To give up on Mike, even what was left of his body, was unthinkable.

He strained his eyes but the darkness was so thick it was almost palpable. How long was this tunnel? How far could a kitten run? For how long could it keep ahead of a dog? The answer came to him callously frank – no time at all. He spoke into the blackness: "Have you seen a kitten? Chased by … maybe … was it your dog?"

There was no answer. He stepped forward but found himself instantly forced back against the wall. The inconvenient way that his eyes were refusing to adapt made no sense but, in spite of being effectively blind, he could appreciate the viciousness that had been in the shove and feel the menacing implacability of whatever it was before him. "I do need to get past," he said. "He's a very young kitten and …"

"… he's probably dead now." A disembodied voice finished the sentence for him. It was not the kind of voice he'd expected. It held no accent and no hint of the colloquial or the uneducated. It stated the fact without emotion. He turned towards it, straining to see. He thought he could make out figures in a loose semicircle. Darker darknesses.

"He's little but he's resourceful," he said. "I think there's a chance, if you'd let me past."

"And how resourceful are you?"

Arthur didn't answer.

"So, what is the price you are prepared to pay to pass? How much will you give the toll keeper ? What price the ferryman?"

Arthur fished in his inside pocket with his least bloodied hand and held out his wallet. He had little in cash and little enough in the bank. His overdraft facility had been withdrawn sometime after he'd lost his job. He endeavoured to explain this, but with his pin number, he pointed out, they could still count the day as one of profit. No-one took the wallet from him. He continued to hold it out.

"Not a fighter, are you?" A slightly different voice.

"I'm sorry. I don't … I mean I've never …" Arthur gave up. It was pointless. They knew. *We are who we are. People never change.* He tried again with the wallet: "It's little enough but it's all I have. Please take it and let me through. I beg you."

There was no reply.

He scanned the darkness helplessly. "It's all I have," he repeated, "except for the kitten. Please … I just want to see …" The arm holding out the wallet fell back to his side. What did he want to see? What was left of Mike? The thought of Mike's poor little body being worried and tossed about by a dog made him feel sick. His whole being trembled and retched at the thought of it. He was barely aware of the taunts that were now coming, or even of his instinctive dread of what was going to happen to him.

"So, now we meet who you really are."

And in that moment, hearing those words, Arthur was suddenly filled with a burning hatred. For his helplessness, his fear, his paralysis. Yes, he knew who he was. What he was. How defeated and hopeless he'd always been. He'd tried to find it within himself to be better, but his boundaries had been laid out long ago, and they were insurmountably hedged with weakness and failure. What he was, he would always be. But, as this hatred burned within him, an incandescent, tripartite flame of anger, fear and self-loathing, it laid waste every boundary he'd ever had until it cleared the way for something of which he had no experience, no real understanding. The part of him that he barely believed existed. From the very centre of his being, uncoiling with a power that had only lately been called forth, the shadow rose like a giant serpent and offered itself.

'Sweet words will not get you through this tunnel, Arthur. You know this. They never have. You must not take the idea that the meek will inherit the earth as a literal truth, my friend. Before you stands every fear you have ever had. The sum of everything that has kept your life at nought. Without what I can offer you, you will die here. They will see to it. You will die of a surfeit of cowardly and self-effacing emptiness. I hold out my hand to you. Take from me what is right and good that a man should have and leave the rest. Take my hand, Arthur, and use what I hold, or remain in the underworld forever.'

Arthur stood transfixed, and the pounding of his heart shook his entire body. He had no idea what to do. What he was meant to do. How to do it. But the cries of those who have spent time in the darkness become powerful for they contain all that has been building for day after day, week after week, year after year. And these cries rose into Arthur's throat and filled his head and screamed for release, and he took the hand of the shadow and stepped forward. And when he opened his mouth, the sound of his frustration, his pain, and his anger filled the air. And it was the cry of the mother for the lost child, and the cry of the soldier for the fallen comrade, and the cry of the soul that has finally learned that if it does not use with wisdom, all that has been granted to it, all that has been offered, right until the moment of death, then it will never have truly lived. And the terrible sound filled the tunnel, and the air was sucked from the place, and the litter rose and whirled, and the walls began to shake like the walls of Jericho. The vortex caught at Arthur, as if he were a leaf on the wind, and swept him up with a power that left him stunned. Flung back to earth, he lay on the ground for long, unconscious moments. Somewhere a jackdaw shrieked … again and again. And then … nothing … no-one …

An adventurous sunbeam crept in and glinted on a puddle. And Arthur got up and began to run.

Beyond the tunnel the ground started to rise, and he scrambled up a slope, slipping and sliding on wet grass, to the ruins of a stone folly. Mike was sitting in front of it, on some sun-warmed steps. He gave a few satisfied sleepy blinks when Arthur arrived, panting and gasping, and dripping blood.

It's nice here on the steps of the Parthenon.

"Parthenon?" Arthur looked up at the ruin. He didn't know whether to be relieved or angry. In truth, he was too drained to be either. He felt increasingly nauseous.

Yes. You know. That Greek place where all the philosophers gathered.

"So you're a philosopher now?"

No. I expect the Parthenon was the stray cat equivalent of Antonucci's Big Breakfasts.

Arthur lowered himself shakily onto the steps. "I can't believe this. I feel as if I just died. As if you just died. In fact, I think I'm going to throw up."

But we didn't die. Either of us. And you got through the tunnel. Which is just as well, because it's the only way back.

"Why do I feel as if I've been through some huge …" Arthur didn't know quite how to describe it, but it had certainly been huge. And terrifying.

I think the word you're looking for is catharsis.

"You don't say …" Arthur gave him a black look. "Then why are you treating it like a walk in the park?"

Because it was a walk in the park. And, once I'd got you here, I felt privy to the outcome.

"You knew?"

Let's just say that I believed more in your Self than you did.

Arthur began to retch.

Mike patted him sympathetically. Just go and get it up. Then it'll all be over.

"All of it?"

Not quite.

"Oh, shit!"

And so Mike sat enjoying moments of winter sun and listening contentedly to Arthur throwing up in the bushes.

Chapter Eighteen

The spring after the freezing, snowbound winter that spanned the years 2010 and 2011 was especially early, warm and beautiful. Arthur, exhausted from his experiences, mostly slept his way into it. And, while he slept, Mary Jacob Park gradually came alive again – busy with new life and young growth and flush with the restorative power of nature. A place rebirthing.

And when Arthur wasn't sleeping he showered, ate food and then slept some more. His mother brought him home-made soups and cleaned the flat, his sister plied him with particularly expensive vitamins, and his father swept up dead leaves and fished them out of the drains. Even Dr. Robinson had been temporarily stimulated into visible response by the sight of Arthur's dog bites. They took him right back to a youthful trip to India in a psychedelic van, when a bite from a dog had involved one of his hippie friends in a month's worth of excruciatingly painful intraperitoneal injections of rabies antiserum. Of course, things were different these days. Better antisera and a good vaccine. And here in London, bites were just about antitetanus, antibiotics and wound management. Barely worth the trouble of a few stitches. He looked quite downcast. Maybe, Arthur had just got off Air India or some freight ship from Africa? No? Happened just up the road? Ah well, that's how it goes sometimes. And as for all the other stuff - well, Arthur had probably picked up a virus. People did when they got made redundant. The upset depressed their immune systems. There was a lot of it about. Somehow, everybody felt inclined to agree.

Arthur would have welcomed the opportunity to have more explicit conversations, but Madame Ibeg Boona's telephone number had suddenly become one of those that was no longer recognised. Before he was sufficiently well to rise from his couch and present himself in person, however, he received a postcard. It bore the image of a splendid white kitten wearing a garland of daisies round its neck, and also an unreadable postmark, a magnificently exotic stamp and very brief message:

Taking a little rest cure myself. You won't need me.
Metaphysical dog bites heal the same way as other dog bites.
Love to you both.
Your friend, Epiphanie Ibeg Boona.

And Mike, knowing that Arthur needed a rest for body and soul with only the commonplace in terms of dreams, and nothing in the way of archetypal manifestations, mostly just sat - alongside his image on the propped-up postcard - and watched him sleep. Then at other times he sat on the kitchen window sill and stared up the basement steps. And he knew, in a more profound way than the way in which animals can predict earthquakes and tsunamis, that something really big was coming. All was not yet finished.

So, one sunny morning, Arthur awoke to find Mike sitting on his chest, staring intently into his face. I've had dreams.

"Really?" Arthur eased himself into a sitting position.

I've been dreaming of springtimes.

"You actually had a dream and remembered it?" Arthur was impressed.

I've had lots of dreams recently. All the same dreams. Of big grass with white and yellow flowers in it. And the old witch there. Picking the flowers and offering them to us.

"Oh, no," groaned Arthur. "Not her again. I thought we were normal now." He paused and, almost reflexly, checked the healed wounds on his arms and hand. Healed wounds but impressive scars. Talk about the unconscious reacting explosively when it needed to! He looked back at Mike. "But I suppose we can't be normal if you're still talking and I'm still answering." He sighed. "So what does this mean?"

I don't know, but we need to do something. Acknowledge the dream physically. Act it out. That way the energy from the unconscious can be integrated into our lives and do what it needs to do.

"You've become very well versed while I was sleeping," said Arthur. "But you're no bigger. How does that work?"

I have no idea. Where will we find lots of grass with yellow and white flowers in it?

"In a park?" suggested Arthur, with a slightly sinking heart. He glanced at his arm again. Mary Jacob Park existed. A place unmapped amongst nameless streets and curious turns. A place you found when you had to.

Mike shook his head. Not a park. Somewhere different.

"Thank God." Relieved, Arthur gave his attention to the problem. So, they just needed to follow a straightforward procedure for acting out dreams in order to produce a psychological integration of their message. "Well... I guess that leaves us with countryside," he said.

And so, they decided upon a picnic in the countryside to honour the dream. Arthur checked the oil, the water, the tyres and the battery on the old Morris and shopped for splendid picnic food and loaded it into the car boot in carrier bags.

He headed for the Chilterns, red kite country and Mike sat in his booster box asking: Are we there yet? Is this real countryside? every time they passed a green space. And then it was real countryside. The fields got bigger and the houses more spread out and the roads much smaller and occasionally confusing.

"I thought we were here," said Arthur, having stopped the car to consult a larger-scale map, "but I think we are more likely here." He held up the map, pointing.

He had eschewed satellite navigation, having had no particular information to put to it. Besides which, the map seemed to chime more satisfactorily with the rather fanciful nature of the outing.

Mike scrambled out of his booster box. I think we're here.

"Where?"

Where we need to be.

"Here?" Arthur looked around. It was a pleasant enough spot. No purple mountain majesty, not even any red kites in the sky, but then this was English countryside and this spot was as representative of it as any other. And picnicking by the roadside had once been a national past time. As it happened, they were right next to a small empty field - a field which, as Arthur confirmed when he got out of the car and hopped the fence, contained a lot of grass plus buttercups and daisies. And, as yellow and white flowers go, buttercups and daisies are as good as any. There were also a few too many thistles so Arthur got out a picnic rug and spread it on the grass. Then he laid out the food.

Mike watched him carefully. Is this how a picnic is done?

"You will find grander picnics," said Arthur. "Picnics that come in fine wicker baskets with plates and cutlery on the inside of the lid. There could be a table and champagne. Unfortunately, we have only supermarket carrier bags, which we must on no account allow to blow away, and non-alcoholic beverages because we have no chauffeur. We are, nevertheless, deeply committed picnickers."

There was fresh salmon and tinned salmon and cold chicken. Egg and cress sandwiches, cheese and tomato sandwiches, scones with jam and cream, sponge cake and chocolate finger biscuits. There was tea in a flask and a full quarter pint of kitten milk. Mike viewed it all with an air of satisfaction. It was certainly an awful lot of food for one man and an exceedingly small cat. But Mike had wanted the dream to be honoured, and Arthur knew of no other way to do it.

If the old witch was going to present them with flowers, then they would present her with food. That seemed only civil. And who knew what sort of food an old witch would want to eat? The important thing was, that she didn't eat them. Arthur suddenly wished he'd picked up cocktail sausages and pork pies. But did, in fact, the presence of the old witch in Mike's dream mean that she would be coming herself, or was she merely representative of something else that would come? And what did the flowers symbolise?

Mike didn't know.

"Well, what did you feel like when she gave them to you?"

I felt ended.

"Could you phrase that a bit better?"

I felt like it was the end.

"The end of what? Like the end of a race when the winner gets presented with a bunch of flowers?"

More like the end of everything.

"That sounds disturbingly apocalyptic." Arthur looked around. The sun was shining, there were bumble bees tumbling amongst the flowers, birds busy in the hedgerows. two squirrels chasing each other up and down the trunk of a nearby beech tree. This was more Field of Dreams than Apocalypse Now. "So have you given much thought to the actual meaning of this dream?" Arthur persisted. "The end of everything doesn't strike me as the most likely interpretation. It's just not the afternoon for it."

Mike didn't answer.

"Well are you, for instance, expecting the witch to arrive in person?" Arthur began to realise that this was a line of questioning that wasn't going to get him very far. Mike was being annoyingly unresponsive. So would anything come at all?

It did.

Mike watched its approach with interest. Is this a cow?

"Observation leads me to believe," said Arthur, "and very strongly, that this is a bull. A bull in full possession of all that a bull can have – including horns." Which struck him as unusual, because in those Sunday drives with his parents that had been followed by interminable country walks, bulls with horns had never featured. As he dimly recalled from his countryside spotters guide, mild-mannered polled Herefords had seemed to be the only free roaming bulls.

Mike stood up. He's coming to see us.

"He most certainly is," agreed Arthur fervently. "And I could have sworn that this field was empty." He stood up, too. "I think we ought to get out of here."

Wouldn't that be rude?

"Mostly smart," said Arthur, mentally assessing the

distance to the fence.

I'm sure he'll be fine.

"Based on what?" asked Arthur. "Your extensive knowledge of those cows in the TV milk adverts?"

He's immense, isn't he? Quite, quite magnificent. I'm so glad we're getting to see him close up like this.

"A thrill that could be very short-lived," pointed out Arthur. "Come on now. We must move." The necessity for doing something was becoming imperative. He bent down to pick Mike up. But Mike didn't want to come. And Arthur found that he was unable to do anything about that. Moreover, he found himself trapped in some hideous frozen moment wondering if he was about to replace his dog bites with a thorough and terminal goring. The end of everything, Mike had said. Was this going to be it? White and yellow flowers for their funeral corsages?

The bull was almost upon them. And as far from those amiable drawings in Arthur's countryside guide as it could possibly have been. Huge beyond any city dweller's computations of bullness, it had giant muscles and superfluous mounds of flesh which wadded out its huge neck and rolled hither and thither as it walked. And its horns! Arthur would not have believed that domestic beasts within the boundaries of the British Isles could be in possession of such horns. They were the horns of other lands and other centuries and men on horseback.

The bull stopped about ten feet from them and blew down its nose. Its flanks, a dull, mottled red colour, rose and fell. It looked at them from large, long lashed eyes.

"We," said Arthur, "are going to die."

Mike gave him an amused look. Just stand still. Do as you are told.

"But this is a bull," protested Arthur with rising desperation.

Not today. Today he's an instrument.

"And he knows this?"

Be reasonable, Arthur. He's a bull, for heaven's sake.

"Was he in the field?"

What field?

"The field in your dream, of course."

It was just grass in my dream. Big grass. And flowers.

Arthur snorted. "So he is… what then? Just an optional extra sort of symbol?"

Actually he's a very powerful symbol. Taurus is one of the most powerful signs of the zodiac and the bull was often a symbol of masculine power in major myths.

"Fascinating," said Arthur heavily. "Absolutely fascinating. I really should've picked up on that." But, try as he might, he couldn't move.

And then suddenly, with a huge sigh, the great beast dropped to its knees followed by a slow and careful settling of its rump to the ground. Once in sternal recumbency it proceeded to contentedly chew the cud.

"Well," exclaimed Arthur with an exhalation of loud relief, "at least he's brought his own food."

Quite a companionable atmosphere developed. Mike ate chicken and Arthur ate egg and cress sandwiches. The bull ground away amiably at his regurgitations.

"What else could he be symbolic of?" Arthur asked presently. "Apart from all flesh is grass and the zodiac thing."

We'll see. Mike moved on from chicken to salmon. Arthur ate a scone with jam and cream. The bull seemed to have gone to sleep, except it was still chewing.

But every feast has to have its spectre and presently he

came, in a rush of black wings. Perching on a section of roadside fence, he cocked his cowled head and observed them with one all-seeing, blue-white eye. Mike turned to look at him. You're not welcome here.

Churlish, churlish, tutted the bird. In view of the way things turned out, we could show a little grace I think.

"Have a scone," said Arthur.

The jackdaw swooped down in a neat easy glide, took the scone from Arthur's fingers and then, with a courteous nod of his head, flew away.

The bull dozed and chewed. Mike cleaned out the cream pot.

"You think this is normal behaviour?" asked an angry voice. "Sharing a picnic with a bull? Don't you know that they are dangerous?"

Arthur leapt to his feet. "I knew they were," he said, "but he wouldn't have it." He pointed accusingly at Mike.

A small, slim woman in a white lab coat with a stethoscope in one pocket looked at him as if he were mad and shook her head in breathless exasperation. "I've had to leave a patient to come and see that you are alright," she said. "A neighbour came crashing into the consulting room to tell me that the bull was about to kill somebody out in the field."

"He's your bull, is he?" asked Arthur for want of something more sensible to say. Mike, meanwhile, was trying to deal with his in-dwelling sensitivity to white lab coats. He'd always known that he was going to have to face one sooner or later, and here was one got slipped into his dream picnic when he wasn't expecting it.

"No, he's not my bull," retorted the woman. "He's just hospitalised after I did a rumenotomy on him yesterday." She pointed to stitches in the bull's flank. "Actually he's chewing the cud nicely, isn't he? That's heartening." She looked suddenly pleased. "But he's not supposed to be out here. We can't leave him with all this lush grass."

Arthur craned his neck to look at the bull's stitches. He was vague about the exact nature of rumenotomies but he had an idea that '...otomies' in general were pretty intrusive procedures, and he confessed inner surprise that a woman so far removed from the ilk of Mrs. Bunce should elect to spend her days re-jigging the insides of immense creatures. It was unaccountably impressive. Mike, on the other hand, was mostly anxious that her frightening proclivities should not spread to him. He remembered the horrid vision he'd had when the old witch had reached out to grab him from Arthur. That gory examination of his innards for female parts that he didn't have. So what was the witch up to now? Where was the bunch of flowers? Jung had been absolutely right about that dream business ... 'I prefer to regard the symbol as the announcement of something unknown, hard to recognise and not to be fully determined'.

"He's a rare breed," said the woman, looking at the bull. "English Longhorn. Very good specimen. Can't risk losing him. We must get him back to his pen." She looked around thoughtfully for a moment or two but, before a plan presented itself, the jackdaw suddenly whooshed down over the bull's head. Startled, the beast got to its feet and began lumbering down the field the way it had come.

"Quickly, quickly!" shouted the woman to Arthur. "We must turn him through that gate over there. Wave your arms at his nose!"

So Arthur ran and waved his arms, and the bull turned and turned again and trotted obligingly into a yard and back into his pen.

"Goodness," panted the woman. "That was a lot easier than it could have been. He could have behaved like a bull with a sore side. I think we've all been very lucky." She bent over as she struggled to get her breath back. "Sorry," she said, "I've been feeling a bit odd today."

"Can I get you anything?" Arthur asked solicitously. "Anything we could help with in order to compensate for dragging you out into the field?"

She shook her head. "I'd have had to come out and get the bull back anyway, because as sod's law would have it there was only me in the surgery, and my neighbour," she gestured up the road, "she's into flower arranging, not bulls. Truthfully, you were a lucky find." She smiled. "I dare say I should let you continue to use the field for your picnic."

Arthur stood irresolute for a moment or two and then he said: "I have no right to ask this, though I'm sure it's just the work of a moment for you. Would you tell me what sex my kitten is? If I brought it …" But as he spoke the words, the jackdaw dropped Mike from a rather mischievous height with a bouncing bomb effect that deposited him right at Arthur's feet.

"Goodness me!" exclaimed the woman. "Did you see that bird?" She twisted her neck to follow the jackdaw's flight. "This is turning into the most extraordinary day. The oddest things have been happening."

"Sometimes they do," said Arthur, bending to pick Mike up.

Mike was a very cross kitten. He'd been snatched unceremoniously from the picnic rug and was covered in buttercup pollen from being bundled through the grass at takeoff. The woman took him gently from Arthur and looked into his face. She looked for such a long time that Arthur began to wonder if she was trying to do this thing by divination. Finally she nodded at Mike - it looked remarkably like a 'by your leave' - and tipped him backwards. "He's a man," she said bringing him back up to the vertical and looking into his face again.

"A male," suggested Arthur.

"Yes." She seemed to be forgetting to give him back.

"He can hear," said Arthur, holding out his hands helpfully.

"I can tell." The woman shook her head, handing him over in a vaguely bewildered way. Then, as Arthur took Mike, she was suddenly all business. "Yes, male kitten, absolutely lovely. Blue-eyed white, of course. He may not be able to hear. It's an unfortunate genetic linkage. You must watch out for that. It can make them a little insecure. Now, I really must get back. You enjoy the rest of your picnic."

"Wait," said Arthur." We must owe you something." He searched in a trouser pocket.

She waved a dismissive hand. "For a fifteen second consultation? I'm a vet, not a lawyer." Before she left she tested the gate of the bull's pen, checking the latch. Clearly she could not understand how the beast had got out.

Arthur shook his head but Mike nodded in silent and grudging acknowledgement. In a tree two fields away, the jackdaw bobbed twice in return and then he spread his black wings one last time and flew off into the westering sun.

"So," said Arthur as he flung himself back down on the picnic rug. "There you are. Boy kitten. Aptly named. It's been bothering you, hasn't it?"

Only off and on. But, inside, Mike knew that it was conclusive. Or rather, that it was in the nature of a conclusion.

"So, the old witch did us a service in the end," said Arthur. "And so did that damned jackdaw. I think I'll have the last of the tea and some more sponge cake to celebrate." He picked up the flask thoughtfully. "You know," he said, as he poured. "You remember your woolly knot garden?"

Mike looked up from his kitten milk. I remember it as a mandala. You said it was a magic circle in Sanskrit.

"Actually, I think it was something else altogether. You remember that it wandered off a bit at two o'clock?"

Mike wasn't entirely certain that he wanted his creation revisualised like this. It had worked out just fine.

"I think," Arthur went on, "that the embellishment at two o'clock was an arrow. And a circle with an arrow going off at the two o'clock point is the biological symbol for maleness."

Now, Mike was interested. That's what the old witch was trying to tell us?

"I think it was. Part of it, anyway. Though it's hard to see why it should have been so significant. Maybe, had we got the whole story …" he shrugged. "Who knows? Maybe things might have been easier. I guess that wisdom always has a hard time getting through to us because mostly we don't want to listen. It's like parental advice, we don't like it and we try to get away from it as fast as we can."

Mike took a last and rather wistful look in the empty cream pot. All done…

Arthur felt a sudden twinge of unease. He looked up from cutting himself the piece of sponge cake. "Why was it so important to you that you were a boy kitten?" he asked.

It was only ever important to you.

"That's ridiculous. A girl kitten would have been fine."

So why did you immediately call me Mike?

Arthur thought. "I guess it's because I always wanted to be

242

called Mike."

Why?

"It's one of those names, isn't it?" And he spoke something of what he had felt at the time. "It's short but strong. Unpretentious but masculine. And it's reliable sounding. Mike is never the bad guy, is he? He's always someone you can depend on. Someone who will get you through. Get the job done."

And yet, you gave this name to a kitten when you must be familiar with the expression 'helpless as a kitten'?

"Yes …" agreed Arthur uncertainly, not entirely confident in what he was agreeing to.

And you looked after this kitten, believed in it as a talisman, loved it, even tried to educate it, and finally overcame tremendous fear in order to give it the chance to live and grow.

"Which you haven't," pointed out Arthur. "Grown, I mean." He joked because his twinge of unease was becoming the conviction that something unforeseen, unpredictable and irrevocable was about to happen. Mike was sounding not at all like Mike. "Still," Arthur hurried on, as if avoiding silence were important, "we must celebrate. It's like some sort of rite of passage, isn't it? Acknowledging the moment - a boy becomes a man, a kitten becomes a …"

A man. The lady said 'man'.

"We'll, yes, but it was a slip of the tongue."

Mike shook his head. It was the writing on the wall, the 'open sesame', the abracadabra word.

Arthur lost interest in the sponge cake. Put down the knife. Felt a tightening in his throat and his chest. Mike looked straight at him with those vivid blue eyes. Sometimes change builds before it becomes apparent but then, when it finally happens, it can be amazing. And the small, white kitten stood up on the picnic rug and stretched.

England, as Arthur had already acknowledged, is not a place of wonder. It no longer has a wildwood, or a magical lake, or an Avalon. Or even the dream of them. It is, both by terrain and temperament, largely and prosaically domestic. A green and pleasant land. So, without the ice palaces of the north, or the burning sands of Africa, or the cloud-covered grandeur of Himalayan peaks, can there be room for the miraculous?

Can transformation take place in the soft light of an April evening, amongst the buttercups and daisies of an English meadow? Can the bleating of lambs and the distant hum of a working tractor be an overture for the unfathomable? The truth is, that transformation will take place wherever it needs to take place. If you want it badly enough, and if you've worked for it.

So, as Mike looked at Arthur and Arthur looked at Mike, the gentle English light started to gain in power and scope, and from the western skyline a brilliance began to advance, moving towards them with dazzling intent. Arthur suddenly felt alive as he had never felt before. He was aware of everything: his heartbeat, his breathing, the pulsating, vibrant energy that was flowing from earth to sky, to tree, to bird, to kitten to man. He closed his eyes against the brightness and gasped in the wonder of it all, and when he opened them again there stood before him on the picnic rug, not a small, white kitten but a young white tiger in the first magnificent flush of full strength. And for a moment, just a moment, he was afraid.

And the tiger said: "It's still me, Arthur. Just as it will still be you."

"But ..." Arthur was lost for words. "But ... you're glowing," he finished weakly.

"You think you can keep reaching for who you really are and not, just for a few seconds, get a glimpse of the brilliance? In Mary Jacob Park, in that tunnel, Arthur, you faced the worst in utter darkness. You think you can look now upon the best and not even blink? Have you learned nothing?"

"Spoon in the kitchen," said Arthur apologetically. "Just a spoon in the kitchen."

"Ah, yes. The great Dr. Jung, via the lovely Mr. Krishna. We could have stood to see a little more of Mr. Krishna." Then the tiger looked around him. "Interesting, isn't it?" He looked back at Arthur. "Remember those Greek Eleusinian Mysteries? According to Dio of Prusa, they ended pretty much how we have : 'wonderful light .... pure regions ... and meadows there to greet you ...' That was the setting for the ekstasis."

"I don't know anything about Eleusinian Mysteries," said Arthur.

"Psht!" The tiger made a noise of tiger admonishment. "I have a distinct impression of staggering around Oxford on a Saturday night, lurching from one student party to another, feeling terrible, while some stoner reading classics held forth about how we were all on a magical Eleusinian Mystery tour. Then somebody called Ricky had an ekstasis all over the floor of that pub ... what was it called now? ... you remember ... we were banned after that."

Arthur rubbed his eyes. "I'm sorry, I just don't ..." He stopped.

The tiger took a moment to survey himself – down his powerful forearms, to his enormous paws and along his shining, rippling flanks. And then he said: "Big white cat,

Arthur. Black stripes. Long swishy tail. And balls, Arthur. Balls. Don't you understand?"

Arthur just looked at him. Obviously he didn't. It was a lot to grasp.

"Think, Arthur. *Think.* We talked a lot about your *anima*, your feminine side, when we talked about love and lust. We also, as I recall, talked about balance. So," the tiger shook his head, "did you never wonder what was actually going on with your *animus*? Your poor old inner masculine? Why his name was barely spoken? Why you were content to have him characterised by those noteworthy absences you so frequently referred to? So, where was he when he should have been a leading character in the search for your Self?"

"You?" blurted Arthur finally. "*You?* I thought you were a talisman. *You* thought you were a talisman!"

The tiger gave a big tiger shrug. "Well, in one sense I was, wasn't I? The word talisman is from the Greek word 'telesma', meaning complete. So, originally, a talisman was any idea or object that completed another and made it whole. You know that, don't you?"

"Do I?" Arthur shook his head. "But you didn't understand this all along, did you? You couldn't have. As I remember it, neither of us appeared to understand anything for quite inordinate periods of time."

"Because it was a quest, Arthur. And a quest is a search. And searches are erratic and confusing things."

"Well, they certainly are when they're led by kittens," said Arthur with feeling. "I mean, did you have to be an animal?"

"Oh, Arthur! There's always an animal! Madame Ibeg Boona understood that perfectly. And why not? As far back as the Palaeolithic times Homo Religious used to end his initiations with a confrontation with the animal master. Half man, half beast, symbolising the underlying unity of everything."

"And I suppose we learned this from an archaeologist on yet another pub crawl?"

The tiger gave an impatient snort. "Primitive initiations, Greek Eleusinian mysteries, Jungian psychological processes, but probably not all pub crawls, are symbolic journeys, Arthur. Journeys that can lead to profound change. It's a whole big symbolic thing, and quite frankly you are rather spoiling the moment with all of these pernickety questions." He shook his head. "So, I'm a tiger, tiger burning bright and some metaphysical hand has helped you shape my awe-inspiring symmetry. Now, no more. There are things that are beyond exhaustive explanation and the human psyche, with its connection to a higher Self and a greater consciousness, is one of them." And he laid back his ears and made a low rumbling noise that came from deep within him. It wasn't a million miles from a low rumbling growl.

Arthur took an involuntary step back. "Well, you've grown a lot anyway," he said uncontroversially. "In every sense."

"Indeed I have. Just needed a bit of time for processing. And still a work in progress, of course, as these things inevitably are. But not a kitten anymore. So always keep your eye on Mike – the man you always wanted to be. That way we will turn out just exactly as we should. Let's promise."

So they did, standing silently for a few moments, taking one last look at each other. And then the tiger gave a great tiger grin and said: "So are you ready for me? Ready for the end of this? The actual, specific moment when you finally man up?"

And Arthur said: "I am." And suddenly there was a catch in his voice and tears in his eyes.

And the tiger crouched and sprang and Arthur opened his arms to receive him.

Chapter Nineteen

Arthur sat on the picnic rug – alone – for a long time after this. If the vet, somehow in passing, noticed him staring up at the sliver of the new moon and the one star that hung beside it, she did not interfere. Which is fortunate, because it's very rarely in a lifetime, if at all, that a man is given such a powerful reminder that he is more than he thought he was, and much more than he imagined he could ever be. These are moments to savour and with them comes a peace – perhaps, although Arthur was not familiar with the expression, it had to do with the 'peace that passeth all understanding'. But, to get peace like that to endure is more than the work of one lifetime. For Arthur, at thirty years old with no money, no job and the love of his life still out of his reach, perfect peace wasn't going to last much beyond that incredible dazzling moment amongst the buttercups and daisies when he was granted a glimpse of the miraculous.

*****

"Where's the body?" demanded his nephew Charlie. Death left behind a body. That's how life worked. Charlie had learned this when a bird had flown full tilt into the side of his mother's new and expensively bespoke conservatory. So, if Mike was dead, Uncle Arthur had to be hiding his body somewhere.

Polly was more concerned with why there should have been a body in the first place. "Who were these vets?" she interrupted litigiously. "What did they give him? And why did you have to go into the back of beyond to some bucolic rustics? What was the matter with a practice in Kensington or St John's Wood?"

"There was nothing that anybody could have given him," said Arthur firmly.

"Why not?" asked Sophie.

"For what he had, what he was, there was no cure. He passed away in his sleep on the way home. It was very peaceful. He's at peace. I assure you. I know."

"Where's the body?" asked Charlie again.

"That was all dealt with out in the countryside." Arthur had to keep repeating himself. Perfect peace was certainly a difficult thing to hang on to.

"You didn't just throw him out of the car window, did you?" asked Polly. She didn't really think that her brother was in any way capable of a drive-by grass verge internment but . . .

"What on earth is the matter with you?" snapped Arthur crossly.

Polly burst into tears.

"I'm sure Arthur buried him nicely," said Mrs. Loveday, in some shock. She'd never seen her daughter cry since a sixth-form boyfriend had scored more than she had on a totally unimportant test. Some equilibrium had been disturbed.

"I always knew that kitten wasn't right," said Mr. Loveday. "He never grew, did he? Poor little thing. He's best off now. I think I should make some sandwiches. Would sandwiches be a good thing?"

"They would be perfect," said Arthur.

*****

It would have been nice for Arthur to have been able to turn these things over with Madame Ibeg Boona. He drove, rather pointlessly, to Hampstead and paused outside her house. There was a sign in the garden. It read: For Sale. Carruthers Sloan, Estate Agents. Arthur sighed. He would at least have liked her to know the ending.

It seemed, however, that she did. Two days later he received another postcard with another exotic stamp and another smudged postmark. There was a picture of white tiger on the front. The card read:

Congratulations. Time to go and live your unlived life. And you know where that process has to start. You have to come to terms with the feminine. She won't wait forever. These things have a time. One day the door will close. Get it done. What I have to do now will keep me occupied some while. Maybe one day we'll meet again. Until then – remember that you probably gained more than you lost. The physicists don't have all the answers.
Your friend, Epiphanie Ibeg Boona.

Although he knew that a visit to Anastasia had to figure prominently in it, Arthur had no very clear-cut ideas on how to begin living his unlived life. Before him lay a world of unburdened possibility. At this point, he felt no great pressure to choose one possibility over another. He was, for the moment, content to wait until something presented itself with an agreeable hint of metier and yes … even destiny. 'Do not hunt for subjects, let them choose you …' And his back garden was the thing that was currently insisting upon being done. The dusty, depleted, clinker-ridden patch of earth could be given a new life with relative ease. And if that pleased no-one else, it would at least come as a big relief to Mike's earthworm.

So Arthur dismantled his dark tower. He had no immediate need of it and when he moved on, as he knew he had to, it would not be a welcome legacy for a subsequent tenant. He filled sacks with rubbish and rubble and drove to the tip. He turned over the exhausted earth and dug in bags of council processed organic matter bought from the nice men in the fluorescent jackets. On their advice, he added handfuls of manure pellets. He consulted a book and administered care to the struggling lilac tree – ignoring the highlighted advice, which was brief and to the point: 'grub it out'. He made a path of clinkers and a crazy paving sitting area from broken slabs.

A neighbour, hugely grateful for the disappearance of the dark tower, arrived at his door with plants - unwanted divisions resulting from his own spring gardening activities. More plants began to arrive – a veritable pied piper flow of appreciative botanical donation from people whose back bedrooms were once more in possession of a view that did not signal the imminent breakdown of society and the end of days.

Arthur's parents, even more thrilled than the neighbours at the dismantling of the dark tower, and immensely relieved to be able to drop words like psychiatrist and voodoo from their routine vocabularies, bought him a garden seat with a memorial to Mike, in brass plate, screwed to the back. The senior Lovedays didn't go in for deep and abundant post-mortem discourse. A brass plate was the thing. His sister, convinced that he was never going to do anything about Anastasia (largely because he refused to listen to what she had to say on the subject) offered to pay for a subscription to a superior matchmaking service. Arthur said he'd prefer a birdbath.

When the garden was finished, he turned his attention to the flat. And, as the old wallpaper was stripped and scraped away, number 29B finally began to give up its pain. Arthur filled and sanded and papered and painted.

He received another postcard. There was a picture of a giant tortoise on the front. The card read:

> *I didn't expect to have to send this.*
> *Has that tiger gone completely to sleep? I'm going to India next. I'd send you a copy of the Kama Sutra from there if I thought it would help. Get it done. It's time.*
> *Yours, Epiphanie Ibeg Boona.*

But deep change needs to be assimilated. Arthur continued to fill and sand and paper and paint in the knowledge that his unconscious mind would be making better decisions than his conscious mind about when the life to come should start to begin.

In the meantime, paper and paint have to be paid for so he took a series of temporary jobs. He was not attempting to build a CV, so he took whatever he could find – the sort of jobs for which the qualifications tended to be minimal but strenuous. He spent a couple of weeks loading bankrupt stock from warehouses onto lorries, and then another two or three weeks with some shop-fitters and, finally, he started labouring for a team of landscapers who were turning a brownfield site into an amenity garden.

All of these things came easily to Arthur, so then he knew that he ought not to keep doing them, but before he really gave himself to a new life, he had one more thing to do. It was time. So, one beautiful autumn morning he caught the tube at Finchley Central, changed onto the Central line at Tottenham Court Road, and got off at St. Paul's.

He knew exactly where he was going because only a couple of days previously, the information had been given to him by none other than Damien Price. In one of those curious coincidences, through which life sometimes seems to give you its blessing, Damien had been passing the brownfield site on the way to cast an eye over a nearby development opportunity.

"Arthur? Oh, my God, *Arthur*!" Damien was astonished. "You're a labourer? You're actually *digging*? Smaller ponds Arthur, smaller ponds, but this is ridiculous!"

And Arthur had laughed, assuring Damien that it was a pretty pleasant pond - when the sun was shining.

"You are unbelievable," said Damien, turning away. And then, as Arthur put the spade in the ground again, he turned back and said: "When you're digging a hole for yourself, Arthur, you really ought to know when to stop." He paused. "I saw Anastasia the other day ..." It sounded very casual, a non-sequitur in fact, but Arthur knew better. Damien didn't do non-sequiturs. He was too focused to have random conversations. "She was asking after you. And she's broken up with that millionaire masterpiece we all thought she was going to marry."

"When?"

"A couple of months or so ago. 106, Exchange Street,

seventh floor. Stop digging now, Arthur. I think you'll find the hole is quite deep enough."

*****

The city's powerhouses were starting to disgorge staff for lunch as Arthur stepped into the twelve-storey glass construction that was 106, Exchange Street. He stood for a moment or two on the travertine marble floor in the immense reception area, and took in the palm trees, the bubbling central fountain and the fish. The place was impressive.

And, though he had no particular consciousness of it, Arthur was looking pretty impressive himself. He was tidily, but not overweeningly, dressed in light-coloured trousers and a dark blue jacket that hung well on his tall frame. He had the leanness of hard work and the casual, contained strength that comes from having done it. A sense of ease sat with him as naturally as breathing. Maybe, he could have had a fresh haircut and a closer shave but he didn't want to appear over-anxious. He still paid attention to some things his sister said.

The security guard, small and stocky, watched him impassively. The formidable lady behind the immense desk, where he was expected to record his visit, patted her stiff curls and smiled as he approached.

"Poliakof Foundation, please," he said, signing his name.

"Seventh floor, sir. The lifts are to your left."

"Thank you."

The seventh floor presented him immediately with another formidable female with her hair in a smart French pleat - a style that is more exacting than stiff curls. It requires patience and manual dexterity and a ritualistic pinning that most people who catch the seven a.m. tube at West Ruislip simply aren't up to of a morning.

Arthur asked if it was possible to see Anastasia Poliakof.

"Is she expecting you? Do you have an appointment? There is no mention of you here." The P.A. scanned a computer screen.

"No. Sorry."

"I'm afraid Miss Poliakof isn't seeing anybody at the moment."

"But she is in her office?"

The P.A. thought about this for a second or two while she studied Arthur. "Yes," she said finally.

"Is she alright ?"

This wasn't deemed entirely appropriate. The P.A. raised her eyebrows. "She's busy."

"Of course," agreed Arthur. "But, if you could just take one minute of her time and tell her that Arthur Loveday has dropped in to say hello and that he will come back whenever suits her, if hello is currently out of the question. If you could just please tell her that …"

"You mean interrupt my employer against her express instructions?"

"Yes," said Arthur. "If you would. Just this once. Tell her I held a gun to your head." He smiled and his heartbeat began to feel just that little unruly.

The P.A. studied him again for a moment or two. "Mr. Loveday, I am paid - and paid well - to resist blandishment. And I have been blandished, on occasion, to the tune of quite large sums. It never works."

"Is there any chance, any chance at all, that you could look upon it as a threat?" suggested Arthur.

The P.A. sighed. "You may be determined, possibly even stubborn, but threatening, I entirely fail to see." She counted herself surprised that the conversation was taking the turn it was. There had been a deterioration into banter that flew in the face of her professionalism. She had no truck with fraternisation. So why was she still talking? "Do you actually know Miss Poliakof?" she asked.

"We worked together for three years at Carruthers Sloan."

"Arthur Loveday, you said?"

"Yes."

"A purely social call?"

"Yes."

Was Anastasia in dire need of a purely social call from a tall, handsome young man? That was the fine point to which the P.A. had, much against her normal inclinations, mentally honed the conversation. It was not in her job description to hone along these lines, but she had been suddenly reminded of another tall, handsome young man who had stood before her in those far off days when she'd just burnt her bra and thought a career was the most important thing in the world for a woman. But now, she'd learned that a career doesn't give you everything and, if it turns out to be a lesser thing than you'd hoped for, then the days become days of nothing but punctuality, perseverance and small thoughts, and the right young man will have passed you by.

So the P.A. took another look at Arthur, then looked at the intercom, then looked down the passageway, and finally got up and walked to the big double doors at the end and opened them sufficiently to insert half of her body. Arthur could not hear what she was saying, but there was a lot more of it than he had initially suggested. Then she came back to her desk, sat down, took another and very thorough look at him and said: "You can go on in."

"Thank you so much," said Arthur. "I really appreciate this."

The P.A. shook her head sadly - aware that this was a state of affairs that probably wasn't going to last for very much longer. Sometimes youth was just wasted on the young. As Arthur moved away, she suddenly caught hold of his sleeve. "Don't give up," she said quietly. "Stick it out."

Anastasia was standing by the floor-to-ceiling glass windows, gazing across the city. She looked elegant and efficient in a dark suit and a white silk shirt. Her hair was coiled into a business-like knot at the nape of her neck and the few softening strands that had escaped served only to highlight a certain tension in her lovely face. She did not turn around until Arthur was well into the room and, when she did, she looked momentarily blank. "Arthur?"

Arthur smiled. "Hello, Anastasia."

Anastasia shook her head. "For a moment there, until you spoke, I wasn't certain that it was you ... You look so ..." She stopped.

"So what?"

"So much the same and yet so very different. An amazingly familiar kind of stranger."

"Sounds like you just forgot me," said Arthur lightly.

"I hadn't." Her voice hardened suddenly. "It was more like one of those annoying 'spot the difference' pictures."

She crossed to her desk and started a desultory tapping at a computer keyboard. Arthur waited in silence while she consulted the screen. Finally, she looked up at him. "So this is entirely a social visit?"

"Entirely."

"It's been a long time coming."

"It has. I have. But the intention has always been there."

"And what is it that has kept you so busy that this intention just wasn't powerful enough to prevail upon you to call in, until now. Have you got another job?"

"I have been working," said Arthur carefully.

"At what?"

"Various things," said Arthur. "Latterly, I've been involved in one of those urban renewal projects."

"Doing what?"

"Digging," said Arthur.

"Digging?"

"Digging and clearing."

"You've been *labouring*?"

Anastasia was clearly unimpressed. Arthur realised that he had either been extremely ingenuous or very stupid to introduce the subject of digging. He could imagine Damien shaking his head in disbelief. The immediate problem with digging was that it was hard to tell which aspect of it was about to give him the greatest trouble: the fact that its very menial nature had actually been something capable of getting between him and his intent to visit Anastasia or …. its very menial nature. He knew his inner tiger had to be sitting with his paws over his eyes. You sailed right into this one, Arthur. Your eyes were on the siren and you just didn't see the rocks.

"It was a very worthwhile project," he said.

"On which you were doing the digging?" Anastasia sounded incredulous.

"Not on my own," said Arthur. "There were a few of us who dug, and we must actually have been pretty impressive because every day an old man and his ancient dog came and sat on a seat nearby and watched us. Finally, one lunchtime, I took my food across and sat next to him, and he ate my Kit-Kat and the dog ate most of my sandwiches, but that's by the by – when the old man had finished the Kit-Kat, he said: 'This is a fine job you're doing. It could put heart and soul back into this community.' And I said: ' I'm just digging ..."'

"Is there a point to this story?" interrupted Anastasia. "Something about 'just digging' that I really need to know?"

"I think so," said Arthur. "So, yes, I told the old man that I was just digging, and I pointed out the landscape architect and the project manager and the chap who was scratching his head over the giant planting plan - and I explained that they were the guys. And the old man nodded and watched and took it all in, and then he said: 'A very long time ago an important man came to visit a huge building site. And he got down off his horse and shook hands with the people in charge – just like Prince Charles would do today – and then he moved along to take a closer look at everything. Nobody handed him a hard hat, by the way, because nobody wore hard hats on building sites in those days. Anyway, while the important man was having his look see, he paused to speak to a workman who was on his knees, and he asked him: 'What are you doing?' And the workman answered: 'I'm dressing stone.' And the important man nodded and smiled and moved on. Presently, he paused again to speak to another. And he asked the same question: 'What are you doing?' And the workman answered: 'I'm mixing mortar'. And the important man nodded and smiled again. Now, the next time he stopped it was beside a very old workman with a shovel and a wheelbarrow, and he asked the same question of him: 'What are you doing?' And the very old workman looked up and said, simply: 'I'm building a cathedral.'"

And then Arthur smiled and it was the most wonderful smile, as full of pleasure and warmth and love as it is possible for a man's smile to be.

And the Tiger took his paws from his eyes and said: 'Okay, good recovery, I think we could be back in the game'.

And the Shadow said: 'Well, he could have just walked in and kissed her. That would've saved a lot of hot air and time.'

And the Tiger gave a tiger snort and said: 'You're the one who eats the marshmallows straight away in the psychology experiments, aren't you?'

'Yes,' said the Shadow. 'Besides which, I never saw an old man with a dog.'

'Because there wasn't one,' said the Tiger. 'It's just a story. Illustrative. Probably originated in Ancient Greece. There's been a lot of that going around lately'.

'Not getting it', said the Shadow.

'It was a way to show her that he felt no shame in just digging.' said the Tiger. 'He doesn't have to have gone away and made his fortune, or discovered that he was the long lost heir to a kingdom. That's not what finding out who you really are is actually about.'

Anastasia didn't say anything for a quite disconcerting period of time and then she asked: "Who did you say you were, again?"

"Arthur," said Arthur.

"I knew Arthur," said Anastasia. "And somehow, somehow you are just not he. I doubt Arthur addressed that many coherent words to me the entire time we worked together."

"There was obviously more to him than either of us realised." said Arthur.

"Not strictly true," said Anastasia. "Much as I despaired of him at times, I always felt, or hoped perhaps, that he could be a sleeping tiger … though I confess myself surprised that it took a relationship with a spade to wake him up."

Arthur forced himself not to dwell upon the obvious questions in her eyes or the moody set of her beautiful mouth. (Or the china loveliness of her skin against the darkness of her hair. Every bit of her just delicious and edible.) He gave them both some time while he ostensibly paid attention to the vast room - taking in the dove grey carpets, the black leather and chrome furniture, and the white marble sculptures on their slate coloured plinths.

"Impressive," he said finally.

"We have the whole floor." Anastasia was dismissive. "Drink?" She nodded towards a trolley.

Arthur didn't think that a drink was necessarily going to resolve the evident tension and the long pauses. Even a drink brewed in an art deco cocktail shaker. "Or maybe," he said levelly, "I need to tell you why I came."

"What made you think that I would be available to tell?"

"Blind optimism," Arthur confessed. "And if you hadn't been here, or had been occupied with someone else, I would have made an appointment for another day. And if you had been merely disinclined to see me, why then I would simply have begged."

"And what is it that you so desperately need to say?"

Now it was time. Or not. It was possible, Arthur thought, that turning down the drink had been a mistake. "Maybe I could take you out to lunch first?"

"You never asked me out to lunch in three years."

"And that was extremely foolish of me," Arthur confessed. "I've been somewhat prone to foolishness but don't think, for one moment, that I haven't paid a very high price for it."

"Well, I have to tell you that this invitation just feels like more of your typical procrastination. I do not want to eat. I want to hear what you have come to say."

So Arthur took a deep breath and decided that it was best

to keep things simple. "I'm in love with you," he said. "I always have been."

And Anastasia looked him straight in the eye and obviously decided that it was best to be honest. "I know," she said. "I always have done."

This response had not featured on Arthur's list of possibles. "You do?"

"Yes. I realised. But it was by no means clear to me that you did."

"I did," protested Arthur, "of course I did, but ..."

'Floundering,' groaned the Shadow. 'I told you. We should just have gone with the walk in and kiss her scenario. You make a decent job of the kiss and what you say afterwards doesn't have to be so smart, because she's not really going to be giving it much attention.'

The Tiger gave one of his tiger snorts, but the qualms were back.

Anastasia ignored Arthur's protests. "I knew it because I could see it," she said. "In your face, in your eyes, in everything you did. And I could feel it. Over the years, Arthur, there has been, quite possibly, an above average number of men prepared to tell me they loved me. One or two of them might even have meant it. But I couldn't feel it in them. But with you, Arthur, it was as if this thing, this incredible thing that has filled books and plays and poems for century after century, actually existed - it wasn't just something that we had invented in order to make it easier to live. There were moments, when you and I were alone and standing next to each other, that it rolled off you in such great waves it was almost uncanny. It was so powerful and compelling that I had to step away. And I thought: 'He has to feel this, he has to understand what it means. How can he not?' And yet you did nothing. Said nothing. I could have spoken out, but whatever barrier it was that held you back, somehow kept me back. At one level, you were a very accessible man - you were always helpful, you covered for my mistakes and on occasion took the blame for them." She paused. "Yes, I was aware of all those things, Arthur, but somehow, at another level, you were ..." Evidently unable to explain it, let alone express it, Anastasia shook her head sadly. "So I waited. I dated other people and I waited some more. After you left Carruthers Sloan, I thought: 'Now he'll realise. He has to miss me. Surely?' And every day since I started here I've looked out at the city from these glass windows, like the Lady of Shallot in her tower with her curse, and told myself: 'It will be today. Today he will come. Three times I've asked him to get in touch. He has to come.'"

Anastasia's gaze was still holding, but her lovely eyes were beginning to glint with tears. "What took you so long, Arthur? *Really?*"

Arthur realised that he had been naive in thinking that he wouldn't have to explain himself. But he'd never appreciated just how much his love had given him away. It was as if he'd kept on making some exceptional promise that he'd repeatedly failed to keep. He'd always planned, should this meeting work out, that he would tell Anastasia how it had been. All of it. But he'd somehow imagined that he would have time. That the explanations would be able to come gradually and naturally. And not today. But she had asked the question, and she was waiting for an answer.

"It's difficult to explain," he said.

"Haven't you got another story?" asked Anastasia.

Arthur smiled, and then he said slowly, "Once upon a time there was this beautiful princess. A princess who was not only beautiful but funny, highly educated and, by all accounts, extremely rich. And she had a lot of handsome, highly educated and extremely rich friends, who, as a matter of record, were not quite as funny. And then there was this swineherd, who was not even particularly good at herding swine, but the one thing he was good at was loving the princess, and doing such small things as lay within his power to make her life run more smoothly and happily.."

"I don't like this story, Arthur," Anastasia protested." Surely, you didn't think that you …"

"Unfortunately, I kind of did," said Arthur. "And it took a bit of time for me to work out that I was actually …" He stopped because Anastasia's tears seemed on the point of spilling over.

'… the dread pirate Robert,' finished the Tiger. 'He was actually the dread pirate Robert.'

'What's he doing?' asked the Shadow in exasperation. 'Calling himself a swineherd? You would think the man had learned nothing at all! And who's this Robert? I thought we were called Arthur … Or maybe Mike.'

'He's explaining the swineherd complex,' said the Tiger. 'Advisedly or otherwise. The solution to which is to find within yourself the wherewithal to be the dread pirate Robert. Except he's not going to be allowed to take it that far. Pity. It could have rounded the thing off nicely.'

'How come," asked the Shadow, 'that it sounds as if I'm the wherewithal for creating the inner Robert, but I've no idea who he is?'

'Movie reference,' said the Tiger. 'The Princess Bride. You never watch movies?'

'I've never been allowed to,' said the Shadow sadly. 'Everybody was always too afraid to take me along.'

'It was a good movie,' said the Tiger. 'Swineherd loves prospective princess but doesn't think he's worthy, leaves farm, becomes the dread pirate Robert – who is really more about image and archetype than piracy – rescues princess from scheming prince, then hands on the mantle of the dread pirate Robert to the next guy because now the swineherd has found the wherewithal to be him he doesn't need to be him. See? The princess, of course, had been in love with him all along - because he was handsome and good and he'd always done for her whatever he said he would do. Even when he was just the swineherd.'

'Not entirely convincing', said the Shadow. 'I can't believe that the princess was in love with him before he found his inner Robert. When did you see this?'

'When we were recovering from the metaphysical dog bites.' said the Tiger. 'It was on the Sky movie channels.'

'I think you could have told me,' said the Shadow sulkily. 'We were supposed to be friends by that time.'

'Anyway', said the Tiger, 'you're wrong, aren't you, because Anastasia has virtually told him that she was in love with him beforehand. Modern women, you know, and that includes the ones in movie audiences, aren't always as thrilled with the inner Robert in the entirety of his naked splendour as *we*, by which I mean *you*, think they ought to be.'

'That's as maybe,' said the Shadow, 'but let's not forget that if it hadn't been for *me*, then *we*, by which I mean *you*, would never have got this far in the first place.'

'But it was always Arthur who needed the inner Robert,' insisted the Tiger. 'Not the princess. Not Anastasia.'

'She needed him,' said the Shadow, darkly. 'Or a few dates down the line she'd have been wondering what sort of a wuss it was that could do nothing else but feed her cups of coffee.'

"I didn't like the swineherd story," said Anastasia to Arthur, eyes still full of tears. "Because all those little things you did for me couldn't have been little at all, because they felt like the care and the grace that made life really worth living. I used to think of you waiting for me at work with the cappuccinos and the muffins and that got the day off to a start ... I could have people bringing me cappuccinos and muffins all day long here but it wouldn't be the same. It hasn't been the same. And all because you thought I was a princess ..." And then the tears spilled over.

The Tiger and the Shadow looked at each other.

"This new Arthur can do cappuccinos and muffins too," said Arthur gently. "In fact I was hoping you would prefer him. After all, he not only loves you but he's prepared to do something about it, over and above muffins."

"Plus," admitted Anastasia with a faint smile through her tears, "the man is smokin' hot."

'See?' said the Shadow smugly.

"And yet he's over here and you keep going over there," Arthur pointed out.

'Too much smoke,' said the Tiger and gave the Shadow a shove.

Anastasia, who had taken up agitated turns round the room, stopped suddenly. "But, now I'm thinking that if you'd really loved me you'd have come sooner. When I asked."

The Tiger and the Shadow groaned in unison.

"Of course, I love you," said Arthur. "You know that. But you must believe me when I tell you that if we start from here, then things will go far, far better than if we had started from there. I promise you."

And he walked across to her and gently lifted back some strands of hair that had fallen over her face and looked into her eyes. And when she smiled he put his arms round her and said: "Now, tell me the rest of it. What else is wrong?"

"This should be a wonderful job, shouldn't it?" she said.

"It certainly looks that way," replied Arthur.

"It's fraught," she said. "The field of charitable endeavour is unexpectedly fraught. But not now, not at this moment, because the birthday of my life is come, my love is come to me."

Arthur closed his eyes. It was unbelievable joy. "Is come?" he asked after a moment or two. "*Is* come?"

"It's Rossetti. We had a romantic poetry club at school."

"We didn't. But I can assure you that I would have been the first to join if we had."

Anastasia lifted her head and gave him a look. "And the important thing about an extensive knowledge of romantic poetry," she said, "is that it leads one to the conclusion that irony should never be part of a long awaited protestation of undying love!"

"Come here," she added, suddenly urgent. "Come to the Foundation and help me. So many times I need, we all need, to be reminded that our ultimate purpose is not to have dramas over estimates and planning and contracts but to build cathedrals."

"It's a lovely idea," said Arthur carefully. "But I'm not sure that this headhunting amongst the lower echelons of the Brown Landscaping Company would meet with all round approval. Besides which," he held her a little tighter to discourage protest, "I'm popular there. My technique with a spade is much admired. I could rise in the firm."

"You don't want to work here? You don't want to work with me?"

"It's a situation that could have more than an average

allotment of pitfalls," replied Arthur. "We are, essentially, new to each other, so let's just take undying love one step at a time. And we could begin, I believe, with something I have thought about since the first moment I saw you. Something that can no longer be postponed ..."

And the swineherd bent his head and kissed the princess.

'Whoa!' said the Tiger.' Did you feel that? Depth charges!'

'Pretty impressive,' agreed the Shadow. 'I think it's even turning my darkness a bit pink.'

The Tiger gave the matter some consideration. 'It works for you, though.'

'Honestly?' asked the Shadow. 'You're not just saying that?'

'That's the thing about love,' said the Tiger. 'It works for everyone. Even you.'

And the Shadow laughed and gathered his new pinkness about him and did a celebratory twirl.

Acknowledgements

There are many, many things for which I have to thank my husband – the most pertinent one being the work he's put into enabling this book to join the ranks of the self-published. If he found the process a tedious waste of time, he never said so, and for that I am more than grateful.

Or, perhaps, he simply didn't dare complain because he gave me the first book by Jung that I ever read: Modern Man In Search Of A Soul. And he never did say why exactly he gave it to me. Nor why other members of the family seemed to think it was a good idea to follow suit. I chose not to ask. Jung isn't always easy to fully comprehend for someone who is not a professional in the field and of works I found helpful in this regard, I would particularly like to mention Ruth Snowden's Jung: The Key Ideas (Teach Yourself series) and also Inner Work by the Jungian analyst Robert A. Johnson.

I would hasten to emphasise, of course, that Jung For Kittens is a work of fiction and when the ideas of great thinkers are processed through redundant estate agents, voodoo priestesses and talking kittens they do not always come out in quite the shape they went in. In short, I would ask you to remember that a small white kitten is responsible for everything you have read.

I would also like to thank my craniosacral therapist Helen Beale for her work on me and her development of the somatic writing process (www.somalogos.com) which has more than a dash of Jungian inspiration about it. I must also mention my sons Max and Todd whose advice to 'go for it' came primarily, I suspect, from an urge to keep me occupied.

Lightning Source UK Ltd.
Milton Keynes UK
UKOW04f1804290515

252586UK00001B/1/P